HUNTER GREEN

by

Debra Deaver

Dedicated to my loving family.
Thanks for being so patient with me.

For whatever was written in former days was written for our instruction, that by steadfastness and by the encouragement of the scriptures we might have hope. Romans 15:4

Prologue

One year ago today, on March 2, 2002, an old man died at Mercy Hospital in Eagle Creek, Wisconsin. He was just a poor man with no family or close friends to mourn his passing. Why do I remember the exact date of something so uneventful to everyone else? It was the day my simple, uncomplicated life turned upside-down all because of a worn piece of paper and a pair of striking green eyes.

Chapter One

March 1, 2002

"Teresa? Jerry wants to see you when you get a chance."

"Oh, okay. Thanks, Jess."

My heart started pounding in my chest and I nearly dropped the clipboard I was carrying as I led a worried mother and her young, feverish son down the maze of hallways to the next available examination room. I'd only been called into the principal's office once in my entire school career, but I recognized this as the same feeling of dread. Being called to the administrator's office couldn't possibly be a good thing. Could it?

As I took the sick boy's vitals—and assured his worried mother the doctor would be in to see them soon—I wondered if there was anything I could have possibly done wrong. In the ten years I'd worked as a nurse at the West Side Health Clinic, I'd never had my professionalism questioned. I prided myself on being thorough and meticulous in my work. I always arrived early and stayed until I was certain all my charting was done and my equipment was properly sanitized and put away. Did the new administrator have something personal against me?

"I can't believe he's making me leave the floor during one of the busiest days," I grumbled to myself as I returned to the nurse's station. Leaning over the counter, I asked the other nurse on duty, "Jess, do you know what this meeting might be about? Can you think of anything I've done wrong to get into trouble with Jerry?"

"Hey," Jess responded in that soothing, motherly voice she used so naturally, "you're the most reliable nurse we have. I can't think of one, solitary thing Jerry can complain about. It's probably nothing, so don't worry so much."

"I am so sorry to leave you hanging like this," I said, taking a glance out at all the people still sitting in the waiting room. I felt guilty for having to leave my post, but I knew Jerry would make sure I felt even guiltier if he had to come looking for me.

"It's not your fault," Jess replied with a dismissive wave of her hand. "When the boss says jump, we gotta jump."

"I promise I'll be back as soon as I can."

I hurried upstairs to the business office and then ended up having to wait for Jerry to finish talking with someone else. I sat in one of the hard plastic chairs in the hallway, my knee bouncing nervously as I stared at the gray, industrial carpeting. 'What did I do wrong? I hope I'm not getting fired,' I thought.

I enjoy my job as a clinic nurse at West Side. The pay isn't the greatest—I could be making more money working at a nursing home, hospital, or in a private clinic on the richer side of town—but I find it more rewarding to help people who may be less fortunate and have limited resources. Most of the patients coming to our clinic are on state insurance or even homeless. Some of those with critical health conditions we get to know well, and it always warms my heart whenever we can help ease their symptoms if not their situation.

The opening door startled me out of my thoughts. Kelly, another clinic nurse, gave me the barest of glances as she left the administrator's office and headed down the hallway toward the stairs. She was scheduled to work the next shift, and the fact that she wasn't wearing her scrubs and still had her coat on wasn't a good sign.

"Miss Billings?"

I looked up at the owner of the nasally voice standing beside me. To me, Jerry always sounded like he had a perpetual cold. He smiled down at me, and I got the impression he liked looking down on people.

"Jerry, we've known each other since kindergarten." I stood up, my eyes lining up with the top of his head. "You don't have to start calling me *Miss* just because the office you work in is higher in altitude than mine."

Forced to tip his head to look up at me, his smile faltered for only a second before a professional one replaced it. "Fine. Teresa. Thanks for coming."

Jerry turned and headed back into his office, leaving the door open as his invitation to follow. Sitting in the cushioned swivel chair, he waited for me to join him, hands clasped primly on top of the papers scattered across his disorganized desk with its 'Mr. J. Newman' nameplate. The years had been kind to Jerry in that he hadn't seemed to age since high school. He probably still got carded at bars even though I could tell the hairline of his short-cropped, dishwater-blond hair was beginning to recede. At least it wasn't hanging down in greasy locks over his forehead anymore.

As I entered the claustrophobic office and sat on the solitary plastic chair, I mentally berated myself for reminding Jerry of our shared past. It was true we'd gone all through school together, but it rubbed me the wrong way when he acted superior to me just because he had a fancier job title than I did. He'd only worked here less than a year and still didn't know some of the employees' names. What I should have remembered before opening my mouth was the number of times I'd spurned him when he'd repeatedly asked me out—yes, he had been the kind of boy who didn't take no for an answer. Now, he held my job in the palm of his hand. If he wanted revenge, he was in the perfect position to give it. Besides, I probably deserved it—both for my dismissal of his feelings in school and my inability to stop sabotaging my life with my big mouth.

Jerry consulted his computer screen as if he'd forgotten why he called me here. "I see you've been working a lot of overtime. You're way over the limit specified in our employee policy."

I sat in silence, not knowing where this conversation was headed. I wanted to point out that Sondra, the one in charge of scheduling the nurses, had been the one to call me, practically begging me to pick up the extra shifts. But since I'd probably already upset him, I didn't want to push my luck and have Jerry think I was being sarcastic as well as disrespectful.

"I know the bigger paychecks might look amazing—"

"I don't pick up the extra shifts for the money," I interrupted.

Jerry continued as if I'd never spoken. "—but we've had complaints that other staff members never get the opportunity to work more hours. There are those who could use a little more help when it comes to paying bills than you do. You know, ones who have rent or mortgages to pay and children to support."

The obvious stab at my living situation and lack of family felt like a physical slap across my face. Even though I shouldn't have to apologize for my secure finances or unsuccessful relationships, Jerry's comment made me feel guilty that I failed in some way. I gritted my teeth, but it didn't stop the words from spilling from my lips. "I probably keep getting called because some of the other nurses either don't answer their phones or say they're too busy to pick up the extra shifts."

Jerry held up his hands in mock surrender. "I know. I know. I've already told them that. But the fact remains we can't have one staff member working that many hours in a pay period."

"Am I in trouble, Jerry?" I blurted out. My fists clenched, barely containing my fear and anger. "Are you firing me for covering for other people?"

He stared at me as if I'd just grown another head. "Whatever gave you that idea? You're one of our best nurses. No. I just wanted to let you know that starting

Monday, I'm having Sondra implement a rotating system for calling. Everyone gets a chance at being called first—except for you. I'm having her put you at the bottom of that list. We all know you don't need the money, and this gives everyone else a fair shot at overtime. Then, when you do get a call to cover a shift, it will be because you were our last choice."

"Last choice?" My words were nothing more than a whisper. I struggled to breathe beneath the crushing tightness in my chest. Logically, I knew what he meant—I would be called as the last option. My subconscious, though, heard the words in the most derogatory way possible—I wasn't good enough.

Jerry gave a resigned sigh before continuing. "That being said, Sondra left for vacation at noon today and we have a staff member out sick. Could you stay and work a double shift to cover for her?"

The irony was not lost on either of us. I sat in stunned silence for a few seconds, still sorting through the absurdity of the whole exchange, then pasted a smile on my face. My cheeks cramped from trying to look pleasant instead of annoyed as I answered, "Of course, Jerry. I'd be happy to help."

"Now, I know it's Friday, so if you have anything like…" Jerry's hands flapped like fish on the ends of his wrists and he licked his lips before continuing, "...a date or anything better to do, I'm sure Jess could handle—"

"Nope. I'm free," I interrupted, knowing he was just digging for information on my dating life. Again. I stood up to leave before I could say anything else self-destructive. "So, I'll just get back to work then."

Jerry called after me, "Next week, though, we'll get that new plan up and running."

I made my escape out of Jerry's office as gracefully as possible. Walking down the hall, I fumed that Jerry actually sounded like he thought he was doing me a favor. On the way back downstairs, I was able to shake off some of the tension that built up during the meeting. Even though the morning shift had been physically and mentally exhausting—especially the meeting with Jerry—I had eight more hours staring me in the face. I couldn't take my frustrations out on the patients or my favorite co-worker, especially when she was pulling a double shift as well.

I found Jess leaning against the doorway to the nurse's station as she waited for the printer to spit out the next patient's paperwork. She looked up at me over the rims of her glasses and asked. "What did Jerry want?"

I didn't want to unload Jerry's issues with my overtime onto her, so I just smiled and said, "Looks like the Dynamic Duo will be together tonight, too."

"Thank heavens," she said, eyes turned skyward. "I don't know what I would've done without you, Teresa. Did you see Kelly? She looked terrible." Jess attached the papers to the next available clipboard. "Probably has what everybody else's been getting. Doesn't it seem like this virus hit earlier and harder than in other years?"

"I think we say that every year," I reminded her, receiving an eye roll in return. "Besides, I couldn't just leave you hanging like that. You've put in almost as much overtime as I have."

"Almost." She held up one hand to stop me when I opened my mouth. "And before you say anything, I don't have my car today, but of course I'll walk home with you. You know you don't even have to ask."

I chuckled at her perceptiveness. Or was I just that easy to read? "We must be working too much overtime together if you're beginning to read my mind," I joked.

"Maybe you're right," Jess agreed with a nod, "but we are the Dynamic Duo, after all." A sly grin tugged at one corner of her lips. "And in payment for my escort services, can you take over for a bit? I have got to get something to eat before I pass out or bite someone's head off."

"Sure," I said plucking the clipboard from her hand. "Go on. Both of those options sound like a lot of paperwork."

"I promise I'll hurry." She gave me a quick, one-armed hug, grabbed her purse, and hurried for the door.

I was still seething from my meeting, and my brain was on autopilot as I called the name on the clipboard. A man stood up from one of the waiting room chairs and followed me down the hallway to an open exam room. I took his temperature, blood pressure, and pulse without even looking him in the face. His complaints were the same as so many others that week; fever, difficulty breathing, deep cough, weakness, and fatigue. All fitting the symptoms of the most recent virus spreading across the country. I was already making my own mental diagnosis that would send him home for rest and the proverbial chicken soup which would have him back to normal in less than a week.

"The doctor will be with you as soon as he can." I finished my entry on the form and finally spared him a glance.

His clothing was old and mended in several places, but it was clean. The thin coat may have fit him when he first purchased it, but now that he was underweight and slightly hunched over, it was much too loose hanging off his narrow shoulders. White stubble covered the bottom half of his sunken cheeks, standing out over his splotchy, feverish skin. His date of birth put him at 61, but he looked haggard and much older, even with the illness.

When our eyes locked, my heart skipped a beat and the most overwhelming sensation of déjà vu washed over me like a tidal wave. His bright green eyes with brown specks looked back at me—eyes that were like looking in a mirror—at myself. I had never seen anyone with eyes so similar to my own.

The man's eyes widened until I could see each and every broken blood vessel around those eerily familiar irises. A huge smile spread across his face, but when he tried to speak, his breath came in short, quick gasps. Clutching at his chest, he began to cough, struggling to get enough air into his lungs. Bright, red splatters of blood spewed from his mouth onto his threadbare pants, and he began to tip dangerously close to the edge of the examining table.

"No, no, no. Please don't fall," I said, pushing him gently, yet firmly, back onto the table.

While he labored to breathe, I grabbed the oxygen mask and hit the call light for help. The oxygen helped ease his coughing, but the clear, plastic mask was soon speckled with red.

"Just take some nice, even breaths…" For the life of me, I couldn't remember his name. "We're going to help you, Sir."

His eyes locked on mine again as he struggled to say something beneath the mask. I leaned closer and took it away so I could hear him better. His hand clutched my arm with surprising strength, pulling me even closer. With my ear just inches from his mouth, I was able to hear what he whispered.

"Who's…your mother?"

It was such an unexpected question, I didn't answer right away. But when I pulled back to look into his face again, I saw his desperate need for an answer.

"Margaret," I answered. "Her name was Margaret."

He shook his head weakly. "Peg," he said in a croaked whisper. "It's Peg."

Surprised, I nodded in assent. Only one person still used my mother's nickname and that was Claire, her best friend from high school and my Godmother. His lips formed the name again and he smiled, eyes slowly closing. His arm fell limp to his side, and he slipped into unconsciousness just as Jess burst into the room.

"I just got back. What's wrong?"

"Get Dr. Peterson and call an ambulance," I ordered, slipping naturally into emergency mode as I grabbed my stethoscope and listened to his erratic heartbeat. "Tell them we have an unconscious, 61-year-old male with arrhythmia and hemoptysis."

Within a half hour, the old man was transported by ambulance to Mercy Hospital without regaining consciousness, and the rest of us went back to our regular routines. It took me longer than normal to shake the rush of adrenaline that made my heart beat harder and my hands tremble. I was unnerved by his question and the odd reaction to my answer. The name, Peg, had given him a sense of peace despite his failing body. Before they rushed him away, I took a closer look at his form.

Benjamin Hunter. The name was slightly familiar. Like something I'd heard long ago and dismissed because it wasn't important—or that my mind had blocked because it didn't want to remember.

Hunter was a word my mother always used to describe my eyes. I remember sitting on her lap as we watched television on one of her good days, a sad expression darkening her face. When I asked what was wrong, she shook her head and gave me a forced smile saying, "You certainly have Hunter-green eyes, my dear."

"You always say that, Mom," I said, snuggling closer and pulling her thin arms around me like a blanket. "But there's a hunter-green paint chip in the art room at school, and my eyes aren't that dark at all."

She'd only held me tighter, kissed my temple, and rocked me back and forth whispering, "They will always be Hunter-green."

~~~~~
~~~~~

"Ready to go?" Jess asked as she teasingly tugged my blonde ponytail.

I shut off my computer and gave her a tired smile as I stretched my aching back. I could still feel the stress of the day deep in my muscles. "Yeah, I'm ready."

We made sure all the lights were off and doors locked before grabbing our things and heading out into the crisp, winter evening. The air was cold with lightly falling snow reflecting the lights of the streetlamps. At least it wasn't enough to make the sidewalks slippery and I wouldn't have to shovel tonight. If it didn't stop before morning, I would hire the teenager across the street to clear the sidewalk and driveway for me. He was always willing to do a little physical labor if there was money involved.

"You were Superwoman today," Jess said as we made our way down the Reynold Street sidewalk together. "Double shift, surviving a meeting with Jerry, and saving a life. Never a dull moment."

"Nope. Never dull," I agreed. "But I wouldn't call myself *super* anything. Would Superwoman need to be walked home when it's only eight blocks? I'm sorry you have to keep doing this. I'm sure you have better things to do."

"Hey, I get it. I was young and pretty once, too." Jess gave me a wink that made me chuckle then she heaved a dramatic sigh. "How pathetic are we? It's a Friday night and neither of us has anything better to do than pick up extra hours. Me, I can see—a divorced mother of two teenagers doesn't have a whole lot of prospects—but you...you're only thirty-two, tall, skinny, and pretty. You should be out there living it up and finding some nice guy who's cute and spoils you rotten."

I blew out a long sigh, my breath hanging like a cloud in the cold air between us. "We do sound pretty pathetic. But I think I'm done with the whole dating scene. I've had enough bad relationships to know Mr. Right is just a figment of my imagination."

"So, you don't even want to look? Never want to get married or have kids? I admit my marriage wasn't the best, but there were good times, too. And my kids…well, I've never regretted having them."

"I'm not saying I'd never get married. I just have to find someone I can stand to be around day after day."

"Well, that's a romantic way of putting it," Jess said sarcastically.

"My parents didn't have that lovey-dovey relationship everyone seems to think you need in order to have a perfect life, so I don't really see what all the fuss is about. All the guys I've dated were either too self-involved, too needy, or too demanding. I'm perfectly happy to concentrate on my work right now and pick up the extra hours for those who need the time off more than I do."

"Well, I still think that's a pretty pessimistic way of thinking, but I guess you have to do what you think is best."

We stopped under the streetlamp at the corner of Baker and Reynold. From here, I only had to pass one more house to make it home. Jessie, on the other hand, would have to backtrack two blocks and follow Hickory Street to get to her apartment.

"I'm sorry you have to go out of your way just because of me," I said. "Thank you so much."

"Would you stop apologizing for everything? It's okay to ask for help when you need it, you know. Nobody's perfect, and no one should apologize for being human. Have a good weekend, and I'll see you bright and early Monday morning."

I watched Jessie walk away—wishing some of her confidence would rub off on me one day—then glanced nervously up and down Reynold Street. Everything was quiet, and the new dusting of glittering snow gave the neighborhood a dream-like quality. In the glow of the curtained windows, the steep roofs, wide porches, towers, and turrets made the old, Victorian-style homes look as quaint as dollhouses. I knew, though, that the harsh light of day revealed roofs that needed updating, cracked stained-glass windows that were too expensive to replace, third floors that were sealed off because they were too hard to heat, and trim that desperately needed repainting but required specialized equipment to reach. It was a neighborhood that wanted to retain the image of the wealthier district from the town's history even though I knew for a fact they were built from Sears and Roebuck kits at the turn of the century.

Digging my keys from my purse, I hurried up the walk to my dark Queen Anne-style house. If I'd known I was going to work so late, I would have left the porch light on to welcome me home. In the limited light, the new, blue vinyl siding looked gray and cold. The three-story, century-old house really was much too big for just me. My grandfather willed his home to me, so I saw no reason to waste money on renting something smaller just because it was more suitable for a single woman.

I remember being surprised when I'd learned Grandpa Bennett left me his house. He'd never seemed very fond of me even though he always sent money in my birthday and holiday cards. Then again, I was his only grandchild. Since the house was where my mother, grandfather, and great-grandfather grew up, I felt obligated to keep the stately relic in the family. I told myself I might get to know my mother better by living in the house she lived happily in as a child. But even I had to admit there were some days I'd rather be at work than home in my lonely, dark, empty, old house.

I paused on the cement steps that led up to the covered wrap-around porch, my keys already poised to unlock the front door. Thinking about my mother made me remember Benjamin Hunter and his episode at the clinic, and I wondered what happened to him after leaving in the ambulance.

Chapter Two

Curiosity got the better of me. I changed course, forgoing the comfort and warmth of the house for the cold, hard seats of the blue Volkswagen Beetle sitting in my driveway. As I waited impatiently for the defrost to loosen the covering of ice I hadn't scraped off in days, I warmed my hands in front of the vent. Even though I always walked to work or the grocery store, I was thankful I'd gotten the Beetle's thermostat fixed before winter started.

My windshield finally scraped clear, I drove to Mercy Hospital on the east side of Eagle Creek, the workplace of my best friend and University of Wisconsin-Madison roommate, Mary Jean Meyers. She smiled up at me, her teeth dazzling white against her dark skin, as I made my way toward her. Her smile faltered a little when I only managed a weak one in return.

"You're looking even paler than usual. What brings you over to my neck of the woods?" she asked.

"Hey, MJ. I'm looking for a man brought in by ambulance this afternoon from the clinic. Name's Benjamin Hunter. Can you find him for me?"

"Sure thing." She gave me a puzzled look as she tapped away at the computer. "The clinic usually doesn't have much to do with patients once they're sent to us. Did he forget something there or do you know this guy?"

I rubbed my aching forehead and sighed. “Would you believe I honestly don’t know if I know him or not? But he seemed to know me.”

“Your family’s been here since horse and buggy days, Ter. Half the city knows you.” She stopped typing and read over what she found, summarizing it for me. “He's been taken to intensive care and his condition is critical. Looks like a serious case of pneumonia, but his heart is giving them the most trouble. It stopped in the ambulance and took three jolts of the defibrillator to get it started again. They nearly lost him again while draining the fluid from his lungs.” MJ shook her head at the unfortunate news. “You going up to see him?”

“Yeah,” I answered absently, trying to process how I felt about his diagnosis. I didn’t know him, so why was it bothering me?

She wrote down his room number on a sticky note and handed it to me. “Stop back before you leave and fill me in.”

As I rode the elevator up to the third floor, I berated myself for getting involved. One of the first things we learned in nursing school was to keep it professional. Involvement with patients on a personal level only leads to heartache.

So, why was I going to see this very sick man? Was it just because he'd asked about my mother? I did the quick math in my head and knew he was too old to have gone to school with her. Was he a distant relative of some kind? Did it have anything to do with his eyes, so similar to my own?

The sight of Benjamin Hunter shouldn't have surprised me as an experienced nurse. However, I still became emotional when I saw all the tubes and wires running from him to the equipment flanking his bed. According to the machines, the man was barely alive.

A nurse breezed in and gave me a bright, rehearsed smile before inspecting the man's monitors. "Oh, good. I'm glad they finally found some family. My name's Susan and I'll be checking in on Benjamin tonight. He's been showing brief periods of alertness, so that's a good sign. Feel free to stay as long as you want, and just let me know if you need anything."

She was gone as suddenly as she appeared, so I didn't have a chance to correct her assumption that I was related. I pulled a chair up next to the bed and studied the man who had shaken my senses. He looked peaceful, but I could see signs of the hard life he must have lived. His hair was gray and thin, his skin was tough and weathered, and there were deep lines around his eyes and forehead as if he spent a lot of time worrying. I looked down at the relaxed hand lying on the clean, white sheets and thought they looked like strong, kind hands. The fingers were long and thin, and his nails were cut short and looked well cared for. Impulsively, I took hold of that hand and felt it curl, weak but warm, around my fingers. I looked up to see him staring at me with those striking, green eyes.

"Peg," he croaked weakly from behind the oxygen mask.

"That's right. How did you know people used to call my mother Peg?" I asked. "Did you live near her or maybe go to the same school?"

He tried to say something, but, with his dry throat and labored breathing, I couldn't understand the whispered response. I spotted a cup of ice chips on the bedside table and gave him a few spoonfuls. He nodded gratefully, then licked his cracked lips and tried again. "They are Hunter-green."

The use of my mother's odd phrase struck me like a punch in the stomach. It took me a few deep breaths before I was able to ask, "What did you say?"

"Your eyes. Hunter-green. Like mine." He smiled and the years melted away from his face. I could tell, even in my confusion, that he must have been a very handsome man in his youth.

"I'm sorry…about back then. I was trying to…make sure."

"Back when? Sure of what?" I was totally confused, and it suddenly seemed important to find out what he was talking about.

He closed his eyes. "Make sure you were her. Didn't mean to…scare you."

Images flashed through my mind like scattered pieces of a puzzle. A strange man grabbing my arm. The smell of alcohol as he leaned close. Crying. A handful of candy. Someone yelling at me to run.

The memory, buried deep since I was a child, now crawled its way to the surface. Forgetting where I was as my mind transported me back in time, I whispered, "Benjamin Hunter."

“Yes,” he answered.

“Detroit,” I added.

“Yes.”

“It was you?” I asked, the blood draining from my face. I wanted to pull my hand from his but I couldn’t move.

He opened his eyes, grasping my hand tighter. “I’m sorry. Didn’t mean to scare you,” he repeated earnestly. “I would never hurt you.”

“Why did you do that?” I demanded, my chest painfully tight and on the verge of a panic attack. "I was just a little girl. Why me?"

He gave a raspy sigh and closed his eyes again. “They didn’t tell you.”

“Tell me what?” The strain of trying to piece the puzzle of my memories and this man together created a distant buzzing sound in my head. It was difficult to breathe, and my vision began to narrow as if I was looking down a long tunnel. “Just who are you, anyway?"

His eyes were sad, yet serious, when he looked at me, hypnotizing me with his gaze. For a brief moment, I wanted to run from the room. Somehow, I knew whatever he said was going to be something I didn’t want to hear.

“I’m your father.”

I couldn’t speak or even move. His voice was calm and steady, and for a minute he didn’t look as sick as I knew him to be. I sat there staring at this man I'd just met hours ago who had somehow managed to upend my stable, sensible life. All I could manage was a slow shake of my head. It couldn't be true. My father was living across town. This was just some old man dying in a hospital bed.

Benjamin's voice was barely above a whisper as his brief surge of strength rapidly waned, and I had trouble hearing it through my shock. "I loved Peg. She left me. The letter. I wanted...to tell you." Each sentence was punctuated by gasping breaths before he finally gave in and slipped back into unconsciousness.

I sat and stared at him for nearly five minutes. The silent blips on the monitor showed his weak and unstable heartbeat. Still in a daze, I left him and went back down the elevator.

"How's he… Ter? Teresa!" Mary Jean called to me from behind the desk. It took longer than it should have for her voice to penetrate the shock and for me to force myself to turn toward her. Her mouth dropped when she saw my face. "Good Lord in heaven." She turned to the male nurse next to her and said, "Barry, I'll be back in a bit, and don't you dare complain with all the smoke breaks you take." MJ grabbed one of my arms and quickly steered me toward the cafeteria.

Feeling strangely numb, I followed her to a corner table in the deserted dining room and obediently sat down while MJ fetched coffee. In the short time she was gone, an odd feeling of cold emptiness crept over me. I suddenly realized I didn't want to be alone.

"By the looks of it, you need something stronger than coffee," she said, setting the disposable cups on the table and sliding into the chair across from me. "But unfortunately, I just started my shift and won't get off until morning. So. Spill it," she ordered. I smiled weakly. It was the same order she'd used all through college whenever she wanted all the juicy details of my dates. I didn't know where to begin, so I sat and sipped the hot coffee in silence.

"Obviously it has something to do with that man from the clinic," MJ prompted, pushing the tightly braided cornrows that slipped forward over her shoulder back where they belonged. "Who is he?"

"His name is Benjamin Hunter," I began, unsure of how I was going to say aloud what I wasn't sure I wanted to admit to myself.

"I know that. And?"

"He said…" In frustration, I flung up my hands and blurted out, "He said he was my father."

She raised one eyebrow at me, unimpressed by this monumental announcement. "That's it? That's what's got you all flustered?" She slouched back in her chair in disappointment. "Lots of people end up with some form of dementia at the end. You probably just remind him of his daughter or something. Heck, he probably said the same thing to every nurse who went into his room. Why is it bothering you so much if you know it isn't true?"

"He said he loved my mother, but she left him. He mentioned a letter and wanting to tell me something."

"So, what made you think he meant you specifically?"

"He apologized for something that happened a long time ago. I'd forgotten about it, but when he brought it up…I remembered. How would he know about that,

MJ?" I paused before revealing the most disturbing part. "And then there's the eyes."

"Eyes? What do you mean?" She sat up straighter, intrigued by the possibility of new evidence.

"We have the same eyes." I could still picture his green eyes clearly in my mind. "And he called them Hunter-green. Just like Mom used to."

"Wow," MJ breathed. She took a drink of coffee as she contemplated the mystery with great interest. A fan of crime novels and soap operas, she loved all those situations that never happened in real life and this was certainly right up her alley. Suddenly, she slammed her empty cup down and looked up excitedly. "I bet your mom had an affair."

"Mary Jean!" I scolded. "That's my mother you're talking about. She would never have cheated on Dad."

"Or maybe they met while she was still engaged and it was too late to call off the wedding, so she had to break it off with him," she continued, thinking aloud.

I propped my overloaded head on one fist and let her ramble on, only half listening as she recalled various plots from her beloved soaps. "During one season, Mickey impersonated his twin, Marty, to trick Jennifer into sleeping with him."

"Benjamin doesn't look anything like Dad," I said absently, staring into my cup.

"Well frankly, Ter, neither do you."

Chapter Three

Mary Jean's statement hit me like a ton of bricks. The question of my parentage was blindingly clear as I suddenly realized I didn't resemble either of my parents. True, I did have my mother's fine blonde hair, but her face was much narrower than mine. The father I'd grown up with had jet-black hair and very broad features. I'd always assumed my features were just a combination of their genes and that my eyes were inherited from one of their ancestors.

I drove home from the hospital in a mental fog, completely oblivious to the late night's freezing temperature. As I reached to unlock my front door, I suddenly froze in shock. I stood there on my porch, staring at the hand still holding the key. Both my parents had short fingers—my mother's had been thin, and my father's were thick. My fingers were long and graceful and an almost exact replica of the hand I'd held at the hospital. Shaking myself back to reality and feeling very exposed under the harsh porch light, I slipped inside and locked the door behind me.

Kicking off my snow-covered boots and hanging up my coat in the small entryway, I crossed the polished wood floor of the front room in my stocking feet. Even though I'd lived in this house long enough to add my own personal touch to the decor, much of it still remained unchanged and outdated. The furniture and wallpaper were from my grandfather's time. Possibly even longer. I just saw no need in spending money to replace things that still served their purpose even if I hardly ever used them. The dining room came complete with a sturdy buffet table and a massive China hutch filled with antiques I never touched. The only room that looked thoroughly modern was the kitchen I renovated shortly after moving in. I replaced the clunky gas stove with a sleek, efficient flattop and installed a dishwasher and microwave. I honestly don't know how anyone lived without them.

A flick of a switch turned on the overhead light in the old-fashioned sitting room my grandmother probably kept immaculate and only used for company. I dropped heavily onto the old couch and pulled a fluffy blanket around me for comfort and to hide the hands I didn't want to think about. My eyes wandered around what I now referred to as my living room, picking out the items I'd kept from my mother and the ones left by those who lived here before me. The only possessions that were solely mine were the self-help books I always felt compelled to buy in an effort to better understand myself. Even the old, upright piano in the corner was the one from my childhood. Although I had a passion for playing the piano, I never took the time to play much anymore.

Fleetingly, I wondered if Benjamin Hunter was a musician, too. No one else in my family played any musical instruments and those long-fingered hands were perfect for the piano. Wouldn't it be great to play with someone instead of always alone? What would it have been like to have Benjamin as a father? Would we have sat side-by-side on the piano bench and played duets while my mother smiled down at us with a look of pure happiness and love? When I realized I was actually wishing for this complete stranger to be my father, I shook my head to clear the thought.

"I can't deal with this right now," I said aloud to the empty living room. "Nope. Not gonna do it. I'll just make something to eat, get a good night's sleep, and deal with this tomorrow."

In the kitchen, I switched on my small radio as a distraction and hummed along with the music as I reheated leftovers in the microwave. The soft jazz of my favorite station calmed my nerves and made me feel safe and comfortable. Mom used to love it as well and listened to her jazz records whenever Dad was at work. For some reason I never understood, my father absolutely hated jazz.

With my stomach filled, I climbed the narrow stairway, my feet tired and heavy. Of the four rooms on the second floor, I only used the master bedroom. The other bedrooms were now merely for storage, so I kept their doors closed all winter to conserve heat. I took a quick shower and crawled under my heated blanket, determined not to think about Benjamin Hunter. Yet try as I might, I could only toss and turn as my mind replayed every scene and what it all could mean.

Before the sun even had a chance to rise, I gave up trying to sleep and decided to head back to the hospital. I got dressed, slipped into my winter coat and boots, and pulled a stocking cap over my unbrushed blonde hair.

When I stepped out onto the porch, I was disappointed to see the fresh blanket of snow covering the neighborhood yards, cars, and roofs. At least the city snowplow and sand truck had already been through so the roads were passable. Unfortunately, there was the inevitable mound of snow across the driveway I knew my Beetle wouldn't be able to break through. I brushed off the three inches of snow from the car and let the engine and defrost warm up as I attacked the dirty lump of street snow, clearing just enough to get out of the driveway. I made myself a mental note to call my neighbor at a more reasonable hour to shovel the rest along with the sidewalk.

MJ was just finishing her overnight shift when I walked through the door of the hospital. She looked me up and down then shook her head as she said, "You look like death warmed over, Girl."

"Thanks a lot," I said, my voice gruff from lack of sleep.

Her voice softened with concern. "You came to see him again, didn't you?"

"Yeah. Is he any better?" I was too distracted to notice the sad look on her face. But when she didn't answer me right away, I knew the reason. I let out a long sigh. "He didn't make it, did he?"

"I was just coming to tell you. And to give you this." She held out a large, manila envelope.

I started to reach for it, then realized what the envelope contained. "Wait a minute. Are those his…" I snatched my hand back as if the innocent-looking envelope held something as dangerous as nitroglycerin. "Why were you bringing me his belongings? Did you steal them? I mean, I was curious about the guy, but not *that* curious."

"Ter. Look." She shoved it closer and tapped one fingernail on it to draw my attention to the neatly printed label. *Benjamin Hunter* was filled in as the deceased, and the recipient's name was *Teresa Billings*.

"But...but..." was all I could manage as I numbly took the envelope. I was so tired and confused. Now, the one person who could help answer the questions my brain fixated on all night was gone.

"I didn't think you'd want the clothes," MJ was saying. "They were pretty shabby and worn. I don't think even Goodwill would've wanted them."

I turned the envelope over and over. There didn't seem to be much in it, but I could hear the muffled jingle of keys rattling inside. MJ watched me carefully. She knew me better than any other person in the world, and it hurt her for me to look so lost. I was usually the stable one, the voice of reason, the one taking control. Now for the second time in less than twelve hours, she took charge and steered me toward her car.

"I hope you don't work today, because you're coming home with me," she announced, daring me to defy her. I didn't even try.

We arrived at her single-story suburban house just as her husband, Ron, was leaving for work. He raised an eyebrow at my disheveled, pale appearance but didn't comment as MJ leaned in his car window to kiss him goodbye. I gave a half-hearted wave as he drove off, then she took my hand and led me into the house like a child.

"Ron's still trying to talk me out of working nights," she said as we stomped the snow from our boots and unbundled ourselves in the small entryway that led directly into the main living area. "He says since he got promoted to Detective III, he's making enough money for me to quit. Not bad for the only African American in the department. Anyway, if I do, then maybe we can finally start working on a family. Time is running out, I guess. We're not getting any younger, are we?"

She rattled on to fill the silence and tension coming from me as she led the way through their tiny, yet neat, living room and into the bright kitchen. She pulled a chair out from the small, butcher-block table as she passed by and I took the implied invitation to drop my numb body onto it. While she bustled around making coffee, I sat staring at the envelope I placed in the middle of the table like the world's saddest centerpiece. When she finally set the coffee cups in front of us, she gave up the small talk and stared at it with me.

"Why me?" I finally ventured, pushing my hair behind my ears instead of hiding behind it. "How did he know my full name? I didn't tell him, and my clinic badge only has my first name on it."

"Maybe he knew who you were longer than you thought." When I still didn't move, she asked, "Want me to open it?"

I shook my head, finally picking it up. As I unlatched the flap, the keys I'd heard before slid out onto the tabletop with a soft clink along with a battered wallet.

No ring or even a watch. Tipping the envelope up and giving it a shake brought out two smaller envelopes; one old and faded, one new and crisp.

I fingered the keys absently. There were only two keys on the ring. The larger one had a number on it, and I assumed it was the key to an apartment. The smaller one looked like a locker or file cabinet key. I left the wallet where it landed. It seemed an invasion of privacy to open such a personal item.

I picked up the faded envelope and saw it was addressed to Benny Hunter in Detroit, Michigan. There was no return address. The new envelope had my name written on it, so I felt I had to read it sooner or later. With a deep breath for strength, I took out the single sheet of paper and read it—silently at first, then aloud for MJ.

Dear Teresa,

I'm glad you came to see me. You must have lots of questions. If I can't talk to you again, you can find all your answers in my apartment.

I never got to tell you how sorry I was about your mother. I wasn't allowed. I never meant to hurt you. I'm proud of you and have always prayed for your happiness.

"It isn't signed," I said.

"Let me see." MJ took the letter and studied the writing. "This is Susan's handwriting. She must've written it for him last night after you left."

"How…I mean, when did he go?"

"About three this morning. His heart just stopped while he was unconscious, so he didn't suffer in the end. They didn't have much hope for him in the first place."

"Did you look at his history? How bad was he?"

"Looked like he had a hard life," she began as she refilled her cup. I hadn't touched mine. "Confidentially speaking, he'd been in for liver complaints a while back, the doctor's note said it was probably alcohol-related. Another time, for chronic cough. They'd suggested he have a scan for lung cancer, but he didn't have insurance. Things like that."

"Great," I moaned, laying my head on my folded arms. I was still hoping this was all a bad dream but knew I wasn't that lucky. "My supposed father was an alcoholic chain smoker."

"You don't know that," she said quickly.

"I guess I won't know anything for sure," I said without raising my head. "I can't very well ask him anymore, can I?"

"Aren't you going to go to his apartment?" she asked in surprise. Her curiosity was something I knew I could never match. When I didn't respond, she said, "At least open the other envelope. They said it was in his coat pocket. Looks like it's been there a long time."

I finally raised my head and reached for the battered envelope. The writing on the paper was barely legible. It looked like it had been folded and unfolded numerous times and was wrinkled badly as if crushed. There were even spots where the ink had bled as if it had gotten wet. As I read, I realized I knew the handwriting very well. It was my mother's neat, careful script. The same writing as on the birthday cards from her I still kept in the bottom of my jewelry box.

Benny,
Your daughter has Hunter-green eyes.
Peg

I sat completely numb staring at the letter until MJ's curiosity got the best of her. She whipped the paper out of my hand and read it herself.

"Wow," was all she could say. When she saw my state of shock, she quickly pulled a bottle from a nearby shelf and poured me a small glass. I mechanically obeyed her order to drink, and the fire burning down my throat woke me more effectively than an entire pot of coffee.

"What are you trying to do, kill me?" I sputtered.

"It worked, didn't it?" she answered over her shoulder as she replaced the bottle of brandy. "Well?" she asked when she returned to the table. "What do you think?"

"I don't know," I said miserably and finished off the rest of the liquor. I knew I'd probably regret drinking it with nothing in my stomach, but I desperately needed a crutch right then. "What do *you* think?"

"I think you should find out what answers he has for you at his apartment. Or at least talk to your dad and see what he says."

"I don't know if I can," I said truthfully. "We barely talk as it is. How can I just show up and ask him something so…personal?"

"True," MJ agreed, nodding her head. "You two act more like acquaintances than father and daughter. Were you closer before he got remarried?"

I thought about my relationship with my remaining parent. Since he sold our house to move in with his new bride and I moved into the ancestral home after graduating college, it felt like the glue holding us together had let go. Without the constant memories of my mom surrounding us, we were just two separate people who used to share the same house. I was invited to holidays but felt it was mostly obligatory and usually ended up working instead.

"I suppose we were, but it's really hard to say. I know Dad was always there for me growing up, and I can't say I ever felt neglected, but I don't remember him ever being as loving as Mom was with me. I would've said that's just how he was, but now I see him being all lovey-dovey with Charlotte and her family and know that's not true. I think that just makes it harder to spend time with him knowing he was capable of showing love but just didn't."

"Is there anyone else you could talk to who knew your mother before you were born?" MJ asked.

I immediately thought of Claire. "There's my Godmother. She was Mom's best friend in high school. She was kind of like a fun aunt when I was growing up, but I haven't talked to her in years. Last I heard she'd moved to Nashville to work at one of the recording studios. I get Christmas and birthday cards from her still, but I don't have her number or anything."

MJ gave a dismissive flip of her hand. "That's no problem. We can just ask Ron for help. What's the good of being married to a police detective if you don't use him now and again?"

Her comment struck me just as she'd intended, and we both burst out laughing. The laughter, combined with the brandy, eased the lingering tension I'd carried since Benny Hunter collapsed at the clinic.

"Alright, I'll think about it," I promised, sliding everything safely back inside the envelope. "I at least want to ask Ron about the legalities of going to Benjamin Hunter's apartment. I mean I didn't even know the guy."

MJ snorted and rolled her eyes. "You've got his keys and written permission. That's pretty much a solid invitation. What more do you need?"

Chapter Four

There was no obituary in the paper that week for Benjamin Hunter. Either he didn't have any family to write one, or they weren't from around Eagle Creek. I called the hospital morgue, but they couldn't give me any more information other than his remains had been released to his power of attorney. Not where he'd been taken or even a name, only that he'd been claimed and was no longer their responsibility.

I felt a pang of regret but wasn't entirely sure why. I wasn't responsible for him, either. Why would I be? Just because he believed we shared the same blood didn't necessarily make it true. Several times a day, I found myself reopening the two letters, staring at them as if they could speak.

"I don't know if you were who you said you were," I told the keys in his absence, "and I don't even know what kind of person you might've been. I'm sorry you didn't have any family to be with you at the end, but…"

The shrill ring of the telephone interrupted my speech and made me jump. I hurried to answer it with my heart beating like a runaway engine, hoping it wasn't MJ reminding me once again of our plans to meet at the Eagle Creek Supper Club tomorrow night. She was more excited than I was to 'get to the bottom of the mystery' as she put it, and talk to Ron while we ate the restaurant's Friday night all-you-can-eat-fish special. The stoic man's voice on the other end was definitely not MJ. I listened carefully, replying in all the right places, all the while inwardly feeling like this had to be a dream. After writing down the pertinent information, I called the clinic.

"Hey, Teresa, what's up?" Jess asked when she picked up the phone.

"Hey, Jess. I hate to do this to you, but I have to take tomorrow off."

"Anything wrong?" she asked, the genuine concern in her voice warming my heart. "You're not getting sick, too, are you?"

"No. I'm fine, I just have an appointment out of town I have to make."

There were a few seconds of silence before she spoke again. "Does this have anything to do with that guy you told me about? The one that almost died here, told you he was your dad, and then gave you his apartment key?"

I couldn't help but smile at how she read my mind so effortlessly. "Unfortunately, yeah, it does. Sorry for the short notice and I'll try to make it up to you somehow. Can you transfer me to Sondra? Hopefully, she can find someone to cover for me so you're not short-staffed."

"Sure. Good luck with whatever it is and let me know if there's anything I can do to help."

Touched by the sentiment and the genuine caring in her voice, I promised I would before she sent my call up to our scheduler's office. After taking five minutes to convince Sondra I honestly had a legitimate reason for not being able to come in, she finally agreed to find someone else to take my hours. Of course, she couldn't agree without making several comments about how difficult it would be at this late notice to make sure I felt as guilty as possible. When I hung up with her, I immediately dialed MJ's number.

"So help me, Ter, if you're calling to cancel on me because you're picking up even more hours at work, I'm going to personally come down there and drag you out by your hair," she warned without even saying hello.

"I'm sorry," I apologized sincerely. "Yes, I'm canceling, but no it's not for work."

"Then why? I thought you wanted our help." She sounded hurt and disappointed, but I couldn't tell if it was for the missed opportunity to talk mystery, or because she knew Ron would try and find an excuse not to waste money going out to eat if I wasn't going to be there.

"I still do," I reassured her. "And I promise to make it up to you, but I have to go out of town tomorrow and I won't make it back in time."

"What for?"

"The reading of Benjamin Hunter's will."

~~~~~

Since it was a seven-hour drive between Eagle Creek and Detroit, I packed a small suitcase and booked a hotel room for the night. My appointment was at 3:00 Friday afternoon, but since I didn't trust the Midwest winter weather, I set my alarm for 5:00 a.m. so I could
~~~~~

be on the road by 6:00. I figured that should give me enough leeway in case the roads were bad and allow for a few stops along the way. Since I didn't have any plans for Saturday, I would have all day to drive home.

I couldn't believe my luck. Not only was the traffic light, but the sprinkling of salt on the streets kept the Volkswagen's tires from slipping on the frost. By my first pitstop for breakfast, the sun broke through the last lingering clouds and warmed the I94 blacktop enough that it was completely clear and dry the rest of the way. It was a long drive around the southern part of Lake Michigan, so I had a lot of time to think. Maybe too much. By the time I reached Detroit, my nerves were strained almost to their limits imagining what Benjamin Hunter's will would reveal.

After checking into the hotel and depositing my belongings, I got directions to the attorney's office from the front desk clerk. I was happy to discover it was a mere four blocks away. The afternoon was unseasonably warm, so I gave my poor, overworked Beetle a break and walked instead. I had more than enough time to saunter along and window-shop, the fresh air and sunshine helping to ease my anxiety. By the time I sat down in the tastefully simple office, I was as calm and clear-headed as I could get under such an unusual circumstance.

The weather the next day, though, reflected my mood perfectly. The gray skies, intermittent sleet, rain, and wind gusts on the drive back from Detroit mirrored my sadness, confusion, exhaustion, and anxiety. After the previous day's meeting and a half-eaten fast-food supper, I tossed and turned all night, only getting two hours of sleep at best. The Saturday interstate was packed with weekend traffic, kicking up road sludge every time they sped past me, causing my windshield washer to run dry before I was halfway home. It took me an extra two hours of tense driving on my trip home due to the weather, traffic, and the need to stop at a small town's Walmart to replenish my washer fluid. Not to mention the extra stops for caffeine to keep me alert, which also required extra restroom stops. By the time I reached my house that evening, it was already dark, and I was both physically and mentally exhausted.

MJ left several voicemail messages reminding me to call her as soon as I got in, but I just couldn't bring myself to spend what would probably be a good hour on the phone with her. Being a detective's wife, she could probably give her husband a run for his money when it came to interrogating. I wanted to leave it until morning, but just as I was climbing into bed, the phone rang and I knew if I tried to ignore it, she would only keep calling and I'd never be able to get to sleep.

"What happened?" MJ asked before I could even say hello.

"Can we please wait to talk about it? I'm just too tired," I said, unashamed of the whine in my voice. "What about tomorrow afternoon?"

"But Ron and I are going to be at his mom's all day tomorrow," she whined back. "It's his nephew's baptism and you know how long those family parties last."

“Then why don’t we meet at Culver's between our shifts Monday? I promise I’ll be much more coherent then.”

She sighed but could tell I was in no mood to change my mind. “As long as you also promise not to get yourself talked into picking up a second shift,” she warned.

“Don’t worry. After what happened during my last double, I’m not planning on picking up another anytime soon, even if they beg me.” As soon as I set the receiver down, I collapsed onto my pillow and was soon fast asleep.

Chapter Five

Mary Jean was waiting for me in the parking lot when I reached the restaurant. Despite the dip in temperature and steady, biting wind, she leaned against her car with a scarf protecting the lower half of her face. I was still in my scrubs and sneakers with my hair up in a bun from work while MJ wore trendy jeans and fur-lined boots because she always changed clothes at the hospital.

"Did you meet any new family members at work today?" she joked as I climbed out of my car. When I gave her a scathing look, she held up her hands in surrender. "Sorry. Obviously too soon yet."

Showing great restraint at least for her, she waited until after we'd ordered our food and found a quiet table in the back corner before demanding the details.

"He left everything to me," I said simply as we removed our coats and hung them on the back of our chairs. "Whatever's in his apartment and a few bank accounts. The lawyer said he was an only child, never married, and had no living relatives that he knew of. His parents died about 15 years ago and that's when Benny made out his will. He hadn't changed a word of it since."

"So it's *Benny* now, is it?"

I rolled my eyes and she smiled, pleased with my reaction. “That’s what the letter and his attorney called him,” I explained. “Somehow I get the feeling it fits him better than *Benjamin*.”

We paused the conversation as our food arrived, then MJ leaned excitedly over her butter burger. “You’re saying the lawyer knew him? Personally? Did he tell you about him? Who he was, what he was like, and the whole secret daughter stuff?”

“Well…” I popped a French fry into my mouth and chewed before answering. MJ gave me a warning look that said if I was going to use my food as a distraction technique, she would dump the entire tray on the floor. I quickly swallowed and continued. “Apparently, he was a musician or something. He came back to Detroit just long enough to take care of his parents’ things, sell their house, make out his will, and was gone again. I drove past the hardware store his parents used to own, but everything in the neighborhood was boarded up and deserted like an urban ghost town. The lawyer didn’t know anything about my mother or what Benny was doing in Eagle Creek, but I found out that the address on his license was current. The will also said he'd been saving money for the daughter he'd never met, and I was given some papers I’ll have to take to the bank to take over his accounts. But, come on, you saw his clothes. He couldn’t have had much money if he dressed like that, didn’t have insurance, and came to West Side Clinic.”

MJ silently chewed her sandwich while she thought about what I'd just told her. “Did the will say the money was to go to you specifically or just his daughter?" she blurted out.

"Both. But the lawyer assured me that as long as I was mentioned specifically, it was all legal—real daughter or not. I don't know if I want to go to the bank," I admitted.

"Why not?" she asked. "He wanted you to have it."

"But he didn't even know me. What am I supposed to do with a stranger's money?"

"What if what he said was true? He wouldn't be a stranger then, would he?" she insisted.

"But I don't know for sure."

"Then donate it to some charity. Give it to a soup kitchen or women's shelter or something. It's legally yours and better than just leaving it unclaimed in the bank."

By the end of our meal, MJ effectively talked me into promising to visit the bank the very next day. I couldn't think of any good reason not to. Just because I had access to whatever Benny had willed to me didn't mean I had to decide what to do with it right away.

Yet when I got home from the bank the next day, I had even more to think about than where to donate a poor man's meager life savings. I made myself a cup of tea and sat staring at the manilla envelope on the kitchen table. It reminded me so much of the one I'd received from the hospital. When the phone rang, I knew who it was even before answering.

"So?" MJ asked. "Tell me quick. I'm on my lunch break, but I just couldn't wait."

“I’m…dumbfounded,” I admitted as I pulled the bank printouts from the envelope and spread them out across the kitchen table. “You won’t believe what I found out.”

I briefly recounted the trip to the bank and my shock when the bank manager first informed me about Benjamin Hunter’s accounts. One was his checking account, which held very little and looked like he only kept enough in it to pay necessary bills. Another was a savings account which looked like it had been steadily dwindling for the last twenty years and was nearly as meager as the checking account. The last account was what shocked me speechless.

“There was another savings account, and it was set up on my first birthday. On my eleventh birthday, the account’s beneficiary was officially changed to…Teresa Billings.”

“Wait! What?”

I unfolded the printout of the account’s progression over the years and scanned through the numbers again. It started out with only a couple hundred dollars for the first few years. Then one enormous deposit that I could only attribute to the sale of his parents’ house. Other than that, the deposits were sporadic. Sometimes twenty dollars, sometimes a hundred or more. Toward the end, the money seemed to trickle in slowly with even a year between deposits. But all that time, the interest grew.

“MJ, there’s hundreds of thousands of dollars sitting in that bank with my name on it.”

There was a clatter from the other line and I heard a muffled, "Jesus, Mary, and Joseph," as she picked up the dropped phone receiver. "Are…are you absolutely certain it's yours? That it wasn't meant for some other Teresa Billings?"

"I asked the bank manager the same question, and she showed me the original paperwork. It not only has my name but my date of birth and social security number. I have no idea how he would have gotten those, and the manager didn't know either. She said it was set up as a trust fund that I wasn't to know about unless he told me himself or it was revealed by the executor of his will."

Looking over the papers again without the initial confusion of shock, I noticed one thing. In all that time, there were no withdrawals from the account with my name on it. Only deposits. Why hadn't he used at least some of that money for himself? It certainly looked like he needed it. He could've at least afforded better clothes and health insurance.

"What are you going to do with all that money?" MJ asked, probably picturing cartoon dollar signs in her head.

Mary Jean had been brought up pinching pennies to save enough to go to college while I came from a prominent, wealthy family. My parents made sure I was never spoiled, but I always had the security that I was well provided for. When my mother got sick, a lot of money was spent on medical bills and my inheritance shrank. Now that we earned our own living, MJ liked to spend her extra money on fine, showy things while I preferred to live much simpler.

"I'm not doing anything with it," I said firmly. "I plan on leaving it there while I sort things out. If I find out I don't actually have any right to that account—that there's some misunderstanding and I'm not the person Benny meant it for—I'll find the one who should. If I can't do that, I can always give it all away to charity."

"When I suggested you give it away, I was thinking of hundreds, not hundreds of thousands. You can't just give all that money away. Some of it, sure, but not *that* much. And you may never find out for sure if this guy actually had another daughter. How long are you planning to let that account sit there?"

"As long as it takes. Although, if you and Ron aren't busy Sunday, I'd like to come over and see if he can give me some investigation tips."

Regardless of MJ's continued debate, leaving the money where it was sounded like a good plan to me, and I was determined to stick to it. If Benny could go thirty years without touching an account meant for me, I could wait until I found out more about him and who really deserved his life savings.

Chapter Six

"Sure, I can poke around and see what I can find. To tell you the truth, MJ already asked, but I told her I wasn't going to pry unless you wanted me to," Ron said, giving his wife a pointed look. She turned her eyes innocently to their living room ceiling and shrugged one shoulder. "But I still think the best way to find out about the life of Benjamin Hunter is to go to his apartment. He told you in that letter your answers would be there."

"It still feels wrong to go into a stranger's apartment and look through his personal things," I argued. "Like violating his privacy or something."

"You have his written permission, key, and a will," he reminded me. "Legally, you have every right to be there. But if you still feel like you want backup, a witness, or just moral support, I'll come with you."

"The sooner the better, I always say," MJ piped up, already getting to her feet and pulling Ron up off the couch after her. "We have the time now. Let's go."

I was still reluctant, but Benny's wallet and keys were in my purse. I handed them both over to Ron and he drove us to the address listed on the driver's license. The air had warmed back above freezing once more, and as we stood on the sidewalk looking at the old brick building, we had to squint against the sunlight reflected off the snow.

"He didn't just live in the neighborhood of the clinic," MJ said, scowling at me as if I'd been keeping secrets from her. "This is the street you walk to and from work. Why didn't you say something?"

"I didn't even put two and two together," I admitted. "I don't really pay attention to building addresses. I just knew it was one of the streets I crossed."

The apartment building on the corner of Reynold and Jameson faced toward the West Side Health Clinic. It was old but not too run-down. Not nearly as nice as the older, stately part of town I lived in, yet there were no broken or boarded-up windows like some buildings on the other side of the clinic.

"I wonder if one of those was his," MJ continued, pointing to the windows overlooking Reynold Street. "He could've been watching you walk by almost every day for the last ten years. I can't believe you lived so close and had no idea he even existed!"

I shivered at the thought of being watched without my knowledge. Maybe my anxiety about walking alone at night was valid after all. As if reading my mind, Ron put a comforting arm around me as he said, "I'm pretty sure he wasn't stalking you, Teresa. If he knew you were the blonde woman walking past his place for so many years and the daughter he saved so much money for, he would've introduced himself long ago. Don't you think?"

Nodding in agreement, I forced my shoulders to relax. His logic made complete sense. How could someone know the person passing their window day after day and not at least attempt bumping into them? Benny had so many chances to tell me who he was and what he was doing. If he knew I was so close, why wouldn't he say something?

"Let's get this over with," I said, leading the way to the main entrance of the apartment building.

Ron paused to hold the door for a young mother struggling to carry a wiggly toddler, diaper bag, and four plastic grocery sacks into the building, and MJ took the opportunity to ask her if she knew where Benny's apartment number was located. Her hands too full to point, she jerked her chin toward the stairway leading down to the basement. We all thanked her as she continued down the hallway, the little girl in her arms giving us a cheery wave. As we walked down the darkened stairs, I shivered even though we were all bundled in coats and the hallway was adequately heated.

"I hope he didn't have a cat or something locked up in there for this long," MJ whispered.

I groaned at the thought. "Why'd you have to say that? I feel guilty enough as it is. I don't want to think about being responsible for killing a pet just because I waited so long to do this."

"I don't smell any animal waste or decay," Ron said in an eerily matter-of-fact way as we followed him down the dimly lit hallway to the last door.

Taking an experimental sniff, the only things I smelled were the dry odor of the dusty carpet and detergent from the laundry room at the other end of the hall. As Ron slipped the key in the lock, MJ and I huddled behind him, holding our breath in anticipation.

"Who're you?"

The gruff voice made me jump guiltily, my heart pounding in my chest. Ron, on the other hand, turned casually to the large man behind us.

"Are you the landlord?" he asked. His tone was polite, but we could tell he was taking mental notes of the man's pit-stained t-shirt and suspenders holding the grimy pants from falling from his sizable girth.

"That's right. What're you up to there? Get outta my building before I call the cops." From the way he looked at MJ and Ron with obvious distrust and arrogance, I could tell he was judging them by their color and felt an instant disgust toward him.

Ron remained calm as he held the key up in plain view. "We're not breaking in. We have the key."

"Where's the old man?" he asked, jabbing a thumb toward the unlocked door.

"I'm afraid he passed away," Ron answered coolly, then nodded his head toward me. "This is his beneficiary. We're here to look over his belongings."

"Well, then take 'em all with you. I need the room." He pointed one stubby finger at us as he added, "But not the appliances or furniture. This was a furnished apartment. I see any of my stuff being carted out, I call the cops."

"Is the rent paid up?"

I could tell Ron was beginning to lose his patience with the landlord by the way he exchanged politeness for directness.

"Well, yeah, but that don't matter now, does it?" the man sneered. "Just get his junk cleared out in the next coupla days so I can fill it again."

Ron's jaw clenched. MJ saw it too, and we both backed a step away from him. He was a tall, well-built man and an officer to boot. If this guy thought Ron could be intimidated just because of his color, that weasel of a landlord didn't know what he was in for. Ron squared his shoulders and put his hands on his hips. As he did so, his coat slid open revealing the badge and gun holster on his belt.

"If the rent is paid until the end of the month, you can't rent it until the end of the month. Miss Billings will pack his things and be gone by then. And I better not hear about you giving her any trouble, either. Understand?"

The landlord visibly shrank at the sight of the domineering policeman who filled the hallway with his imposing presence, staring at him so intently. He mumbled a half-hearted threat that I'd better be or else he'd change the locks, then scurried off down the hall, leaving us in peace.

Once we were inside the apartment with the door shut, I released my breath and relaxed. "Thanks, Ron. If you hadn't been here, I'd have probably just up and left." He smiled brightly, showing no trace of the ruthless cop he'd been earlier. Dropping the keyring in my hand, he gave me a wink before going off to search the bedroom.

"See?" MJ said, nudging me. "What'd I tell you? What's the use of having him if you don't use him?" We laughed, and I could see in her eyes how much pride and love she had for her husband.

There were only two rooms in the apartment, not including the extremely tiny bathroom. The bedroom was through a door off to the left, the kitchen was in the main living area. There was a bowl and spoon lying on a dish towel next to the sink, clean and dry and waiting for their owner to put them away. Other than that, the small counter was bare. Tacked to one of the two cupboard doors above the sink was a piece of paper, the writing so faded I had to walk closer to be able to read the words.

> *I love thee, O Lord, my strength. The Lord is my rock, my fortress, and my deliverer, my God is my rock, in whom I take refuge, my shield, and the horn of my salvation, my stronghold. Psalm 18*

Two small, street-level windows on one wall let in a minimal amount of light and only provided a view of people's feet as they walked down the sidewalk. A third window on another wall faced the neighboring building across the alley and was partially blocked by a dumpster. The only furnishings were a ragtag sofa and a second-hand easy chair, nothing I would consider as priceless as the landlord inferred. A make-shift bookshelf of wooden planks and empty milk crates held a small collection of books and a larger one of vinyl records with an old portable turntable propped open on a coffee table beside it.

What caught my full attention was what dominated the middle of the room. It was a collection of various musical instruments. From a shiny baby grand piano all the way down to a clarinet, there were at least a dozen of them in all. They looked well cared for, but you could tell they'd also been well used. I walked around gazing at them, not daring to touch anything.

"Nothing much in there," Ron said, returning from the bedroom. He handed me a book, which I took automatically. "Only this on the floor next to a small bed. Nothing under the bed. No closet. There was a dresser, but not much in there, either. This guy didn't even have a TV. Did he say what you were supposed to look for?"

I shook my head as I turned the book over in my hands. It took me a few seconds to realize the old, worn cover was that of a well-used Bible. Opening the front cover, MJ looked over my shoulder, reading aloud what had been written inside, the penmanship neat and beautiful.

Rejoice in your hope, be patient in
tribulation, be constant in prayer.
Romans 12:12.

"Well, at least he was a Christian. He couldn't have been too bad of a guy, then," she added, obviously trying to make me feel better.

I raised one eyebrow skeptically at her. "People have done horrible things and still claimed to be Christians, MJ. If anything were to convince me he was a decent man at this point, it's the instruments. I've never met a bad person who loved music as much as he must've."

MJ just shrugged her shoulders as she wandered off to look for anything interesting. I continued to walk around with my arms folded around the Bible, reading the titles of a few of the books and albums. It was like I was spying on someone's private life, and I wasn't comfortable with it at all. The tiny room felt like it was getting even smaller, so I opened one of the windows for some fresh air to push back the threat of claustrophobia. It was then I realized that at this angle Benny could have seen me pass by. Did he know who I was? If he did, why didn't he say something earlier? Why did he wait until it was too late for him to answer my questions?

"I think I found something," MJ called to us from the far corner of the room. She'd moved a laundry hamper to reveal a two-drawer filing cabinet. Ron and I joined her, but neither MJ nor I wanted to open it. Ron gave a sigh and muttered something that sounded suspiciously like 'women' and tugged on the handles.

"Locked. Do you have a key?" he asked me. I rummaged in my purse for the keyring he'd given back to me. The smaller key fit the lock on the cabinet and Ron opened the top drawer.

The drawer was filled with sheet music. As I thumbed through it, I noticed it was mostly jazz, and some must have been Benny's own compositions. I would've been content to spend time studying the music closer, but MJ interrupted my perusing.

"I don't think a bunch of music is what he meant to answer your questions. What's in the other one."

The bottom drawer contained hanging folders, neatly labeled by years. Looking in one of them, I saw check stubs, receipts, and tax information. At least he was well organized, I thought. Opening the drawer further, I saw behind the files were several composition notebooks. Pulling the first one out, I briefly noted a number and date on the front before opening it to read the first page aloud.

July 4, 1970
So my daughter will know the truth.
Benjamin Hunter

For whatever was written in former days
was written for our instruction, that by
steadfastness and by the encouragement of
the scriptures we might have hope.
Romans 15:4

"He must've really liked quoting Romans," I muttered.

"There must be almost a dozen notebooks back there," MJ exclaimed, looking over my shoulder. She reached in, excited about what they might contain, but I held her hand back.

"What do you think I should do, Ron? You're the detective."

I carefully replaced the notebook and stood up, unconsciously wiping my hands on my pants as if I'd just handled incriminating evidence. Ron wandered around the small room with a serious look on his face. I could imagine him doing the exact thing at a crime scene.

"Well," he began, suddenly very business-like, "since he died of natural causes at the hospital, there's no reason for the police to be involved. You have the legal right to everything that belonged to him. My professional suggestion is to clean out the apartment as soon as possible to avoid any more confrontations with that sorry excuse for a landlord. If you don't want to keep something, sell it or give it away."

I looked around at the books, records, and gleaming instruments. This was all too overwhelming for me. How could I be responsible for the treasured possessions of a man I never knew? Ron saw how troubled I was and put an arm around my shoulders, giving me a gentle squeeze.

"On a personal note, I suggest you talk to your mother's friend and your dad, read those journals, and find out the truth once and for all. It's the only way to put your mind at ease."

I nodded and heaved a deep sigh. He was right. I'd have to know the truth about Benny Hunter and my mother before I could sleep well again. As it was, my dreams had been taken over by glimpses of the past as my subconscious tried to answer the questions I couldn't even contemplate while awake. More often than not, I woke up with the memory of my last meeting with Benny still fresh in my mind as if it had happened only hours before.

Chapter Seven

It still took a few days to clean Benjamin's meager belongings out of the apartment since I refused to work on it alone. The three of us could only meet for a few hours after my day shift and before MJ's night shift. She helped me pack up clothes and utensils for Goodwill, and Ron enlisted his new partner's help to haul the rest of the boxes to my house when they got off work.

"Teresa, this is William. William, Teresa," Ron said, making the briefest of introductions as they removed their coats and added them to the pile already on the kitchen counter.

William held out his hand and I shook it, surprised at how warm the long fingers felt and how gentle his hold was even though the muscles showing under his tight, long-sleeved t-shirt professed he could have crushed my fingers to jelly. He was also taller than I was, with my eyes only coming up to his chin, so I had to tip my head back slightly to look up at him. He gave me a small smile and I found myself smiling back.

"Sorry for your loss," he said. "I had to clean out my grandma's place after she passed away last year and I know how hard it is to have to see their entire lives reduced to boxes labeled keep, donate, and toss."

"Um, thanks," I said, my mind going completely blank as I found myself staring into the most beautiful brown eyes framed by a fall of dark hair over his forehead and the longest lashes I'd ever seen on a man. "William, was it? Or do you go by Will or maybe Bill?"

"Actually, my nickname is Liam," he answered, his smile spreading enough to highlight the dimple on his right cheek. "William is usually just for work. But I pretty much answer to anything."

Finally finding the power to release his hand, I stepped back, and Liam joined Ron at the lineup of packed boxes along one wall. He easily hefted the one Ron assigned to him and I would have been blind not to appreciate the way his biceps tightened as he carried the box out of the apartment to Ron's waiting car.

"So? What do you think?" MJ whispered in my ear as she tugged playfully on my ponytail. I'd been so mesmerized by Liam's physique that I hadn't even heard her coming up behind me. "Ron's had him over to the house a few times and I pronounce him a great catch. He's thirty-five, originally from Michigan but has since converted to a Packer fan. He's cute, nice, funny, easy to talk to…and best yet, he's single."

I groaned, realizing their asking for his help was just a setup. "I'm not looking for anyone right now, MJ," I insisted. "Especially while I'm trying to figure out who I am."

"Sometimes you have to stop looking and just let it happen," she replied. "Come on, at least give him a chance. What do you have to lose?"

"How about my time, effort, and possible heartbreak?" I grumbled. "He can't be as nice as you think and look that good, too. Especially being single.

There's probably something he's really good at hiding, or there's some other really good reason he's still single. I just can't deal with the complications of a new man in my life on top of everything else right now."

MJ gave me a look that said I was being totally unreasonable. "I'm not telling you to marry the guy. I'm just saying he's a good guy who's fun to spend time with. What's wrong with that?"

I sighed at her persistence and went back to continue working my way through the records on the shelf. I heard the men return, but stubbornly refused to turn around to look at him again. I told myself I didn't need Ron and MJ setting me up. I didn't need anyone adding to my messed-up life right now. He couldn't be as great as MJ seemed to think because I'd been disappointed too many times already by handsome-looking men.

"Wow! What a nice-looking Steinway."

Liam's excitement caught my attention and I found myself looking over my shoulder despite my inner scolding. Liam was standing next to the baby grand piano, carefully lifting the lid to inspect the inside.

"You play?" I asked.

He gave me a grin and stood before the keyboard. Without even looking at the keys, he began to play and sing the chorus to Billy Joel's *Piano Man*. Perfectly. As if hypnotically drawn toward him, I wandered over to the piano, leaning against the side as I watched his fingers dance over the keys. It wasn't often I got to watch someone else play and his voice was so easy to listen to. Even when he finished and Ron and MJ loudly applauded, I continued to stare at the keyboard imagining a different set of fingers running up and down the keys. Ones that would no longer be able to play. Forcing myself back to the present, I pasted a smile on my lips.

"That was great. You're really good."

He lowered his head as if embarrassed by the praise and smiled what I could only call a boyish grin. While endearing, it also made me question if it was a genuine reaction, or one just made to look humble.

"Liam plays in a band," MJ offered, giving me a gentle poke in the side with her elbow.

"It's just a group of friends who like to get together and sing other people's songs," Liam said in answer to MJ. He then turned his attention to me. "Do you like music?"

Still mesmerized by his inhuman good looks, I honestly forgot he asked a question, so MJ answered for me. "She plays piano, mostly jazz, and she's really good."

"Really? Maybe I could hear you play sometime."

"Oh, um, maybe sometime," I answered, hoping he didn't insist on me playing that very minute because I couldn't remember one single song and wasn't even sure I could feel my fingers, anyway.

"What do you want to do about all these instruments?" MJ asked, holding up a trumpet and a set of drumsticks. "You don't know how to play any of these. And that piano is huge. It isn't going to fit in any of our cars."

I forced myself to look away from Liam and ran a hand along the polished surface of the tall, upright bass. I'd intentionally left the musical instruments for last because it was the hardest decision for me to make.

"I doubt Goodwill would want them. You could try selling them," MJ suggested.

"If you do that," Liam said, "could I put in a bid for the Yamaha set? Our drummer would love an upgrade, and this looks like it's barely been used."

"You could always donate the rest to a school," Ron suggested. "Music programs always seem to have tight budgets."

My head was shaking before I even realized I was doing it. "No. I can't deal with them right now. Liam, if you want the drums, you can have them. I'll decide about the rest later, but I'm keeping the piano." I resolutely closed the cover over the keys. "We'll just pack up what we can, and I'll call a moving company tomorrow to pick up the rest. They'll know the best way to move it out of here."

MJ shook her head and shrugged her shoulders. "Good thing you have that big ol' house and a lot of extra space."

The last thing we moved out was the filing cabinet. While the rest of the boxes were stowed away upstairs in the guest bedroom, I had Ron and Liam set the filing cabinet in the large doorway between the sitting and dining rooms. When choosing its new home, I didn't intentionally plan on having to walk past it every day, but it may have been my subconscious wanting it continuously visible, knowing I would have to deal with it eventually.

"Do you want us to move anything around so that the piano has a place to go?" Ron asked.

I walked around, trying to visualize the best place not only for it to fit, but would sound the best and have the best lighting. "Since I already have the upright in the living room, I think it should go in the dining room. If we move the China cabinet over to that wall and slide the table over, I think it'll go perfectly in that corner."

The two strong men easily switched everything around for me and I was ready for the final items left from Benjamin Hunter's life to blend into mine whether I was ready to accept them or not. I laid a hand on the top of the filing cabinet, both curious and skeptical about what I might discover inside its locked drawers.

"Do you need anything else?" Liam asked wiping a small amount of sweat from his forehead with the back of his hand.

"You were a big help," MJ interjected when I didn't answer right away. "Thanks so much."

"Yeah, thanks," I said, pulling myself back to the present again. "Sorry Ron dragged you along to help with my mess."

"I don't feel like I did a whole lot. I was kinda expecting to haul a trailer full of boxes. You must've moved quite a bit of it yourself."

I shook my head. "What you saw was pretty much all there was."

His eyebrows furrowed in doubt or curiosity, but he didn't comment, which raised him up in my perspective of him a bit. "Where would you like the wall hanging?"

"Wall hanging? I don't remember seeing anything on the apartment walls at all."

"Yeah, this one," Ron added, holding up a poster-sized, framed print. "It was in the bedroom."

I ran my fingers along the etched, wooden frame and realized the picture was not dulled by age but by a layer of dust. Scrubbing the heel of my hand across the glass, I studied the rolling black script printed over the background of a sunrise landscape.

"*And after you have suffered a little while, the God of all grace, who has called you to his eternal glory in Christ, will himself restore, establish, and strengthen you. 1 Peter 5:10.*"

I jumped slightly at the smooth, deep voice just behind me as Liam read the verse over my shoulder. I took a step to the side, nervous to be so close to him because he seemed too perfect, and I didn't trust it.

"Deep stuff," he continued, either ignoring my need to distance or thinking I was just giving him a better view of the print. "If it was the only thing on his walls and it was in his bedroom, it must've been really important to him. Like he wanted to remind himself every morning and every night that whatever happened to him was worth it. Probably brought him a lot of comfort, don't you think?"

"Now you're just showing off, Detective Olson," Ron joked, noticing the pinched look on my face and deflecting Liam's attention away from me. He leaned the frame against the wall and gave the other man a friendly punch in the shoulder. “Promote a guy to detective and suddenly he’s seeing clues and motives everywhere.”

“Well, I don’t know about you two detectives, but I think Teresa looks beat. Let’s get out of her hair and let her start going through things.” She tapped the top of the file cabinet on the last three words, giving me a pointed look. She’d offered to help me read through the journals, but I’d told her I wanted to do it myself.

“Hey, I’m sorry,” Liam apologized, already backing toward the door following Ron and MJ. “I didn’t mean anything by that. I really do like that verse.” He paused at the door, and I found myself staring into his intense eyes once more. “Sorry again for your loss. And I know people always say to let them know if they need anything, even when they don’t mean it…but I really do mean it. If you need anything…” He held out a business card to me, not letting go until he finished his sentence. “...anything at all—help with something or just need to talk—let me know.”

He went down the porch steps, turned and gave me a little wave, then climbed into the back seat of Ron’s car. I closed the front door and looked down at the card, a typical business card with Detective William Olson’s phone number and extension at the police station. But below the typed information was a personal phone number written in blue ink.

I sighed. “Great. That’s all I need right now. More complications in my life.”

Chapter Eight

I hadn't worked up the courage to open the bottom drawer of the filing cabinet again until nearly a month after Ron and Liam hauled it into my house. I contented myself instead with playing some of the pieces found in the top drawer on my new baby grand, rationalizing I was easing myself into the private life of Benjamin Hunter.

Each night after work, I would look through the songs and pick one to practice. Some I remembered from when I was young, some I recognized from the radio, some were written for other instruments I couldn't play, and some weren't even finished. I knew I was just procrastinating reading the journals, but still didn't feel I was ready to face whatever they possibly contained. Then one night, I came across an unfinished piece titled *Peg and Teresa.*

The sight of our names shook me, and I could only sit and stare at them at the top of the penciled-in sheet music. Knowing I just had to hear it, I sat at the piano and carefully laid it out on the music holder. After a brief study of the notes on the paper, I placed my hands on the piano keys and began the song.

It was beautiful. In the beginning, it was light and playful, then it turned soft and sultry. By the middle, I noticed the notes turned a little sad, then sharp and desperate. There was a bridge connecting the next part of the song, and it flowed into a quicker, livelier tune that I could only describe as proud. I was just coming to really enjoy the music when it suddenly stopped in the middle of a run. Obviously, he never got a chance to finish it.

When the notes stopped on the page, I froze with my fingers hovering over the keys. If the music and the title went together, Benny was very much in love with Peg, my mother, and proud of Teresa, his daughter.

At that moment, I knew I was ready to admit to the possibility of Benjamin Hunter being my father. That was when I finally opened the bottom drawer of the filing cabinet.

~~~~~

May 15, 2002

It took several more months to piece together all the information I could about Benny and my mother because I wanted it from every angle possible. Ron helped, discreetly finding everything I asked of him, and even found the phone number of my mother's friend, Claire.

"Teresa? It's great to hear from you," Claire exclaimed in happy surprise when I called. "How's my favorite Godchild?"

"Aren't I your only Godchild?" I asked, playing into our long-standing joke.

"Even if you weren't, you'd still be my favorite," she insisted as usual. "I haven't seen you since your college graduation. How have you been? Is everything okay? Are you okay?"
~~~~~

"I'm fine," I reassured her. "I just need to talk to you about Mom. And Detroit. Do you have time?"

There was a slight pause before she answered. "Um. Sure. But I don't know what…"

"I know about Benjamin Hunter."

There was silence on Claire's end of the line. I gripped my phone so hard, that I could barely feel my fingers as I waited for her reply. Finally, I heard her sigh. "I tried to get Peg to tell you the truth before she passed, but she made me promise never to talk about it."

"Mom's gone, Claire," I reminded her. "And now Benny's gone, too. I read his journals, so I know his side of the story. Now, I need to know hers, and you're the only one who can help me. I want to know everything."

"Teresa…" she began to argue, then stopped herself. "You know what? You're right. I think you should know…at least whatever I can tell you from my end. But not over the phone. I'll come up to Wisconsin this weekend. I can visit my parents and tell you everything I know."

Chapter Nine

July 1, 2002

It was a lot harder than I expected to track down the friends Benny wrote about in his journal. I didn't feel like I had to speak to them to confirm what he'd written, I just had an overwhelming desire to talk with someone who had known Benny personally. There had to be someone other than his deceased parents who should be told about his passing. It was just too sad to think he had no one else who cared about him.

The first person I had Ron search for was a minister. I figured he'd be the easiest one to track since there had to be records of which church he was assigned to or an obvious trail if he'd switched from the one Benny mentioned to another. The good news was Ron was able to find his name in the Michigan church registry. The bad news was that the man had passed away years ago. Without me even having to ask, Ron sent an email with an announcement of Benny's death to the church in Detroit, just in case someone remembered him.

Ron found it more difficult to track down the other person Benny mentioned the most in his journals and told me to give him a few days to work on it. I decided after two days to stop by his office at the police station after work to see how his search was going. If he was still running into dead ends, I was going to have him give up and tell myself I was satisfied with the facts I'd collected in my notebook so far.

I entered the police station and immediately sighed at the air-conditioned relief from the stagnant, humid, 90-degree heat outside. I'd changed into a pair of shorts and tank top before I left work. My scrubs were too damp after so many hours in a clinic without central air and we weren't allowed to wear street clothes no matter how much we sweat and complained. Now my skin celebrated the open, cool air and I already didn't look forward to going back outside into the unforgiving summer sun and humidity.

"Teresa!"

I slowly turned, already recognizing the voice coming from across the room. Liam was walking down the aisle of desks, carrying two coffee cups. He was wearing a short-sleeved, button-down shirt in a light tan color that made his eyes and eyelashes even more captivating below the locks of hair across his forehead. His dress slacks fit his strong legs as if made specifically for him and his tie was slightly loosened, and the top button undone framing the hollow just below his Adam's apple. He looked even more handsome than the tight t-shirt and jeans I'd last seen him in.

"Liam. Hi." I tried to push the stray strands of hair that had escaped my bun during work back behind my ears, self-consciously wishing I was wearing something a little less revealing.

"I was hoping I'd see you again. Are you here to talk to Ron?"

"Yeah, he was checking on something for me. Is he busy?"

"He's got someone in his office right now," he said, holding up the coffee cups as evidence. "Can I get you anything?" I smiled at his thoughtfulness as I shook my head. "Then I'll just let him know you're here. You can have a seat at my desk."

He nodded his head toward a neat and orderly desk just outside of Ron's office. I perched on the edge of the solid, wooden chair beside it, hoping I wouldn't end up with embarrassing marks on the backs of my legs. Liam delivered the coffee and returned just seconds later to sit in his padded swivel chair.

"So, how have the interviews been going?" he asked. When I raised my eyebrows in surprise, he gave me an embarrassed grin. "Yeah, Ron told me a little about what you're doing. I thought it was a little odd that you were cleaning out your dad's apartment but looked so confused by everything in it. I get it now and told Ron I'd help in any way I could."

"Just don't let MJ find out you might know more about things than she does," I warned. "I told her I wanted to wait until I got the whole story before telling her."

He raised his right hand. "I already swore an oath to Ron."

We fell into an awkward silence for a minute while I watched the other officers doing various tasks at their own desks.

"I'm glad I saw you," Liam said, bringing my attention back to him. He held out a flyer and I took it, reading the advertisement for the July 4th police benefit. "I wondered if you wanted to come to this. The band I'm in is going to be playing…if you're interested in hearing us, that is. Scott will be using the drums we got from you," he added as if it might sway my decision.

Since I no longer got called to cover shifts at the clinic, I actually had the holiday off for once. MJ had already insisted I go, and now I knew why. So I could see Liam's band. I had to admit that after reading Benny's journals, I was curious about what they would play.

"I already told Ron and Mary Jean I'd go with them," I said and felt a little pang of regret when Liam's smile faltered.

"Teresa," Ron called from his office doorway. "Come on in."

I stood up and smiled down at Liam, handing him back the flyer. "But I'll see you there." A smile of genuine happiness spread across his face before I turned to join Ron.

"That was one helluva smile," Ron whispered with a teasing wink as he closed the door, cutting us off from Liam and the rest of the officers. I scowled at him, and he wisely mimed locking his lips and throwing away the key. He sat at his desk and folded his hands together on top of the scattering of manilla folders, suddenly all business. "I have to admit, this one was a lot harder than I thought it would be. I don't know how many places I called only to get another place to try. So many dead ends. Then I finally struck gold," he added, his lips stretching into a wide grin.

"You found him?" I couldn't keep the excitement from my voice as I slid forward on my chair.

"Now, I talked to this guy's daughter, and she said he doesn't hear very well anymore so it's too hard for him to talk on the phone. Even if you flew down to the nursing home in New Orleans, it would still probably be hard to communicate with him."

"Oh, great," I groaned. "All that work you did to find him, and I still won't be able to get any answers. He's probably too old to remember Benny, anyway."

Ron held up one hand to stop my pity party. "But she said if you want to mail your questions to him, he can read them and write you back. Said his eyesight is good and his mind is as sharp as ever. Would that work for you?"

It was exactly the ray of sunshine I needed right then. "Thank you! Thank you!" I jumped up and ran around the desk to wrap my arms around his shoulders. He stiffened at the unexpected show of affection but patted my arm in an awkward response. "That's perfect! I couldn't have done this without all your help, Ron. Thank you so much!"

Chapter Ten

The Independence Day Benefit Picnic was the police department's biggest event of the year, raising money for the families of disabled and fallen officers as well as updating their technology. One year they even earned enough through raffle sales to be able to start a K-9 unit. The city park was filled with families enjoying the various bands playing on the erected stage, eating food from the lineup of stands, watching the little league baseball tournament, or playing games set up for all ages. The uncomfortable heat wave of the previous days had ebbed enough to be tolerable, and there was a slight breeze that not only drove the humidity down but kept the mosquitoes and gnats at bay.

MJ and I grabbed our meals, consisting of brats with sauerkraut, potato salad, fruit salad, and root beer, and found a table close enough to the stage to be able to see the performers, yet far enough away from the speaker system to still be able to hold a conversation. I settled on the plastic chairs, wishing I'd worn capris instead of shorts because my legs would inevitably be sticking to the seat before we were done eating. Luckily, I'd worn my hair in a high bun so the wind wouldn't blow it around my face all day.

"I heard you and Liam were chatting at the station," MJ said, feigning innocence as she dug her plastic spoon into her pile of potato salad.

I groaned, mentally taking back the hug I'd given Ron that day. He obviously didn't understand exactly what the locking lips gesture meant. Then again, I also reminded myself of how MJ always seemed to know when someone was keeping juicy information from her and how to most effectively get that information from said someone.

Ignoring my childish response, she continued, "You know I wouldn't mind if you two wanted to spend the day together. I actually wish you would. Then you could see what a nice guy he is."

"I told him I'd see him here," I admitted, "but I don't want anyone—especially you—thinking this is a date. I still have that nagging feeling that he's just too good to be true. I'll bet by the end of the day I'll figure out why."

"Good luck with that," she grumbled with a snort.

I was looking forward to taking the first bite of my brat when I saw Liam and his band come on stage, setting up instruments and moving microphone stands where they were needed. They were all dressed in black jeans and dark blue t-shirts with Eagle Creek Police Department printed on the back in white letters and I wondered if they were all police officers or were just wearing the shirts to promote the occasion.

I couldn't seem to stop watching Liam as I ate. He moved with such confident ease and the smile he gave his bandmates was so relaxed and genuine as they joked around, clearly excited to play their music for the gathering audience. As he tested the volume on his keyboard, he looked out over the crowd and caught my eye, giving me a smile that showed off his dimple. I was about to suggest to MJ that we move to closer seats when Liam's attention was drawn to something to the left of us and his face positively lit up with happiness. Jumping from the raised platform, he ran around the tables and people to throw his arms around the tall brunette who was running toward him. He picked her feet up off the ground and spun her around as they both laughed, her athletic, tanned legs bent up and her thick, wavy hair flowing around them like a chocolate cloud.

"I didn't think you were going to make it," we could hear Liam say to her. He finally let her stand on her own, still holding onto her upper arms as if needing to assure himself she was actually there.

"Neither did I," the brunette admitted. "Holiday flight delays are the worst!"

"You must be exhausted. I can give you my keys if you want to take your stuff to my apartment and get some rest."

"Are you kidding? And miss your show? No way! You know how much I love hearing you play."

"Well, that didn't take all day," I grumbled, my mood plummeting with my appetite as I dropped my plastic fork onto the half-empty paper plate and pushed it away from me. "Mission accomplished."

MJ looked dumbstruck. "He never said anything about a girlfriend. Especially one serious enough to just move right into his apartment the minute she gets into town."

Outwardly, I schooled myself to look vaguely interested while Liam's band played. I hated to admit it, but they were really good as they sang covers of 70s and 80s rock bands, the songs all having an American theme to them. Inwardly, I alternately fumed that he was a snake just like every other man and rejoiced that I'd discovered it early enough not to get hurt by him. I was justified in my original assessment and tried to tell myself I didn't hate that pretty woman with the long, dark hair who sat down at the table right in front of Liam's keyboard, smiling up at him.

I made myself wait until the band was finished, then grabbed our plates and stalked off to throw them away as the rest of the audience applauded. I realized how petty I was being and chastised myself for even caring who this new woman was.

"Teresa! Mary Jean!"

Liam was striding toward us, his face positively glowing with happiness under the gleam of sweat that made his hair stick to his forehead and the back of his neck. Beside him, their hands firmly linked together, was the brunette, easily keeping stride with him because they were the same height. I could hear MJ sigh behind me as I pasted a smile on my face, determined to show him I didn't care at all who he lived with.

"I want you to meet somebody," he said, still trying to catch his breath from their performance.

He put his arm around the other woman's shoulders, beaming at her with obvious love and affection. I couldn't help but notice how devastatingly handsome it made him look and wished someone would gaze at me with such open adoration.

"Lilah, this is Mary Jean, Ron's wife…and Teresa. Mary Jean, Teresa, this is Lilah. My sister."

"His much younger, better-looking sister," she added, offering her hand to MJ first.

"Younger by twelve minutes but definitely better looking," he agreed.

She held her hand out to me and I automatically shook it, still trying to process what they'd just said. "Twins?"

"That's right," Lilah said, sliding her arm around the back of his waist. "Two peas in a pod they always called us. I can't tell you how nice it is to finally meet the people he's been telling me about. Mary Jean, I especially wanted to say thanks to you and Ron. Liam said you two have been so nice and welcoming to him."

"It was our pleasure," MJ said, and I could tell she was relieved to discover Liam wasn't the lowlife we'd thought all during his performance.

"Lilah," he groaned, rolling his eyes. "You make it sound like they adopted me as a pet."

"Well—" she drawled, giving him a teasing sideways grin only a sister could pull off. She then turned her attention to me, and I wondered how I missed their obvious resemblance before when she looked at me with the same brown eyes, long eyelashes, and dimpled smile. "And I'm very glad to meet you, Teresa."

"Okay, I think that's enough introductions for today," Liam interrupted before I could question why his sister was glad to meet me. "Don't mind her, I think the jetlag is affecting her mouth. She just flew in from Hong Kong to visit for a week. I'm going to get her settled at my place, change, and be right back." He gave me an imploring look and I realized he stressed the last part because he was afraid I might leave.

"We'll be here," I assured him, linking my arm with MJ's so he knew I wasn't staying just for him. "Nice to meet you, Lilah."

"See?" MJ said as soon as the siblings were out of earshot. "Sister. Not girlfriend. You're going to have to try harder to find something wrong with that man."

When Liam returned alone, changed into cooler shorts and a red-white-and-blue tank top, he explained his sister was going to join us later after she'd had a chance to rest and freshen up after the long plane ride. I also learned she was a vocal coach in Hong Kong, so they hadn't been able to see each other for the last three years.

"So, you're both into music," MJ commented as we waited in line to get dishes of strawberry shortcake and ice cream. "Is that a twin thing?"

"Our parents used to play together all the time, mostly gospel music. I guess we both just naturally fell into it, too. We were playing and singing together at church since we were just little kids. She's just the one who was able to make a living out of it." Liam turned to me. "Was that the same way you started playing piano? Because your parents played?"

I glanced at MJ, not wanting to give away anything I'd recently learned before I was ready. "Not really. But I was really young when I begged my dad to let me take piano lessons. Somehow Mom convinced him to let me try and he rented a piano for me to practice on, hoping I'd get bored of it and quit. When I took to the piano like a duck to water, he finally gave in and bought the upright I still have today. He praised me whenever I performed at school, but I could tell Dad didn't really like me playing. Mom, on the other hand, was sick a lot and loved sitting and listening to me practice for hours. She said it made her feel better. I asked her once why Dad didn't like the piano, but she wouldn't give me a straight answer." I didn't add that I now realized the reason.

Ron was finally able to join us after putting in his time grilling brats and burgers. We all spent the rest of the afternoon playing games, eating, and talking. I had to admit—only to myself, of course—that MJ was right. Liam was funny and easy to talk to and I found myself wanting to believe he was interested in me enough to overlook my flaws. If only I could shake that inner voice that kept asking why such a good guy was still single.

Lilah joined us in time for the fireworks and she was just as funny and easy to talk to as her brother. She told us about being an American in Hong Kong and what she missed about being so far from home. The first, of course, was Liam even though they seemed to take every opportunity to tease one another. I envied their close relationship since I'd never had a sibling or even any cousins.

"You don't live very far from here. Did you walk?" Liam asked once the last of the booming rockets faded away, leaving our ears ringing.

I immediately tensed, hating the reaction of even thinking about walking alone at night. "I did, but I'll get a ride home from Mary Jean."

"Teresa doesn't feel safe walking alone at night," MJ offered, earning her an angry glare from me. "Never has."

"But you live in the other direction," Liam pointed out. "And the traffic is bottlenecked with everyone trying to leave at once." He turned to me. "Why don't you let me walk you home?"

"What about Lilah?" I asked, not knowing if I wanted to be so alone with him as the five-block walk back to my house in the dark. Not because I didn't trust him, but because it seemed a little more intimate than I was ready for.

"I'm perfectly happy to head back to the apartment," she announced. "You two go on."

As everyone else turned and left me standing, open-mouthed with Liam, I knew I had no choice. I couldn't make a fool out of myself begging someone else to take me and I couldn't just walk by myself. I was stuck with Liam.

"Is there a specific reason you don't like walking alone?" Liam asked with genuine concern as we started wandering through the crowd heading for their cars. "Were you attacked?"

My chest began to tighten as it always did when thinking about this particular phobia. "Not exactly.

There was something that happened when I was young, but I've recently discovered it was all a misunderstanding. That doesn't stop the fear, though, as irrational as it might be."

"I don't believe fear is ever irrational. It may be based on a lack of knowledge, but it could also be a deep-seated memory of an incident that put you at risk. In any case, fear helps to keep us safe as a part of the fight or flight response. You can learn to deal with it or fight through what you're afraid of, but I don't think you can ever completely get rid of it. And whatever keeps you safe can't be a bad thing, right?"

I stared at him in disbelief. Not only was he accepting my phobia, he was actually making it sound logical. We made it across the busy street backed up with cars all trying to leave the grounds at the same time before he asked, "Was there some reason you didn't want to walk home with me? I couldn't help but notice a sort of panicked look when everyone left us alone."

I sighed, knowing I had to give him some kind of rational reason. "Look, I know you're probably a nice guy…I mean from what I've seen you are…but I really don't know enough about you yet."

"Wow," he said after a few seconds of stunned silence. "I guess that's fair although I've never had anyone distrust me before. You must not think me as bad as all that since you chose me over being alone."

I stopped walking and he took a couple of steps before realizing I wasn't beside him and turned to face me. He looked almost hurt. I decided I had to figure out his secret before we went any further.

"I've never had good luck with guys. They always seem to be hiding something, but I find out eventually. I'm just waiting to figure out what your secret is because honestly, you're a little too good to be true."

He stood as still as a statue except for his eyes which blinked in surprise. Finally, he took a deep breath. "Ouch. I didn't expect that to sting as much as it did. I guess I thought I was pretty much an open book. I don't think I've ever been interrogated by someone I'm not officially dating…but go ahead. Ask me anything."

I started walking past him and he fell in step beside me. Now that I had the opportunity and permission to ask whatever I wanted, I wasn't quite sure where to begin. We walked half a block before I said, "If you're such a great guy, then why aren't you married?"

"Are you asking if there's something women find out about me that makes them run for the hills?" he asked, trying for humor but failing. He cleared his throat nervously. "I was married. Right out of high school. It was a mistake and didn't even last two years. Since then, I've probably been about as critical of women as it seems like you are of men."

"What happened?" Even as the words came out of my mouth, I realized how personal they were but couldn't take them back now.

"Let's just say it didn't work out. Not because of anything I did," he added hastily. "I guess we were just too young to realize what marriage really meant. If I'd known then what I know now…" He let the statement die away as he shoved his hands in his pockets and watched his feet as we kept walking.

"Any kids?" I asked quietly. He didn't look up when he shook his head and I could tell just by the tightness in his shoulders that it was a tender subject for him, either because he really wanted them or really didn't.

We were almost at my house, and I no longer felt like prying into his past because I realized it was more awkward than I anticipated. After reading through Benny's journals, I knew better how painful memories could be. Just as we reached my driveway, he stopped walking, so I stopped as well.

"I get it," he said, finally breaking his silence. "We don't know enough about each other and neither one of us wants to be hurt again because we've blindly trusted another human being. I noticed when we were helping move Benny's things that you have a lot of self-help books in your house. I went through a stretch where I tried to fix myself, too. Then someone helped me realize I was never broken to begin with, and I didn't have to blame myself when a relationship didn't work out because of the other person's shortcomings. I've already worked through most of my cynicism, but it sounds like you're still dealing with yours. I like you, Teresa. And I'm willing to take a chance to get to know each other better and see if we can build that trust. That's what dating is all about, isn't it? So, if you feel I'm worth getting to know better, can we at least give it a try? Because I think you are worth it."

I tore my eyes away from his raw, pleading gaze and looked down at my fingers, clenched together in uncertainty. "I can't promise I'm worth it, and I can't promise I'll stop waiting for something bad to happen."

"I'm not asking you to." His voice was as soft and comforting as a security blanket but also held a tension as if he were holding his breath.

I looked back up into his expectant face. "I have a lot I'm working through with Benny and…everything. But I think I'd like to know you better, too."

His wide smile brought out his dimple and his eyes brightened in the light of the streetlight. "Right now, that's all I ask."

Chapter Eleven

July 28, 2002

It took several rounds of letters to get through all the questions I had for Benny's friend that Ron found in New Orleans. Bo and his daughter, Cheri, were very courteous and helpful. He was sad to hear of Benny's passing and his condolences were more comforting than I'd expected. Even after he'd answered all my questions, he added pages of stories he remembered and pictures Cheri had unearthed in his stored belongings, all helping to flesh out the life of Benjamin Hunter. I sent him a picture of myself and his reply to it was that I looked exactly like he'd imagined.

When I thought I had all the rest of the information in place, one last mystery had to be solved. How did the man I thought of as my father fit into the story? The only way I could find the answer was to ask him myself. But since we weren't very close, I wasn't sure the best way to approach him.

I stood on the front porch of the house David Billings now called home, working up the courage to ring the doorbell. The craftsman-style design was a definite step up from where we lived before I left for college. The split-level modular home I grew up in on Birchwood Drive was part of a new development of houses at the edge of town. Previously nothing but a dense forest, the mass construction accommodated the ever-growing city of Eagle Creek. The only distinctions between the cookie-cutter buildings were their paint colors and how well their lawns were cared for and adorned inside their white picket fences. The area has since progressively expanded several times throughout the years with newer and bigger homes stretching out until my childhood suburban home was closer to urban than rural.

Where my neighborhood of Victorian homes gave the impression of old family wealth, the house where my father lived with his second wife implied nouveau riche. The yards were all large and immaculately groomed with rock-walled flowerbeds and stone paths from their two-car garages to the porches deep enough for Amish patio gliders. The sturdy, hand-crafted architecture was solid, energy efficient, and artistically unique from the other designs around them.

Before I could reach my hand out to press the doorbell, my father's face appeared in the decorative leaded-glass window just inches from my face. Even through the distortion, I could tell he was smiling before he opened the door.

"Teresa! I thought that was your car. What a surprise. Come on in," David said, backing away from the door to give me room to enter. Behind the smile, there was a tightness in his jaw that confirmed his shock at my sudden appearance on a random Sunday afternoon. As he led the way into the living room, I realized he looked slimmer and healthier than I'd ever seen him in his cargo shorts and polo shirt, although there were more gray hairs than I remembered. "Would you like something to drink? I could make you a cup of coffee or we have iced tea."

"Iced tea sounds great," I said, sinking into the overstuffed couch as he hustled off to the kitchen. It wasn't that I necessarily wanted the tea, but it gave me an excuse for more time to gain enough confidence to ask what I needed to know.

As I waited, I looked around the cozy room, expertly decorated by his wife who had exquisite taste, yet managed to make their home look warm and inviting. The exposed wood beams and framework were highlighted by the sand-toned walls and masonry of the fireplace. An area rug of neutral-colored blocks kept the furniture off the polished wood floor which gleamed in the sunlight from the large bay window. Actual paintings of landscapes and hand-crafted pottery gave the room an artistic and authentic touch. I guessed with both of them working at the courthouse, they were doing pretty well financially for themselves now that both of their children were adults, but neither of them was the kind who flaunted their wealth. I looked over the framed pictures prominently displayed on the fireplace mantle—the happy, blue-eyed, dark-haired couple; Charlotte's son and his brunette wife; three laughing, brown-eyed grandchildren. The one picture of me with my father, taken shortly after my college graduation, looked conspicuously out of place. Not only was I the lone family member with blonde hair, but my tight-lipped smile stuck out like a sore thumb among all these beaming grins.

"You look bothered by something," he said, handing me a glass and sitting in a chair facing the couch. "Is anything wrong? Do you need money? I know you can't make that much working at the clinic—"

"I don't need money, Dad," I said, taking a drink from the sweating glass and licking my lips, cold from the clinking ice. I set the glass on one of the handy coasters laid out on the coffee table and took a deep breath before blurting out, "I want to know why you married Mom when she was pregnant with another man's child."

He flinched as if he'd just been slapped, and I instantly regretted my lack of tact. He'd frozen with his glass halfway to his lips, then placed it carefully on another coaster. Without looking at me, he stood up and crossed the room toward the stairway. He stood with his hand on the banister, and I was afraid he was going to leave me sitting there without an answer. After a few seconds, he turned and walked back to me.

"Let's talk about this outside," he whispered, and I realized he'd been listening to see if Charlotte had heard my question, not running away from it. He led the way toward a vine-covered gazebo in the backyard, a good enough distance from the house and anyone who might overhear us. We sat on the padded bench, and I twisted my hair over one shoulder to keep it from blowing around in the warm breeze and distracting me.

"How did you find out?" He waved his hands to stop me from answering before I'd even opened my mouth. “Never mind. It doesn’t really matter, does it? Whatever you’ve heard, I want you to know we both did what we thought was best at the time. For you. Understand?”

I nodded. “Can you tell me everything?”

He proceeded to tell me the bare truth about my mother and how he'd entered into the secret kept from me since birth. He spoke with more emotion than I'd ever heard, showing the love he felt for us, the pain of losing her, and the frustration he bore from the whole situation. It seemed like the man sitting next to me in the cool shade of the gazebo and the one I'd called *Dad* for all this time were two different men. When he finished talking, I just sat there, silently absorbing what he'd said. He took my hand and squeezed it reassuringly.

“I’m sorry Teresa. I know the secret I swore to keep prevented me from being a real, affectionate father. It probably would've been easier for everyone if we came out with the truth in the beginning—at least a lot easier for your poor mother. I’m sure she would’ve loved to tell you all the times you reminded her of him. But times were different then, understand, and although it seems a bit cruel now, we thought this was the only way.”

“Well, thanks for finally telling me the truth,” I automatically replied, still numb with shock from what he’d told me. “The little notes she wrote in my birthday cards certainly make a lot more sense now. Sorry I had to bother you with this.”

“You are never a bother to me,” he said earnestly, taking both my hands in his. “I know I was never able to show you in the past, but please believe me when I say

I've always loved you as my own daughter. I guess I always thought if we got too close, I'd end up doing or saying something out of guilt to make you suspicious. It seemed easier, especially as you got older, to keep each other at arm's length. You're my only daughter and I wish we were closer. But now that you know the truth, I'll understand if you want to find and get closer to your real father."

"He's dead," I said softly.

"Who?" he asked.

"My biological father, Benjamin Hunter," I sighed. "He came into the clinic four months ago and died at the hospital that night. All he got to say to me was that I was his daughter, and he loved my mother. The rest I found out from what he left me in his will and from Claire."

"Then you know about the savings account?" I stared at him in surprise, and he laughed. "Yes, I knew about it. In fact, he even asked me for permission to add you as his beneficiary. Your mother made me promise not to tell you the truth, but she didn't say anything about planning for your future," he added, a sly twinkle in his eye I never dreamed I'd see there.

"I'm sorry you didn't get to know him," he continued. "We only met a few times—and they weren't under the friendliest of circumstances—but from what I understand, you're a lot like him. Maybe you were too young to remember, but you met him once, too."

"Not clearly, but after reading about it in his journals, more and more images are coming back," I admitted.

"Well, then let me fill you in on the side he probably didn't know about." He then proceeded to tell me what had been left out of Benny's journals as I sat and listened in silence, more pieces of the puzzle clicking into place. When he finished, he said, "Your grandfather wasn't the nicest person in the world, but I can understand him a little better now than I did back then. I wasn't just being polite when I said I wished you could've known Benjamin. He probably didn't realize it but I watched him play one night. He was good. Really good. And I saw a lot of you in him."

I was touched by his truthfulness, and at that moment he felt more like a father than ever. As he walked me back to the house, I mourned all the lost years between us. But unlike Benjamin Hunter, this father was still alive.

"I'm sorry for everything that happened back then…and for being so distant," I said, giving him a spontaneous hug. "I promise to come by more often."

He hugged me tightly back, and I could feel his relief as if his muscles were finally letting go of long-held tension. "I'm just glad everything's finally out in the open and you don't hate me for keeping it from you. I always wished we were closer." He let me go and laid a palm against my cheek. "Guess late is better than never."

As I drove off, I vowed to put in the extra effort to close the gap between me and my dad…even if he wasn't my father by blood.

Chapter Twelve

August 1, 2002

"It's about time," MJ said when I answered the doorbell.

"What do you mean? It only took me like ten seconds to open the door."

She breezed past me and dropped her oversized purse in the nearest chair. "Not that. I mean I've been waiting for months for you to tell me everything you found out about your mom and Benny. I don't know why it had to be such a big secret, anyway. You even made Ron promise not to tell me what he was helping you with. Do you know how irritating it is to have your husband know something about your best friend that she won't even tell you about?"

"Nice to see you, too, MJ. I'm glad you could make it on your night off. Come on in and make yourself comfortable," I said as I closed the door, earning a raised eyebrow for my sarcasm. "Look, I'm sorry I kept you in the dark, okay? I just had to get as much information as I could possibly get and piece it all together in my head before I told anyone. There's only one side of the story I couldn't get, and that was my mom's, but I think everyone I talked to was able to fill in her part of it. If it makes you feel any better, Ron only heard a small fraction of the story, so you're actually the first one to hear the whole thing."

She took a few seconds to contemplate it before she smiled. "Yeah. Oddly enough that does make me feel better."

"Too bad Ron's out of town tonight or he could've come with and heard the whole thing, too."

"Oh, no you don't. I'm your best friend. I get dibs on the juicy stuff first. I can fill Ron in on the highlights…if I feel like it," she added with a cheeky grin. She then pulled two bottles of wine out of her purse. "We can use one of these if the story is happy, both if it isn't. Now, let's dig into that lasagna you made so we can get down to it."

I laughed at her foresight as I led the way through the house. "Trust me, I'm not the one with the sad ending."

The kitchen was too stuffy from the hot oven, so MJ helped me bring all the food into the dining room. A rotating fan in the doorway of the living room kept the coolness from the window air conditioner circulating around us comfortably. As we enjoyed our supper of lasagna, green salad, garlic bread, and mixed fruit, MJ took the opportunity to grill me about Liam.

"So, you never did tell me what happened after the fireworks."

I choked on a crumb of bread, and she had to wait for me to drink half a glass of water to clear it before answering. "Sorry," I apologized. "I just— It's like— You'll understand better later."

She tapped her fork on the edge of her plate while she waited for my answer.

"Nothing happened," I assured her. "He walked me home, we talked on the way, that's it."

"And? You have to give me more than that! Have you been seeing each other since? Have you figured out what a great guy he is?"

"He's nice, and we agreed to date and see where it goes, but we haven't really had much time to spend together yet. His sister was here, I was working on this story, and then work picked up with everyone trying to get vacations in before school started again. We've only gone out to eat a couple of times and I still have this horrible feeling he's got a secret I'm going to find out about that shatters his whole perfect persona." I leaned closer to her over my plate. "Did you know he's divorced? Or did you conveniently keep that piece of information to yourself? If he couldn't make that relationship work why would ours be any different? What else do you know about him that you haven't told me yet?"

MJ kept her eyes on her food as she picked at her lettuce which was a dead giveaway that she had something to say but wasn't sure how I was going to react. After glancing up to see how serious I looked, she set the fork down and sat back in her chair.

"Fine. I think he should be the one to tell you, but it might be easier for you to understand him a little better and easier on him not to have to watch you react when he finally does tell you."

"I knew it," I said, dropping my own fork and slumping back in my chair while heaving a deep sigh. "Might as well let the other shoe drop and get this over with."

She gave me a look that warned me if I was going to be negative about it, she'd keep the information to herself. I waved my hand to tell her to go on and tell me what she had to.

"Yes, he told Ron he was married before, but it has nothing to do with what kind of man he is today. So, promise me you'll listen with an open mind and think about what he's been through and what he's like now before you judge. Okay?"

My stomach dropped. Although I suspected there was something he wasn't telling me, actually getting to hear about it was an entirely different matter. I nodded my head and tried to prepare myself for anything.

"Liam married his high school sweetheart only a few months after graduation. As you can imagine, both their parents objected, telling them they were too young, they should go to college first, they shouldn't rush into things, and so on. But they were eighteen and convinced they were in love, so they got married at the courthouse and moved into a tiny apartment above a bar. He said it was apparent within the first few months that their parents had probably been right because they found living together wasn't as fun as dating, but they were both stubborn and didn't want to be proven wrong.

"He said when his wife became pregnant, he thought it would bring them closer together and it worked…for a while. Then she lost the baby."

"Oh, no." I thought about the way his shoulders tensed when I asked if he had any children and felt heartbroken for him. He obviously did want them but had suffered through losing one.

"After that happened, she told him she was glad she had a miscarriage because she hadn't wanted kids anyway. She decided this was her second chance to go out and live the life she hadn't been able to since he was the only guy she'd dated. She left him so she could go out partying without having the proverbial ball and chain weighing her down."

"That's horrible. No wonder he didn't want to tell me about that," I said, then noticed MJ pinching her lips together as if trying to decide whether to tell me the next part. "There's more, isn't there?"

She nodded. "When she left him, Liam got really mad and really depressed. He told Ron that he wouldn't tell him everything he'd done during that time but admitted to getting blackout drunk nearly every night and burning all the things she'd left in the apartment. I can't even imagine him doing that, so I have no clue what else he might have done, but something landed him in hot water with the police. While he was locked up, there were some really nice officers who knew him and sympathized with what he'd been through with losing his family. They sat him down and talked to him, helping him get back on track and even hooked him up with a minister who gave grief counseling sessions. After a few months, he was able to get back on his feet, divorce his wayward wife, and go to college to become a police officer. And the rest, as they say, is history. So, now you can see he is the good guy we know him to be, he's just had to go through some suffering to get there and has a hard time talking about it."

I looked down at the clenched hands in my lap and willed myself to relax them. It certainly wasn't the story I'd expected, but now I understood his comment about being hurt again and being able to work through his cynicism.

"*After you have suffered...God will restore, establish and strengthen you,*" I said aloud to myself, then looked up at MJ. "That's why he knew and liked that Bible verse Benny had on his wall. He'd been through suffering, too." I couldn't stop the smile that spread across my face.

"And that's something to be happy about?" she asked, clearly confused by my reaction to something so sad.

My smile turned to snickers that I attempted to dampen as I waved my hand to dismiss my behavior. "It's not that. Really. I just can't believe… It's like… Liam's just… Oh, MJ, you are not going to understand until after you hear the story, and I don't want to spoil it for you by telling things out of order.

"Then let's get on with it," she declared, picking up our plates and carrying them into the kitchen to signal the meal was over. "Like I said before, it's about time!"

Now that I was actually going to be telling the whole story out loud, I was more nervous than I thought I might be. As we cleared the table, put away leftovers, and washed dishes, I dropped two spoons on the floor and almost absentmindedly put the lasagna pan back into the oven instead of the refrigerator. Retiring to the sitting room, I switched off the fan and air conditioner. The room was comfortable enough and I didn't want to have to compete with their constant hum. I sat in my grandfather's leather recliner, tucking my feet under me and setting my notebook on the arm of the chair. I wanted to be sure I didn't forget any part of my story, although with as many times as I wrote and rewrote the entire story in my head, I knew I probably wouldn't look at the carefully planned notes at all. MJ sat on the couch with an open bottle of wine and filled two wine glasses.

"So," MJ prompted, handing me a full glass and taking one for herself, "spill it."

Chapter Thirteen

June 3, 1969

Margaret Bennett, Peg to her high school friends, laid on the sitting room couch wrapped in her favorite afghan, her head resting on David's leg in the darkened room. They'd been dating for years but broke it off just a few weeks earlier. He was a year older and had already finished his first year of college in La Crosse, she had just graduated from high school and planned to attend an all-girls college in Milwaukee. One year of trying to make a long-distance relationship work was enough for both of them to realize their feelings for each other weren't strong enough to bother keeping it alive.

Even though they were no longer a couple, they were still friends and David didn't hesitate when a crying Peg called asking him to come over to keep her company. While she curled up beside him, usually drifting in and out of sleep because she'd been plagued recently with nightmares, David watched whatever was on the one television channel the small black and white set was able to pull in. He lazily ran his fingers through her long, blonde hair more out of habit and comfort than a desire to touch his ex. He was just glad he could be here for her after she'd lost her mother in a car accident a week before graduation. What should have been the happiest time of her life for an eighteen-year-old transitioning into a full-fledged adult turned out to be a time of darkness and depression. Even a week after the funeral, Peg was going through her days in a fog and was frightened awake several times at night.

"What in God's good name is going on in here?"

The booming voice startled them both and they separated guiltily, even though they hadn't been doing anything intimate. Judge Bennett stood in the sitting room doorway, hands on his considerable hips, filling the space with his girth. His sharp blue eyes flashed with righteous anger at finding his only daughter with her head in a boy's lap, his frown framed perfectly by the horseshoe mustache on either side of his mouth.

"Nothing, Dad," Peg promised. "I just couldn't stand being alone all day, so I asked David to come over and keep me company. We weren't doing anything, I swear."

The Judge continued to frown down at them, taking in his daughter's hair, mussed from sleep, and puffy eyes, still red from crying. His intent gaze shifted to David, taking in the dark spot on his shoulder, still slightly damp with Peg's tears, and how his crisp, button-down shirt was still tucked neatly into his pristine, white pants. Satisfied she was telling the truth, he walked over to the window and threw the drapes aside to let in the afternoon sunlight before sitting down in the smaller chair next to the matching couch. Still frowning at his daughter, his fingers started tapping against the arm of the chair.

"You can't be calling boys over here when I'm at work just because you're lonely," he said, his drumming fingers curling into a fist. "What would the neighbors think?"

"But it's David," she argued. "He's been coming over for years."

His eyes bored into David's and David pressed himself further into the back of the couch. "Not while unchaperoned, I trust."

"No," David answered, shaking his head emphatically. "Never, sir."

Her father gave a deep sigh and turned his attention back to his daughter. "I've been thinking," he began, drumming his fingers once more. "You've had a hard time dealing with the loss of your mother. I miss her, too, but you can't spend your entire summer feeling sorry for yourself. Perhaps a change of scenery to lift your spirits and get you in the right mindset before heading off to college. After the funeral, Muriel offered to have you come visit and I think we'll take her up on it."

"But I don't want to go to Aunt Muriel and Uncle Peter's," Peg whined. "I want to stay here surrounded by Mom's things so I don't forget her."

The Judge continued as if she hadn't spoken. "You can spend some time with your cousin, see some of the Detroit sites, and come back all refreshed and ready to face the world again. I'll go call her right now." He pushed himself up out of the chair with a small amount of difficulty, but Peg was already on her feet, blocking his exit.

"I don't want to go to Detroit," she said, emphasizing each word to make her point.

"Can she take someone along with her?"

They both turned to stare at David. Peg looked surprised at the suggestion while her father looked positively murderous. David held up his hands in surrender.

"I didn't mean me. I meant one of her other friends," he clarified.

Her father nodded in agreement. "I'm certain Muriel would be fine with that as long as they don't cause her any trouble."

"Fine," she said, lifting her chin in defiance. "Then I want Claire to come with me."

He frowned and shook his head. "I don't like that girl. I think she's a bad influence on you with all her radical, feminist thinking." Believing she'd found the perfect loophole to be able to stay home, Peg smiled triumphantly, only to fade when her father continued. "But if that's what it takes to pull you out of this bad mood, then so be it. At least you'll be under Muriel's watchful eye. She won't let Claire talk you into getting into any mischief."

As it turned out, Margaret's cousin, Allison, ended up being the one to show the other two girls how to sneak out of the house after her parents had gone to bed. An expert at escaping her home undetected, Ali regaled them with stories of all the parties and clubs she frequented before returning to her bedroom by daybreak.

"Jack's already planning to pick me up tonight. You should come along," Ali said, applying a generous amount of eyeshadow while watching out the window for the light in her clueless parents' bedroom to go out.

"You're a genius, Ali! I think that sounds like a blast," Claire exclaimed, bouncing excitedly on the edge of the bed. "What do you say, Peg? Let's go see what kind of nightlife Detroit has to offer. It's gotta be better than Eagle Creek."

"I don't really feel like it," Peg said, absently picking at the fur from one of Ali's worn teddy bears. "You two go without me."

Claire grabbed the stuffed toy from her hands and tossed it behind her. "The whole point of us coming here is to get your mind off of being sad all the time, right? So, let us help you do it. Come with us tonight. Have some drinks, meet new people, maybe even dance and have some laughs. Then, if you don't want to do it again you can stay behind next time. But at least give it a try. Deal?"

Despite Peg's hesitations, the other girls soon had her climbing down the vine-covered trellis and creeping across the backyard with them. The night was cool for June and Peg donned the sweater she insisted on bringing even though the other girls wore sleeveless mini-skirt dresses. As they crouched behind the row of bushes lining the road, she attempted once more to be the voice of reason.

"Are you sure this is safe?" she whispered. "I mean do you trust this guy? Do you know where he's taking us? Maybe we should've left a note in case something bad happens."

"Don't worry about her," Claire told Ali as she fluffed up her short, brown hair to give it more volume behind her headband. "She's just a product of a sheltered, Catholic childhood and a strict, right-wing father who also happens to be a prosecuting judge. Typical paranoia of someone who never does anything against her parent's wishes."

"A goodie-two-shoes. Yeah, I can see that," Ali replied, looking Peg up and down.

Peg held her temper and ignored their insults, especially since they were true. "I was just brought up with a deep belief of right and wrong…and sneaking around definitely feels wrong."

"If you're going to be a downer all night just turn around and go back to bed." Ali looked like she was going to say more but at that moment a rusty van, spraypainted in colorful swirls, pulled up beside them. She pointed a warning finger at Peg. "Just don't spoil it for the rest of us."

Jack turned out to be a gangly man with long, greasy hair and his van was already half-filled with oddly dressed characters. There weren't many hippies in a rural city like Eagle Creek, but as they climbed into the smoky vehicle, Claire and Peg recognized them instantly. They all wore brightly colored bell bottoms and tie-dyed shirts, and with their long hair, neither could immediately decide if some of them were men or women.

When they reached the bar district of town, Peter found an empty parking spot and they all piled out. Peg was grateful to escape the stuffy, hot confines of the van and was feeling slightly light-headed from whatever it was they were smoking.

The group paused and deliberated outside each bar as they searched for one they wanted to enter. Each place either exuded the wrong kind of music or the wrong kind of people for their tastes. When they finally found one to their liking, Peg spent the entire time huddled in a corner, trying to ignore the blaring amateur band and nursing a warm bottle of beer to have an excuse not to join the already crowded dance floor.

Peg was relieved when they decided to look for another club. Her ears were ringing, and she had a headache from the noise and wanted nothing more than to go back to Ali's house to sleep. They'd only walked half of a block when they met up with another group of Jack's friends. As they stood on the sidewalk talking about the merits of the local clubs, Peg caught the upbeat strains of jazz music coming from the bar on the corner. Wandering away from Claire, she inched her way toward the doorway to catch a glimpse of the band.

The room was dark, but a spotlight shone on the stage and reflected off the instruments playing a lively tune. Most of the musicians were old and dark-skinned, but the one playing the piano was young and white. He looked only a bit older than she was, but he played with a passion that outshone the others.

"What are you doing?" Claire snapped, grabbing her arm to pull her back to where the group waited halfway down the block. "Don't go wandering off on your own. Your dad would kill me if I lost you."

"I just wanted to listen to the band," Peg explained.

"You actually wanted to listen to jazz?" Claire sighed in frustration. "I will never understand what you like about such boring music."

"Hurry up," Ali called, waving them forward. "Jack's gonna give us a ride back home."

"Already?" Claire whined. "We only got to go to one place."

Ali rolled her eyes. "I know, but there are no good vibes tonight. I promise you we'll come back this weekend. That's when all the good parties happen."

Chapter Fourteen

June 8, 1969

Peg was relieved they wouldn't be sneaking out for at least a few nights. She was uncomfortable with the whole business but didn't dare try to talk the others out of it. Claire, on the other hand, pouted and sulked. She was Peg's best friend, but even Peg reconsidered the wisdom of bringing her along. They had little in common but were like opposite ends of a magnet—together they seemed to make sense. Some of Peg's positive charge kept Claire down to earth while some of Claire's negative charge brought Peg out of her shell.

To help keep her mind off her grief, Peg's aunt and uncle took the girls around to see the sights of Detroit. Ali was bored since she'd seen it all before, but the other two enjoyed anything that was not their quiet hometown. Peg was especially excited when they went to listen to a concert in the park that featured jazz music. To her surprise, she saw a familiar face.

"I saw him before," she said excitedly to the other girls. "Look over there at the piano player. Isn't he great?"

"Where did you see him, dear?" Aunt Muriel asked. Peg tried to think quickly while Ali and Claire glared at her. She'd nearly given away their secret.

"I don't remember," she mumbled.

They settled down on blankets to listen, and even Ali and Claire had to admit the band was good even if they didn't particularly like that kind of music. Peg let the sound wash over her as she watched the talented piano player. In the light of day, she realized he was also very good-looking. He was tall and thin with shiny blond hair and soft features. Even from a distance, she could see how long his fingers were as they ran up and down the keys.

To her surprise and delight, he was not only good at playing piano, but he could also play every instrument on stage. During one song, he jumped from one place to another as he was featured playing the trumpet, saxophone, trombone, clarinet, bass, and then ended with the piano. As he finished the song with a quick run up the keys, sweat rolled down his face and she could just imagine how exhausted he would be. Instead, he looked like he was high on adrenaline and the success of a perfect number. He smiled wide as they all bowed together and then jumped gracefully off the stage and ran over to the drink stand.

Peg couldn't take her eyes off him as he received a large cup of lemonade and finished the entire thing in one long drink. He casually tossed the Styrofoam cup into the trashcan and jogged back to help the rest of the band pack up their instruments.

"Well, I'm certainly impressed with that young man," Uncle Peter said as they gathered up their blankets and walked back toward the car. "His parents were worried at first about him playing at that darky club, but it doesn't seem to have changed him a bit. He still works hard at the store, and you can tell how much he loves his music."

Peg wanted to ask her uncle more about the good-looking musician but knew it would throw up a red flag. According to Ali, Peter was very old-fashioned just like her father, and believed that boys should show interest in girls, not the other way around. She waited until that night when they were once again crouched behind the bushes to ask her cousin about him.

"Benny?" Ali exclaimed in surprise. "Yeah, I know who he is. He works at his dad's store during the day and plays at that black jazz club at night. That's really the only interesting thing about him. He's so old and boring."

"I want to go to that jazz club," Peg blurted out.

"No way," Ali said. "I'm not wasting my night there. It's so square."

"Then drop me off there and pick me up when you're ready to come back," she said, her voice calm even though her heart beat wild from anxious excitement.

"Come on, Peg," Claire pleaded. "You're the one who's always saying it's a bad idea to go off on your own, and now you want to split us up? We can meet some guys and have a lot of fun together."

"I don't want to 'meet some guys'," she snapped. "I don't want to spend my summer sneaking out to party at places I don't want to go and with people I don't have anything in common with. I want to go and listen to jazz music. If you don't want to come with me, you two can do whatever you want."

Claire raised her eyebrows at the uncharacteristic sound of defiance in her friend's voice. "Wow. Okay. Look who finally found her backbone." A smile suddenly spread across her face. "Good for you, girl. I may have rubbed off on you after all."

"Fine," Ali grumbled. "Go hang out with the senior citizens for all I care. At least you won't be dead weight like last time."

"Just remember to pick me up again before you come home," Peg continued.

"What if we forget?" Ali sneered. "What if we just leave you there?"

"Then I'll have to call Uncle Peter for a ride home," Peg threatened. "And what do you think he'll do when he finds out what you've been doing behind their backs?" Both girls stared at her, open-mouthed, with new respect.

"We'll pick you up by one," Ali promised grudgingly as their ride pulled up. This time it was a big boat of a car with the top down. There were only two people inside tonight and Peg was glad. She hated being squished together with strangers.

"I like this new Peg," Claire whispered and squeezed her hand. "I like her a lot."

When they pulled up in front of the jazz club as Ali directed, she made the driver promise out loud they would return for Peg by one o'clock. As they drove off, Peg walked into the club, her head held high with new confidence and a determination to have a good time by herself.

The room was dark with spotlights directed at the stage, just as she remembered from her brief look before. As she let her eyes adjust, she became painfully aware that all the customers drinking and listening to the music were older and black, some staring at her as if wondering how this young, white girl could be so lost. Suddenly self-conscious, she tried to make herself small and inconspicuous as she quickly made her way to the corner of the room. She chose a table next to the window where she could watch for Ali and Claire yet still have a clear view of the band on stage. Especially the piano.

"Welcome to The Corner Club. What'll it be, Honey?"

Peg was startled by the voice beside her and looked up to see a tall, buxom waitress, the whites of her teeth and eyes gleaming in her dark face. Struck dumb by the pleasant smile and attention focused solely on her, Peg couldn't think of the name of any drinks except what her mother always ordered on the rare occasions they went out to a supper club. "I'd like a Harvey Wallbanger, please," Peg said, hoping her timid voice carried enough over the music.

"Closest we got is a screwdriver, Sugar. That work for ya?" the waitress drawled.

Peg nodded and soon a glass of the sweet, orange drink was set on the table before her. She sat back and idly played with her tiny straw as she watched the band. Benny played with as much energy and passion as he had the other times she'd seen him. Somehow, he drew her into the music until she wasn't only listening to the notes but feeling the drive behind them.

It was nearly midnight when the band finally took a break. The waitress was delivering drinks to the next table, and with her blocking the view, Peg couldn't see the stage. By the time she moved, a new person was taking a seat at the piano for a solo act and Benny had disappeared.

Without Benny to keep her attention riveted to the stage, Peg sat back and stared out the window at the people passing back and forth. Suddenly, she recognized the song being played. It was a slow, sad song from a record her mother used to play on rainy days. She didn't know its name, but it painfully reminded her of how much she missed her mother. By the time the song ended, tears were streaming down her cheeks. Blindly, she grabbed her purse to hunt for a tissue.

"That song gets to me, too." The deep male voice made her jump, and she was surprised to see a handkerchief being handed to her.

"Thanks," she mumbled as she gratefully took it to wipe at her face and clear her blurry eyes. As she looked up to hand it back, she froze in shock at the sight of the man standing next to her.

"May I sit?" Benny asked politely, waving a hand at the chair across the table from her. She nodded numbly and he slid gracefully into the empty seat. "Now, I know I'd notice if I saw you in here before," he said with a smile and looked out over the audience of dark faces. His deep rolling voice and joking manner helped put her at ease.

"I guess I do kinda stand out, don't I?" she said with a smile, following his gaze.

"So, what brings you here, of all places?" he asked, bringing his eyes back to hers. Up close, she noticed he had the most interesting eyes she'd ever seen. Even in the dim light, she could see they were a bright green and she found herself wondering how they would look in the sunlight. Catching herself staring, she quickly looked down at her glass of melting ice.

"The music, I guess," she answered just loud enough for him to hear over the conversing crowd.

"You like jazz?" he asked as he motioned for the waitress. Peg nodded. "You don't know how refreshing that is to hear."

"This seems like a great place," Peg added, trying not to babble incoherently. "I mean, not that I've been to many jazz clubs, but it seems...great."

Benny smiled fondly at the familiar sights around him—the intimate stage, the tiny bar, the simple wooden tables and chairs, and the pictures of jazz musicians on the walls. "Yeah, it is. It's no Grande Ballroom, Twenty Grand, or Your Place Lounge, but it's getting a little more popular. The Corner Club's been my home away from home for years."

Peg waited as the waitress sat his drink in front of him, declined a refill of her own, and watched her walk away before saying, "I saw you play in the park the other day. I really liked it."

He drained half of the amber liquid in the glass and wiped his lips with the back of his hand before answering. "Thanks. Sometimes that means more to us than the money. Especially when the money isn't that great," he added with a laugh.

A couple stopped to talk to Benny, praising his talent and suggesting more songs they wanted to hear the band play. Peg sipped her watery drink and watched him easily banter back and forth with them. After shaking their hands, he turned his complete attention back to her.

"I was wondering," she began, leaning forward and looking around to make sure she wouldn't be overheard. "Is it hard to be the only white guy in a black band?"

“I’m white?” he asked, startled as he held his long-fingered hands up as if seeing them for the first time. Then a slow smile spread across his face and Peg had to cover her mouth not to laugh out loud at the joke he’d undoubtedly used several times before. He curved his long fingers around the glass in front of him and shrugged. “I guess it was at first,” he admitted, also leaning forward until their faces were just a foot apart. “I almost got booed off the stage before my first gig. But when I started playing, everyone stopped looking at my skin and started listening to the soul of the music.”

"Yo! Benny!" One of the band members called out to him and he waved back. He quickly finished his drink and stood up.

“We’re starting again so I gotta go.” He walked a few steps, then paused and came back. “By the way, my name’s Benny Hunter,” he said and held out his hand.

“Peg Bennett,” she replied as she offered her own. His hand was warm and strong and made her want to keep hers tucked comfortably there. He stood staring into her blue eyes with his green ones until they called for him again.

“Hope we can talk again,” he said and let go of her hand. The band was starting to play, and he ran back to jump up onto the stage to join them. He wanted to look back into the corner to see if she was watching but wasn’t able to until the end of the song. When he finally did, she was gone.

Chapter Fifteen

June 13, 1969

"You're welcome, Mr. Halverson," Benny called with a wave as the old, rusty truck pulled away from the back of Hunter's Hardware Store. He absently watched the rain fall for a minute before walking slowly back to the storeroom. The weather matched his mood perfectly. Picking up his clipboard, he tried once more to focus on the monthly inventory check. After counting the same boxes for the third time, he gave up and sat down on a wooden crate.

"Seems like you've been a little out of it for the past few days, son," his father said from the doorway. "What's up?"

"I don't know." Benny sighed and rubbed his forehead. "I just can't seem to concentrate on anything. Can't seem to get into my music lately, either."

"Something bothering you?" Howard Hunter sat down next to his son, worry plain on his face. "You in some kind of trouble?"

"No," Benny said quickly, "I'm not in any trouble."

“Well, there must be something on your mind.”

"Not something...someone."

He told his father about the girl from the club. Her blonde hair and blue eyes were burned into his mind like the afterimage of a camera flash. And for some reason, he kept hearing her soft voice wherever he went.

“And I haven't seen her since. I don't even know where to look for her,” he finished with a dejected sigh.

“You said her name was Peg Bennett?” his father asked and rubbed his chin in thought.

“Yeah. I wish I would've asked for her number or where she lived.” He stood up and began pacing the small storeroom.

“I don’t recognize the name. But if she said she liked jazz, she’ll find you. Have a little faith, Son.” His father stood up and clapped him fondly on the back.

“Yeah, right,” Benny scoffed. “Like that’s all it takes.” His father was heading toward the door when an awful thought occurred to Benny. “What if she was just passing through? What if she left town right after we met? I’d never see her again.”

“Then it wasn’t meant to be, and someone even better will come along,” his father answered gently. “Why don’t you take the rest of the afternoon off? Business is slow enough with all this rain. Go up and get some rest before you go in tonight. You look like you haven't been getting much sleep lately."

"No, I haven't," he admitted. "Because every time I close my eyes, I see her face, and it depresses me because it isn't the real thing. But I suppose it's worth a try. Thanks, Dad."

As he climbed the steps to his apartment above the store, he tried to convince himself his father was right. Not the part about faith—he didn't believe things happened just because people believed they would. It was the part about if it was meant to be, he would see her again. At least that thought gave him hope. If not...well, at least he still had his music.

The apartment above his father's store had been his since he graduated high school, even when he was away at college. Their agreement was that instead of paying rent he would work in the store, and he promised not to play his instruments during store hours. They hadn't originally approved of him joining an all-black jazz band at the age of nineteen, but he'd managed to dispel their worries when the band started headlining at popular jazz clubs in town, steadily working their way toward the big time.

Benny laid down to rest, but it was no use with those blue eyes haunting him. Pounding his bed in frustration, he jumped up and went out to stand on his small balcony. The rain was letting up, but the clouds still hung heavy overhead as he looked down at the lazy street below. He was nearly twenty-nine years old and was beginning to feel ten years of living alone was long enough. But he'd never been attracted to any girl as he was to Peg Bennett. He desperately wanted to get to know her better and wondered if his life would be able to go on normally if he never saw her again.

Benny went to work in a foul mood that night. He hadn't been able to rest after all and wasn't able to escape through his music because the store was still open. After a while, he couldn't even stand the sight of his empty apartment. So, he'd left and walked around town in the dwindling showers until he had to show up at the club. By the time he got there, the rain had completely stopped, but he was soaked through and in a worse mood than when he'd started. He tried everything he could think of to dispel the thought of Peg from his mind, but she was lodged in there too deep.

"You look awful, man," Bo said as they dressed in their matching suits. Bo was the only other band member who was under forty years old, and the closest thing Benny had to a best friend. Not many of the boys he graduated high school with were interested in his kind of music, and with two jobs, he didn't have much time for a social life. Even though he and Benny had the same interest in music, Bo was married with kids, and they had little else in common.

"Yeah, well, I feel awful," Benny sighed as he put on his jacket in The Corner Club's cramped dressing room. Since the other band members were already dressed and tuning their instruments on stage, he didn't have to fight for space in front of the mirror to run a comb through his towel-dried hair.

"She'll come back," Bo announced as if reading his mind. "I can feel it."

"Have you been working some of that voodoo black magic, Bo?" Benny asked and they both laughed. It was an ongoing joke between them for a long time now. Bo's mother was originally from Jamaica and Bo loved threatening people she would put a hex on them. Benny knew she wasn't capable of hexing anyone. Mama was a devout Christian and the kindest, wisest person he knew.

"Seriously, man," Bo said as their laughter died down. "I just know she'll come back here soon. Maybe even tonight."

"How can you be so sure?"

"Like I said," Bo said as he headed toward the dressing room door, "I can feel it. Besides, if she's affected you this much, think of what you've probably done to her." With a smile and a wink, he disappeared out into the hallway.

Benny turned back toward the mirror to fix his tie. He'd never thought of it that way. He wondered if she'd felt the same current of electricity he had when they shook hands. Was she just as tormented as he was? The thought made him smile and relax for the first time in days. If she felt the same, she just had to return to the club. If not...then his father was right, and they weren't meant to be together. If so, he'd just have to try harder to forget her.

Playing piano helped to relieve some of his tension as he gave himself over to the music. Even Bo noticed it and gave him a knowing smile and nod. He'd always told Benny he needed to find a lady friend. "It ain't healthy to have that much passion and only have musical instruments to hold," Bo told him on several occasions, but Benny thought it sounded more like something Bo's mother would say.

The band was playing the last song before their first break of the night when Bo spied a pale face with blonde hair coming through the door. Still playing his trumpet, he caught Benny's eye and nodded toward the audience. It didn't take Benny long to spot her since she stood out like a sore thumb, and Bo nearly broke out in laughter at how quickly Benny's mood changed. He smiled wide at Bo and nearly lost the rest of the band as he picked up the tempo in an effort to end the song sooner.

Chapter Sixteen

As the song finished and the audience applauded, Benny left the rest of the band gasping for breath as he jumped down from the stage and rushed to join Peg at the same corner table. Bo took the band aside to point out the couple and make some special arrangements.

"I never thought I'd see you again," Benny blurted out breathlessly as he slid into the chair across from Peg without bothering to ask first.

"I tried," Peg answered with her own breathless smile, "but I wasn't able to come until tonight." Benny was happy and relieved to see she seemed as excited to see him as he was her.

"I knew I should've gotten your number." Their reunion was interrupted as the same tall, pretty waitress set two glasses on the table between them and, with a knowing smile, filled them with bubbly champagne. "We didn't order this, Maddy," he said, confused.

"You didn't, Sugar," she said slyly and nodded her head toward the band. "They also sent a message."

"Oh? And what's that?" he asked, knowing Bo had to be behind this.

"They said you're fired." Then she leaned down to whisper something in his ear before turning to stroll back toward the bar. Benny laughed, but Peg looked horror-stricken.

"What did she say? Why did they fire you? Oh, my God! It wasn't because of me, was it? Maybe I shouldn't be here."

Panic gripped him as she started to stand, and he imagined losing her once again. "No! Don't go."

He impulsively grabbed her hand and felt the same shock of electricity from her soft skin as before and marveled that it wasn't accompanied by visible sparks that lit up the room. He could tell in her face she felt the same connection between them as she stared down at his hand, her lips slightly parted as if she'd just taken a sharp gasp of air. But when her eyes followed the length of his arm up to his, he saw uncertainty and concern written on her face, and his heart both melted and soared at the same time.

"I'm not really fired," Benny admitted, giving her a reassuring smile and gently tugging her hand until she sat down once more. "It's just Bo's way of giving me the night off."

"You mean you're not playing tonight?"

He saw disappointment cast a shadow over her bright blue eyes and his soaring mood started to plummet. Could he have misread her excitement earlier? Was she really only interested in his playing after all? Was the reaction and look she gave him after grabbing her hand actually panic from his outburst and embarrassment at his touch? He looked down at where his larger hand still engulfed her smaller one but couldn't bring himself to release her for fear she'd disappear again the moment they were no longer touching.

"Only if you really want me to," he said hesitantly, trying to force his voice into sounding indifferent and failing. "But, to tell you the truth, I'd much rather be here talking to you."

She smiled brightly then, turning her hand to clasp his, and his worries were dispelled. He felt like shouting for joy that the one person he wanted to be with also wanted to be with him but didn't want to risk scaring her away. It took great restraint to settle for merely holding her tiny hand in his.

"So, tell me about yourself," Benny said as they sipped the champagne.

Peg rubbed her nose where the popping bubbles tickled it. "What do you want to know?"

"Everything."

She looked at him skeptically, then smiled when she realized he wasn't joking. "I've never had anyone ask me that before."

He raised his eyebrows in surprise. "You've never had anyone interested in getting to know you? I find that hard to believe."

"It's not that. It's just that back home everybody already knows everything about everybody else because our families have been there for generations."

"Wait a minute," Benny interrupted, a small ember of panic lighting in his stomach. "You don't live in Detroit?"

"No. I'm from Eagle Creek, Wisconsin."

Benny took a sip from his glass as he processed this depressing bit of news, his fear that she'd just been passing through town now becoming a reality. Although Wisconsin bordered Michigan, it still felt to him like the other side of the country. "So, what brings you here?"

A sadness fell over her face. "I'm just visiting my aunt and uncle for a couple months..." she paused slightly before continuing, "...after my mom died a few weeks ago."

"I'm so sorry to hear that," he said, feeling a pain in his heart for her grief. He unconsciously began to rub his thumb against her hand offering what comfort he could. She gave him a sad smile in return. "Were you two really close?"

"We were, and it hit me really hard, especially since the accident happened right before graduation. My dad thought getting out of town for a bit would cheer me up before I have to start college this fall."

Benny's thumb paused when he realized just what she'd just disclosed. Not only was she in mourning and here for such a short amount of time—much too short for any kind of serious relationship—but she was younger than she looked.

"You just graduated…high school?" he asked, hoping he'd misinterpreted her.

She nodded absently as her attention was called back to the stage where the band started playing without him. Benny felt his dreams shatter. Peg was beautiful, loved jazz, and obviously attracted to him…but she was so young. He looked down at their linked hands and felt like a cradle robber. He was trying to think of a way to pull away from her without hurting her feelings when Maddy walked by and gave them a teasing wink.

"She seems friendly," Peg commented dryly, tightening her fingers around his. Benny looked closer and chuckled when he realized the look on her face and the proprietary hold on his hand were out of jealousy. It warmed his heart to know she had those kinds of feelings for him. Maybe their age difference didn't bother her as much as it did him.

"Maddy? She's a hopeless romantic. She's been trying to marry me off to every white girl she meets. Some black ones, too," he whispered confidentially.

Peg laughed nervously with him, and he noticed a definite redness of embarrassment creeping into her cheeks. He loved the way she blushed. The color brought out her fine features and widened her eyes. She tried to pull her hand from his and look away, but he tugged her hand closer to him across the table. With the other hand, he reached over to gently take her chin and force her to look up at him.

"Do you know how cute you look when you blush?" The redness deepened, but she relaxed as she realized he'd been teasing her.

He released her chin and kissed her hand before letting that go, too. She covered her heated cheeks with her palms. The combination of the champagne and his teasing made her skin irresistible, and he didn't trust himself not to reach for her. He needed to remember how young she was.

"Actually..." he paused as he thought hard, "I'd say it's probably been five years since I even had a date. My God, that sounds pitiful," he added and drank the last of the champagne in his glass. Now that he thought about it, it was an extremely depressing thought.

"Was that a high school sweetheart?" she asked, teasingly.

"No," he answered nervously, realizing she had no idea just how old he was. He rubbed his suddenly moist palms on his pant legs, wishing he didn't have to tell her the truth. "Actually, it was just after grad school."

The look on her face struck him like a knife in the stomach. He'd have given anything, even his musical talent, to be ten years younger right at that very moment.

"I...I thought you were younger than that," she said quietly. He could feel her already pulling away from him and suddenly wished he'd lied about his age. Then he shook his head, knowing he couldn't have done that to her anyway.

"I thought you were older," he admitted sadly, absently rubbing a finger around the rim of his empty glass. "You don't look like you just graduated high school." They sat in uncomfortable silence as they each tried to work through their emotions. He could think of nothing to say that would take them back to the way they'd started the night. All he could do was hope she was willing to see past their ages. Even if she had to leave in a couple of months and they could be nothing more than friends, he'd take what he could get just to get to know her better. Then maybe, in a few years, the difference won't be so noticeable.

Just then a sharp rapping sounded on the window next to them. Two girls were standing on the other side of the glass, gesturing frantically at Peg.

"That's my ride. I've got to go," she said and stood up to leave.

"Wait." Benny stood to block her exit. He towered over her with the top of her head barely reaching his shoulder and she looked so small and young next to him making them even more aware of their differences. With a sigh, he decided he didn't care how they looked and was determined to convince her of that as well.

"Benny—" she began awkwardly, but he didn't let her finish as he took her face in his hands and locked her eyes with his.

"I don't care how old we are," he said defiantly. "I want to spend time with you. The question is, do you want to spend time with me? I hope to God the answer is yes."

Her blue eyes flitted back and forth from one green eye to the other. "This isn't just some kind of pick-up line, is it?"

All he could manage was to slowly shake his head and let his face show his honesty. He knew the moment she made up her mind to trust him when her smile lit up her whole face. She nodded between his hands and his heart soared. Very slowly, giving her plenty of time to protest, he bent low to give her a light kiss. When she kissed him back, he knew if it hadn't been for the persistent rapping on the window, he wouldn't have been able to let her go, even if they were probably drawing the attention of every eye in the club.

"Can I call you?" he asked as he walked her to the door. Her eyes flicked uncertainly from Benny to the impatiently waiting girls.

"Maybe you shouldn't," she said. "My aunt and uncle don't know I'm here, and having you call for me for no apparent reason could get us all into trouble."

He cast his eyes about frantically looking for inspiration to solve their problem when he caught sight of one of the many posters pinned to the corkboard just inside the door. When he smiled, she followed his gaze.

"There's another concert in the park tomorrow," Benny said.

"I could just say I met you there," Peg continued, picking up on his train of thought. "That's brilliant!"

The door flew open and the two girls both grabbed her arms and pulled her outside before he could say or do anything but watch her go. Peg watched him from over her shoulder as she was steered toward a waiting car and gave him a wave from the backseat before they sped away.

"The band is gonna take a short break," Bo was announcing just as Benny let the door close and turned his back to it in a daze. "We'll be back in a few with more of your favorites, so order another drink and stay where you are."

Suddenly feeling like part of him was missing, Benny automatically headed for the stage and the piano that had become his island of safety and solace. He didn't need the spotlight or the rest of the instruments to show the world how he was feeling. He let his music do it for him. His fingers caressed and danced over the keys as he closed his eyes and poured his emotions and soul into the song.

As the last notes rang out and died away, Benny became aware of the silence that had replaced the normal background conversation and laughter that always accompanied their playing. Opening his eyes, he looked out over the crowd. No one spoke or even moved. They had sat in stunned silence, listening to the passionate song played by the lone man on the piano, and Benny noticed more than one person wipe tears from their eyes. It was only a moment later when they burst into roaring applause. But to Benny, that moment of silence meant more to him than all the applause in the world.

Chapter Seventeen

"Wow," Mary Jean breathed as I paused my story to make a pot of coffee. We'd already finished off one of the bottles, and I still had a lot more to tell her. I didn't dare open the second bottle yet. I knew we would both need it later.

"Should I make leaded or unleaded?" I asked.

"I think you'd better have the caffeine. I'm used to these hours, but you're not." She joined me in the kitchen and bustled about getting us both a bowl of ice cream while we waited for the coffee. "So did they meet at the park?"

"Claire said she didn't actually see it because she and Ali decided to go to a movie instead of spending another afternoon listening to jazz music, but she did help Mom plan their 'accidental' meeting—she volunteers to get her aunt and uncle some lemonade, they meet by chance at the refreshment stand, he offers to help her carry the cups back like a gentleman, and voila, they have their proper and very public introduction even her uncle couldn't argue with. According to Benny's journal, it worked like a charm. They acted as if they'd never met and let her aunt introduce them. He even pulled her uncle aside to ask if he could call on her sometime, although he warned Benny not to get too involved because of her age and her short stay in Detroit. They never suspected a thing."

"So, what happened? I mean, I know what happened," she said, waving her hand up and down to indicate my obvious existence and the inferred reason for it. "But *how* did it happen?"

"Well, it seems they saw each other at every possible opportunity. They went out together when he didn't have to work; and when he did, she tried everything to be with him. She offered to help him at the store and went to all the daytime concerts he played. Mom even asked her aunt and uncle if she could go to the club to watch him play, but they refused, saying it was no place for a proper, white, young lady. So, she snuck out whenever she could."

"Did she ever get caught?" MJ asked.

"Not once, according to Claire," I answered, pouring the coffee into a thermos to take back to the living room. "Although one time she and Ali lost track of whoever gave them a ride to a party just outside of town. They had to walk two miles to get back to Benny's club, and by the time they got there it was empty and there was no sign of my mom. When they hadn't come by the time the club closed, Benny gave her a ride back. By the time the other two had walked back to Ali's and found Mom sound asleep in her bed, Ali's parents were just waking up and the girls had to pretend they'd just gotten up early," I said laughing at the image in my mind. "They didn't get a chance to sleep all day and were too tired to go back out that night. Claire said she'd never been so tired in all her life."

MJ laughed along with me as we went back to our comfortable chairs in the sitting room. When we were settled with our cups, she brought me back to her original question.

"So, when did you happen? Did the journals say anything about it?"

"Oh, yes," I said, rolling my eyes. "Almost more than I wanted to know."

Chapter Eighteen

June 29, 1969

"Do you think they'd let you come to a Fourth of July picnic?" Benny asked as they walked, hand in hand, through the park. He'd just finished another strenuous set and the sweat made his blond hair curl around his ears and forehead. He normally would've been exhausted, but when Peg was by his side, he always felt strangely energized.

"I'm not sure." She glanced back to where her aunt and uncle were sitting and saw them smiling in their direction. "Maybe. Where is it?"

"It's at Bo's house. Every year they have a big get-together on the Fourth. There's always a ton of food and all kinds of music. They even have their own fireworks."

"Sounds like fun," she said, excited by the idea. "And we could be together for a whole day for once."

Even though they tried to spend as much time as possible together, neither felt it was nearly enough. They were never alone. They had to settle for walks in the park, dinner at restaurants, working together at his father's store, and ten-minute breaks at the club. He loved to whisper his need to be alone with her and watch her blush. There were so many things they wanted to say to each other but couldn't as long as there were people around.

They walked back, and Benny politely asked her uncle's permission to take her to the picnic. Her uncle asked all the important questions he thought he needed to know as her stand-in guardian, and Benny gave all the right answers.

"It's really just an old-fashioned family picnic with a lot of kids running around and our band playing a few songs for entertainment."

"Well, I guess it'd be all right," Uncle Peter said, finally giving his consent. "Even your father couldn't complain with that many chaperones."

"Would you like to help with the games?" Benny asked Peg. "They usually have egg races, gunny sack races, water balloon toss...things like that."

"I'd love to."

Benny could tell she was forcing more enthusiasm than she felt into her voice. Playing games with children she didn't even know wasn't how she wanted to spend their time together, but her aunt and uncle were watching so she was playing her part.

"Let's go tell Bo. I know he'll be grateful for the extra hands." They excused themselves and walked back toward the stage. "Maybe I should have been an actor instead of a musician," he said, gazing into the sky reflectively.

"You mean you're not going to make me help with the games?" she asked hopefully, then started to laugh when he winked at her. "Are you telling me you lied, Benny Hunter?" she scolded, giving him a playful slap on the arm.

"I most certainly did not," he answered, trying to look offended. "There will be games and tons of kids there, but I'm not letting you out of my sight any more than I have to. I told Bo I was willing to do one set…then we're on our own."

"Oh, Benny, do you mean it?" she asked and laid her head on his arm since he was too tall for her to reach his shoulder.

"We can either stay there and get lost in the woods or..." he paused, not sure how she would take his suggestion, "...we could go somewhere else. Like…maybe back to my place."

He could feel her tense beside him at the mention of his apartment. She complained they always seemed to be watched, but should they really be *that* alone? Although she smiled at him, her initial involuntary reaction reminded him just how young, inexperienced, and naive she was. He silently berated himself for suggesting it, knowing if they ever were that alone, it would take a Herculean effort on his part to keep her safe from him. He opened his mouth to rescind the invitation when Bo joined them.

"There you are at last, Benny," he joked slapping the younger man on the back. "Perfect timing as ever since we're almost done packing up.

The least you could do is load your own piano." As Benny reluctantly left to do his part, Bo turned his attention to Peg. "Did Benny tell you about the tour?"

Peg had been watching Benny expertly handle the old piano mounted on makeshift scooters so it could be rolled easily up and down the ramps from stage to truck, but Bo's question startled her. "Tour? What tour?"

"We were able to book the band at festivals, fairs, and clubs all around Michigan, Ohio, and Indiana. We'll be gone for three weeks and the only reason my wife isn't throwing a massive fit is because we'll be making more in those three weeks than we could in three months at the club. My boy Benny there is pretty popular in jazz circles and a big selling point for us. I mean you don't often find a talented white boy that plays jazz like he can."

"No, he didn't tell me." Her smile faltered a little, but she forced it back up again. "That sounds like a great opportunity. When do you leave?"

"A couple weeks after the party. You are coming to my party, aren't you? I mean you're not plotting to steal him away and deprive my guests of his talent, now, are you?" he added, giving her a sly wink.

"I wouldn't dream of it," she laughed. "Wouldn't want to get on your bad side, after all."

Bo loved that Peg had a sense of humor. He'd had to ruffle Benny's feathers now and then himself when his friend started looking too anxious and had a good feeling this little girl would be able to handle that job now.

"Wise choice," he said with a sage nod. "Because he's never missed one of my parties, and if he did because you two decided to skip out on it, everyone would know why. The talk would be all over town." Her eyes widened in shock and followed his pointed look to where her aunt and uncle were waiting. "Then again," he continued, leaning down and talking just loud enough for her to hear, "I have a big place. Many people have gotten lost for hours roaming around there together. That's how I met my wife." He gave her a wink and waggled his eyebrows making her laugh out loud.

"Whatever he's telling you, you can be sure it's a lie," Benny said as he took Peg's hand to pull her away from Bo. Peg was blushing prettily, and he was jealous someone else was able to put it there.

"Not at all, my man," Bo said, amused by his obvious envy. "I always speak the God's-honest truth." Then he laughed and patted Benny's shoulder before he got in his truck to haul their gear back to the club.

"What was that all about? What did he say?"

"Oh, nothing," she said, still blushing.

Benny had to restrain himself from kissing her pink cheeks to feel their warmth against his lips because they were in public and in full view of her aunt and uncle. As they slowly wandered back toward her uncle's car, Peg suddenly stopped walking.

"Why didn't you tell me about the tour?"

Benny inwardly groaned, vowing to give Bo a piece of his mind the first chance he got. "I didn't tell you because I decided not to go. I just hadn't talked to the band yet."

Peg's eyebrows drew together making worry lines just above the bridge of her nose. "But Bo said you were the selling point for the band. Can you just not go?"

"Bo said that?" Benny was surprised. No one told him he was being used as the hook to book their band and wasn't sure if it was due to his talent or color. He supposed it probably was a novelty to see a white man playing in a black band, but he preferred to think music was blind and people only heard how they sounded.

"He also said you'd be making a lot more money. Isn't everyone counting on that?"

"You sound like you don't want me to stay," Benny said carefully, hoping it wasn't true.

Peg looked down at their clasped hands. "I don't want you to go, but I don't think you should stay, either. The band is counting on you."

Benny could feel how hard it was for her to give up seeing him for three whole weeks but was impressed and proud of her for being considerate of the livelihood of his friends. He lifted her hand up to his lips to make her look up at him. "Then we'll just have to make the most of our time together before I have to go." Staring intently into her eyes, he let his breath play across her soft skin as he whispered, "I can't wait to be alone with you on the Fourth."

That night, Peg confided in Claire.

"Bo said we'd be able to be alone together on his farm during the picnic, but Benny also mentioned going back to his place. I'm just so nervous and don't know what I should do. On the one hand, I want to spend time with just the two of us since there've always been people around when we're together. On the other hand…I'm not sure if I'm ready to be alone with him. He's so much older and experienced and I'm…well…not."

"You mean you and David never…"

"No!" Peg interrupted.

Claire gave her a skeptical look. "You dated David all through high school…even last year when he was off at college. You two went to every dance and high school sporting event possible and he was at your house all those Saturday nights and you still didn't—"

"Of course not! We're both Catholic, Claire. We've kissed, but nothing…serious." Claire raised one eyebrow in doubt. "We're both saving ourselves for marriage."

"He's either got the strongest self-control in a man I've ever heard of or he's the most boring man in history."

"Well," Peg said with a sigh, "I admit last year got to be a bit…routine. I was still doing all my high school things, and whenever he came home all he could talk about was how much he loved his classes at business school. I think he kept coming over out of habit more than anything else. That's when we decided to officially break it off. I just couldn't imagine spending the rest of my life with him. I'm pretty sure he felt the same way. Still, he was there for me after Mom died and I really appreciated it."

Claire nodded in understanding. "Benny may not be my cup of tea, but at least he's a step up from David. I never saw David look at you with the same intensity Benny does. I don't think you understand how much that man wants you. The question is, do you trust Benny enough to be alone with him? I mean *really* alone...with just him? He's not David, you know."

Peg opened her mouth, then closed it again as her eyebrows drew together in deep thought. After a minute, she looked Claire in the eyes with the most intense surety she'd ever seen in her timid friend. A smile of amazement brightened her face and tears of happiness shone in her eyes.

"I trust him, Claire," Peg said, grasping her hand excitedly. "Not only do I trust him...I love him."

Claire couldn't help but be happy along with her. "Then you're going to need something great to wear." She bounded off the bed and flung open the closet to root through Ali's clothes. "And definitely something that doesn't wrinkle. That's important."

Chapter Nineteen

July 4, 1969

Benny arrived to pick Peg up at ten o'clock and was forced to sit and talk with Peg's uncle as Ali and Claire put the final touches on her outfit. She had her hair pushed back away from her face with a headband and was wearing Ali's belt and miniskirt, Claire's boots, and even her aunt's scarf, which was around her neck and tucked into the neckline of her sleeveless knitted top since Peg felt it a bit too revealing. She was nervous but happy with what she saw in the mirror.

When Benny caught sight of Peg coming down the stairs, his breath caught in his throat. She looked beautiful and mature as she gracefully walked to his side. He tried to continue making small talk with Peter but was anxious to be on their way to the picnic. All he wanted now was to move the clock ahead to when they could finally be alone.

"You're unusually quiet," Peg commented after they'd driven in silence for almost ten minutes.

Benny noticed she was gripping her hands together and could feel nervous energy coming off her in waves. It made him feel guilty for the thoughts he'd been thinking ever since inviting her to Bo's picnic. Even though she looked so much older in makeup and the short skirt that highlighted her delicious legs, he had to keep reminding himself she'd been a senior in high school a little over a month ago. He never felt more like a cradle robber than he did right then...and touched that she went to all the trouble to look older for him.

"It's nothing," he reassured her, giving her what he hoped was a confident smile. He reached over to take her hand to hopefully put her at ease. "Just thinking is all."

"What about?"

"Do you really want to know?" he joked, giving her a mischievous wink. She blushed right on cue, and he chuckled happily as he kissed the back of her hand.

He pulled his blue Rambler American onto the quarter-mile-long driveway already lined with vehicles and guests making their way toward the party dressed in festive red, white, and blue. Peg looked eagerly around at the fields of wheat and corn on either side and the simple, two-story house at the edge of a dense forest.

"I can't believe Bo has time to take care of this farm and still play in the band almost every night," Peg commented.

"He's got a hardworking and *very* supportive family."

Even though people were still arriving—walking up the driveway carrying picnic baskets, bowls, or casserole dishes—a large number of families were already milling about the yard. Peg gasped at the biggest spread of food she'd ever seen, the wide variety of dishes almost completely hiding what appeared to be colorful bed sheets as makeshift tablecloths covering a flatbed wagon.

"There's enough food there to feed an army," Peg exclaimed in amazement, as he parked his car beside the house where he could unload the electric piano tucked in the back seat when they were ready to set up on Bo's homemade stage.

"Believe it or not," he said, "it'll be empty by the end of the night."

"Still, you should've told me it was a potluck. I would've made something."

"You're my guest," he argued. "I wasn't going to invite you and then make you cook. Besides, I'm providing entertainment. Food for the soul instead of the stomach." She rolled her eyes, and he laughed as he got out and rounded the vehicle to open her door. "Come on, I'll show you around."

Although the temperature of the previous days had reached into the 90s, a cooler breeze had rolled in to keep the day to a pleasant 80 degrees. Fluffy, white clouds drifted by overhead casting moving shadows across the fields, and the smells of soil, crops, and plentiful food mixed together in an inviting way that made them even hungrier.

Benny took her into the house full of women trying to put the finishing touches on the dishes that hadn't made it out to the wagon yet. One woman looked up and gave them a welcoming smile as she came to greet them, giving Benny a big hug.

"Peg, I want you to meet Bo's wife, Virginia," he said when she finally released him.

"Well, it's about time. I've heard so much about you," Virginia said, pulling her into an identical hug. "But, please, call me Ginny. I'm just so happy our Benny finally found himself a girl! And such a pretty, young one, too," she added, jabbing him playfully in the stomach as he dramatically doubled over in mock pain.

"Let mi see." The elderly woman belonging to the lilting Jamaican accent brushed Ginny aside with her knobby wooden cane and looked Peg up and down through her small, thick glasses.

"And this," Benny said, affectionately giving the woman a hug around her hunched shoulders, "is Bo's mother. Everyone just calls her Mama."

"If mi yuh real mama, yuh not be all skin 'n bones," she declared, presenting her cheek for a kiss, which Benny dutifully provided. Mama opened her arms and Benny gave Peg an encouraging nod before she stepped into another big hug. "Mi 'appy to see ya. Benny been alone too long. Mi tell 'im always to find 'im a wife."

Benny couldn't stop the color that crept into his cheeks. Peg laughed and he could tell she was enjoying seeing him blush and be embarrassed for once.

"And on that note, I think it's time to go help Bo get set up. Do you want to come and watch?" he asked, giving Peg an excuse to flee their attention with him.

Peg looked around at the chaos of busy women around them—bustling about mixing salads, frying chicken, reprimanding children for sneaking cookies, and giving orders to the men who happened to wander within sight all while working like a well-oiled machine—and shook her head as she sat down beside Bo's mother and picked up a butter knife.

"That's okay. You go ahead. I'll help out in here."

"Yea, be off wid yuh," the old woman ordered in that beautiful Jamaican voice, flicking her own knife toward the door. "We ave women thing tuh duh."

Benny gave Peg a quick peck on the cheek and gratefully slipped out the door, marveling at how the vivacious women could work and still keep up a steady stream of conversation. Through the screen, he heard one woman declare, "So, I told him if he thought he was gonna spend his weekend lying around drinking beer, he better think again," followed by, "If my man dared do that, I got a good cast iron frying pan to change his mind," while the rest agreed that only a no-good-bum would ever consider doing something so despicable.

Benny sighed, feeling sorry for their husbands if they even thought about crossing their wives. He was still shaking his head when he reached the stage area.

"Have they picked out your China patterns yet?" Bo joked as Benny joined him in setting up rows of folding chairs borrowed from Bo's church basement.

"By now, they've probably picked out names for our children," Benny said. "I just hope they don't make Peg any more nervous than she already is. I don't think she's ever been around so many colored people before."

Offended, Bo stopped and put his hands on his hips. "You think she's scared of us?"

"No," Benny answered. "I think she's scared they won't like her, and she knows how important you all are to me."

A huge smile broke out on Bo's face. "Right back atcha, Benny my boy. But if I were you, I'd be more worried about the ideas they'll put in her head."

Benny groaned and headed toward the house, fearing what stories they could be filling her head with about their ideas on how to handle men. He certainly didn't want her to feel like she needed to go out and buy a cast iron pan. But when he neared the screen door, the sound of Bo's mother caused him to pause just out of sight and listen.

"That a right gud man yuh ave there, miss," she was saying. "If mi was yuh, mi be keepin' him happy tuh stay at home."

"Mama, don't be bothering that young thing," Ginny scolded. "She don't need no advice from you."

"*Yuh* tuk mi advice and now mi ave da most beautiful grambabies." She laughed heartily and several other women joined in.

"I don't think there's a woman here who ain't heard your advice, Mama," Ginny said, her voice dying away as she moved further into the house.

"That right. Now mi gi *you* mi advice, miss. Yuh kno makin' 'im happy will mek yuh happy, suh nuh worry. Happy people always be togetha. Now, tek dis here out wid di rest an' den guh find yuh man."

"God bless you, Mama," Benny thought to himself as Peg came out through the screen door carrying a large basket of buttered buns. Since she was focused on getting them safely to the wagon, she didn't see him standing behind the door. As quietly as he could, he followed her across the yard, and as soon as she took her hands off the basket, he wrapped his arms around her. She jumped and let out a small squeak of surprise. When she turned her head to look back at him, he claimed her lips in a tender kiss.

"Benny," she scolded when the kiss ended, trying to squirm out of his embrace, "people are watching."

"Let them," he laughed and dropped another kiss on her nose. "If you hadn't noticed, we're not in the park with your aunt and uncle watching us like hawks."

Peg glanced nervously to either side of them and gasped at the number of people around the yard displaying various degrees of affection in full view of everyone—couples holding hands, exchanging kisses, and holding each other close as they watched their children play.

"I've never seen anything like this," Peg whispered. "People are so much more... conservative...where I come from."

"They love each other and want the whole world to know it. As it should be, don't you think?" Benny asked, hugging her tight against his chest as he rested his chin on the top of her head. Just then, Ginny came out of the house and began ringing a big, old-fashioned schoolhouse bell. "Looks like it's time to eat."

After they loaded their plates with more food than they could possibly eat, Benny grabbed a blanket from the back seat of his car and led Peg over to the edge of the woods. They sat in the shade, leaning against the trunk of a large tree. While they ate, Benny pointed out some of the families he knew, most of them being Bo's brothers and sisters. As he talked, he made little gestures of affection he couldn't do before—playing with her hair, stroking her arm, wiping her mouth with his napkin, tapping his knee against hers, kissing her fingers and especially her lips.

"Do you trust me?" he asked suddenly.

Peg looked around as if trying to figure out the catch. "Yes, I trust you."

"Then close your eyes." Obediently, she closed them. "Now open your mouth," he prompted.

She gave a little giggle but opened her mouth just wide enough for Benny to stick the item he'd speared on the end of his fork between her lips. She chewed with her eyes still shut, her eyebrows raising in surprise as she tried to figure out the odd combination of flavors.

"I like that. What is it?"

"A chunk of pineapple dipped in a little marinara sauce from the lasagna. I like that mix of sweet and tangy. Good, isn't it?" Before she could answer, he claimed her mouth with his, tasting her lips and tongue before suddenly pulling away and sitting back against the tree as if the kiss never happened. She stared at him in shock, but he just popped another pineapple in his mouth and smiled. "You had a little sauce on your lips there, and I didn't want to let it go to waste."

She gave him a playful swat which he pretended to dodge, and they both laughed. When they'd eaten as much as they could stand, he put their plates aside and pulled her over to lean back against him with his arms encircling her. Since she was so small, she fit perfectly under his chin. The air was so warm and the slight breeze so refreshing, he closed his eyes and sighed happily. Every now and then, he would kiss the top of her head or run his thumb back and forth over her arm. They sat that way in comfortable silence until Bo called Benny to join them on stage to play for everyone.

"Time to earn our meal," he sighed and helped her up from the ground. "I'll be playing for about an hour, so you can wander around and see all they've got going on. I think I'll be able to pick you out of the crowd," he added with a playful wink. They both stood out here just as much as they did back at the club. "I'll find you when I'm done, and then we can go for a walk." He gave her a deep kiss before they hurried over to where an impatient Bo was waiting.

Whenever he could, Benny looked out over the yard to watch Peg walk among the other guests, listening to the music but also watching the older men playing cards or checkers and the younger children gathering to begin their games. He saw Ginny take her arm and steer her back toward the house and Benny gave Bo a dirty look. Bo shrugged back while continuing to play as if to say he had no control over whatever his wife had in mind.

It took two more songs before he lost himself in the music and stopped looking for Peg. When their set was finally done, Benny was surprised to discover two hours had passed. He jumped down from the stage, but Bo held him back from rushing into the house.

"I'll go get her for you. Don't want you going in and seeing her in domestic bliss, after all. It gives a man ideas."

Bo walked through the house, peeking into different rooms where the women were gathered in the lazy breeze of several electric fans. They worked on various projects of needlework and knitting all the while gossiping and talking about husbands, babies, television shows, and current events. He knew his wife would treat Peg as part of the family, so Bo headed for the back room where she would be in the company of others her age, though most of them were newly married with small children.

"Now that's a pretty picture."

Bo's voice startled Peg and she jumped despite the sleeping baby in her arms, his tiny hand curled around her finger. The image looked so natural, he suspected it wouldn't be long before she had her own babe in her arms. He just prayed it wouldn't mean losing Benny in the band.

"You almost made me wake the baby," she whispered sternly.

"Not a chance," he chuckled. "You happen to be holding little Nathan. The house could fall down around his ears, and he'd still be sound asleep. But you'll have to give him up now because I've come to fetch you."

She handed the baby to the woman sitting next to her and followed Bo out through the kitchen. Benny was waiting for her outside, watching a couple of older men playing a bluesy tune on their guitars. Bo clapped him on the shoulder and shook his head.

"I knew they'd have her there. Ginny put her in the 'young wives' room holding babies, hoping it would rub off on her."

Benny pulled Peg into a tight hug, and they watched Bo wander off to where the children were getting ready for what promised to be a massive water fight.

"And what if it did rub off on me?" she teased, looking up into his face and smiling. He was surprised to see there was no pink in her cheeks whatsoever.

"You're not blushing," he accused, and she laughed. "My God! I'd better get you away from here before you start talking like Mama."

Chapter Twenty

He grabbed up their blanket from beside the stage, took her hand, and led her to the side of the house where Peg trustingly followed him right into the large cornfield. The top of the corn was nearly waist-high heralding a good growing season. The leaves had to have been tickling her bare legs, but she never complained as she followed behind him between the rows. Now and then, Benny would steer them diagonally across several rows before choosing another row to follow. Suddenly he stopped, pulled her close, and whispered in her ear.

"Cover your ears."

Peg looked confused but did what she was told just in time to protect her ears from loud, snapping sounds coming from several yards in front of them. She jumped and leaned around Benny to see what was going on.

Two teenage heads suddenly appeared over the tops of the corn. The boy looked completely embarrassed, but the girl started yelling and ran after what they assumed was her younger brother who'd interrupted them with his firecrackers. The girl threatened the little boy with considerable bodily harm, but he was quicker and disappeared into the house before she could reach the edge of the field.

Benny laughed at both the prank and Peg's reaction and soon she joined him, her sweet laughter ringing out over the field hiding the trysts of several young couples from the eyes of their parents.

"Is that why you brought me to this field, Benny Hunter?" she accused, still laughing at the sight of the furious girl chasing her brother. He wrapped his arms around her from behind to pull her against his chest, kissing the top of her head.

"Welcome to Bo's version of Lover's Lane," he whispered in her ear. "The skinny dipping doesn't start until after the fireworks," he joked impishly.

Peg playfully jabbed her elbow into his ribs, and he dramatically fell backward onto the ground, making sure he landed on the blanket to save his tan pants and light blue shirt from the rich, black soil. He lay on his back, surrounded by corn stalks, and looked up at her through the long, curling leaves. With a huge smile, he lifted one foot and caught her just behind her knees. Her legs buckled and she fell forward into Benny's waiting arms. He turned until they were lying side by side on the blanket, forced close by the rows of corn on either side of them. Looking around, she saw they were completely hidden from view and shaded from the sun by the lush vegetation, and all she could see besides the corn was the clear blue sky above and Benny beside her.

"Now, this is better," he sighed brushing her hair back over her shoulder. "I finally have you all to myself. Sorry it took me so long to get back to you, but..."

"You lost track of the time," she finished. "Ginny said you would."

"Oh, she did, did she?" he chuckled. He ran his thumb back and forth across her bottom lip and the laughter burned away as his eyes intensely followed its slow progress. "I wish I could stop time right now. Do you realize how beautiful you are?"

Without waiting for an answer, Benny replaced his thumb with his lips. The kissing started out gentle and hesitant, wanting to give her plenty of opportunities to pull away. When her hands snaked up his neck and her fingers plunged into his hair, pulling him even closer, his resolve shattered. They delved into each other's mouths, tasting inside and out as their breathing deepened. Benny's hand started at the back of her head, holding it in place or guiding it to the right angle as they found their best fit. Before he realized it, his palm had found its way under the knitted top and was resting at the small of her back. He couldn't tell if Peg approved or just hadn't noticed yet as he inched along her spine, reveling in the warmest, softest flesh he'd ever felt.

Wanting to give her another chance to object, Benny slid his lips off hers and laid a trail of light kisses across her cheek to the indentation at the end of her jaw just below her ear. Peg sucked in a sharp gasp but stretched her neck to the side to give him better access. He continued to kiss down her neck as his fingers slid up along her spine under her bra strap. As he dipped his head lower, he encountered the scarf barring his way to the area he wanted to taste.

He was both frustrated and thankful that the filmy barrier brought him back to the edge of his senses and he began to question what they were doing. How far was he willing to take this out here in the middle of a cornfield? How far was she willing to go? Should he stop it here and now before they did something they might regret? Could he stop now even if he wanted to?

As he debated on which direction his lips and hand would take next, Peg's lips found the racing pulse on the side of his neck, and he froze. He couldn't even breathe as she kissed lower, nudging his chin out of the way as she worked her way down to the hollow at the base of his throat. He stretched his head back to give her better access and she continued her trail up over his Adam's apple and along the bottom of his jaw, her fingers clenching around the opening of his shirt as she pulled him closer so she could reach his other ear.

Just as she sucked his earlobe between her lips and he slid his hand out from under the bra strap, intending to follow the garment to the front, another volley of firecrackers exploded from somewhere close by. They both jumped guiltily, Benny's hand jerking back as if burned and Peg hiding her face against his chest. Childish laughter sounded several yards away followed closely by the thunder of running feet and the brush of leaves only a couple of rows away as the perpetrators tried to escape their prey. This time the threats were yelled by a boy to his screaming younger sisters. After the initial shock, Benny and Peg started to laugh, both at the prank and out of embarrassment.

Benny took a deep breath in an attempt to stop his heart from beating so fast and hard, not sure if it was from their kissing, the surprise, or a combination of both. “Well, that was a little too close.”

“I hope he doesn’t catch them,” Peg replied, still laughing as she tipped her head back to look up at him.

Although her cheeks were the prettiest color of blush, he was distracted by the white of the skin showing between her top and miniskirt. Before he could allow himself to forget where they were again, he tugged the knitted fabric back into place and leaned back away from her. The slightly cooler breeze that now drifted between them only reminded him of how good the warmth of her body felt against his.

“Sorry about that,” he said, waving his hand in the direction the children had run. “And about…” he waved his hand above her now respectably covered torso, “...that.”

She looked seriously up at him, her gaze darting from one of his eyes to the other as if making sure he was really looking back at her…as if he could tear his eyes away from hers even if he wanted to. "I'm not sorry," she said, her voice soft yet firm enough that he believed her.

Benny wanted to cry, scream, and shout for joy all at the same time. He wanted to continue kissing her—he wanted to do much more—but he settled for hugging her tight, not even trusting himself to kiss her head for fear of letting it get out of hand again. As it was, his lower body was much too aware of how close they were lying. Shifting into a more comfortable position, he rolled onto his back, pulling her up so she could use his chest as a pillow while he laced his fingers safely behind his head. Instead, she propped herself up on one elbow, smiling down at him as she studied his face.

"I love the color of your eyes," Benny said. "They're like a bright, cloudless day."

"I love yours." She traced one finger along each eyebrow sending a shiver down his spine. "I noticed your dad has the same color green."

"All the men in my family do. My dad calls it 'Hunter-green' even though it's not that exact shade."

"I love the small brown flecks," she added just before a large yawn overtook her.

Benny could have taken the entire afternoon to list all the things he loved about Peg, but now that their burst of endorphins and adrenaline was wearing off, he realized how tired he was as well.

Peg laid her cheek on his chest directly over his heart and sighed happily as her eyes drifted shut. He also sighed and watched the way her head rose and fell with his chest, mesmerized by the fringe of her delicate lashes lying against her cheek. Before long, he let his own eyes close and soon they were both lulled to sleep by the warmth of the sun, coolness of the shade, and their own rhythmic breathing.

They'd only been asleep for half an hour when they were startled awake by the insistent clanging of a bell.

"Time to eat again," Benny said and kissed Peg on the nose. He stood up and stretched his arms high above his head.

"You've got to be kidding. I don't think I'll need to eat for a week," she moaned, but let him help her to her feet and lead her back toward the house.

This time the food wagon was full of sweets. Cake, cookies, pies of all kinds, and even homemade ice cream. Although she claimed she wasn't very hungry, Peg filled her plate again and they sat to listen to the music. Some of the younger generations had taken over the stage and were singing the newer rock and roll songs. She noticed some of the older people shaking their heads at what they considered 'noise', but all the children were happily dancing and singing along.

When a slow song started, Benny took Peg's hand and pulled her over to the dancing area.

Instead of the prim and old-fashioned waltz steps where couples held each other at a distance, Benny held her close against him and swayed to the beat of the music. Peg was startled until she noticed all the other dancers were doing the same thing. Before long, she relaxed against him and enjoyed herself. Even though they were such different heights, they still fit together perfectly, but it was still somehow not enough for him.

"We can go now," he whispered into her ear. She looked up at him in surprise.

"I thought we were going to stay for the fireworks," she whispered back in disappointment. "Why do you want to leave so early?"

There was no way for him to hide the way his heartbeat raced, and his breathing quickened with his desire for her, but he wanted to be absolutely sure she understood how she made him feel. He nuzzled her ear with his nose and let his warm breath play down her neck and inside the blasted scarf that hid all that perfect skin.

"I'd rather watch fireworks from somewhere else. Somewhere I don't have to share you at all."

Her own breath caught in her throat, and she shivered slightly beneath his hand on her back. After a few agonizing seconds, she nodded against his chest just as the song was ending.

"Meet me at the car," he said, reluctantly pulling away from her. "I'll let Bo know we're leaving."

"Shouldn't I say goodbye, too?"

"Do you really want to hear what Bo and Ginny think about us leaving their party early?" Her eyes darted back and forth, and a blush spread up her cheeks. "Good," he said, kissing the warmed skin. "I was afraid Mama stole that blush away."

He didn't wait for her to follow his instructions, not wanting to waste another second without her by his side. He pulled Bo away from where he was reprimanding one of his boys for something involving an errant water balloon and told him they weren't staying for the rest of the festivities.

Bo sighed. "Well, can't say I'm surprised, but I do feel like I need to give you a little friendly advice. She's pretty young, Benny." He waved away whatever argument Benny was going to give. "I'm not saying you two weren't meant to be together…any fool can see that just by the way you look at each other. I just want you to use that space between your ears before you do anything you can't take back."

Benny nodded, momentarily sobered by the fatherly warning. Bo had been a mentor and friend to him for years and he valued his opinion more than anyone else. He believed Bo knew him better than anyone else as well, even his own father.

"I know. Trust me, I am," he promised, but couldn't stop his excited smile. After studying Benny's face, Bo smiled along with him, giving him a happy slap on the back.

“Finally! Here,” he said, pushing a Mason jar into Benny’s hands. “Good luck, man.”

Chapter Twenty-one

It had only been a couple of minutes since leaving Peg, but on the way to the car, Benny dreaded the thought that she'd changed her mind about leaving. Yet when he climbed in beside her, she gave him a happy, although nervous, smile of encouragement. He handed her the gift from Bo and maneuvered the vehicle down the driveway, spraying rocks behind them as he sped out onto the main road.

"What's this?" Peg asked, holding the glass jar up to let the waning sunlight filter through it.

"Homemade wine. They open dozens of them during the fireworks. Bo gave us one since we weren't going to be here."

"And…where are we…going?" He could tell she was trying to be nonchalant—as if men drove her away from parties to be alone all the time—but he could still hear the hesitation in her voice, and she was clutching the jar tight enough to turn her knuckles white. He reached over to coax one hand free and laced their fingers together, wishing she would slide closer across the bench seat so he could put his arm around her.

"Do you trust me?" He glanced over at her and then back to the road a few times before he saw her nod her head.

"I trust you," she answered, and he released the breath he didn't realize he'd been holding.

"Let's go to my apartment."

He watched her out of the corner of his eye almost expecting her to protest. To call him a cad and demand he take her back to the picnic or her uncle's house. To tell him he was moving too fast for her because he was so much older and that she didn't want to be alone with him after all.

But then she smiled, tightening her fingers around his, and he realized she really wanted to be with him, too.

The sun was nearing the horizon when they pulled up behind Hunter's Hardware. Benny cut the engine, but neither one moved to get out. He stared over at her, and she stared down at the jar in her hands. Gently, he took her chin and turned her toward him. All day, he'd kept telling himself how young she was, but now he didn't seem to see her age at all. Before him, he saw someone he loved deeply and never wanted to be parted from.

"There's a great view from the balcony upstairs," Benny said carefully, letting her know he was giving her total control. "Would you like to watch the city's fireworks from there, or do you want to go somewhere else?"

"I want to stay here," she said, giving him the full trust he hoped to always deserve.

Without speaking, they went up the back steps to his apartment. He left Peg in the living room while he went to the kitchen with the jar of wine. He came back shortly with two full glasses and found her looking through his vast album collection.

"Sorry, I don't have any fancy glasses," he apologized, handing her one. "Is there anything you want to listen to?"

"Do you have any slow music like they were playing at Bo's," she asked.

He picked out his favorite LP and started it playing on his turntable. Soft music filled the small apartment. He forced himself to stand back and let her continue to investigate the pieces of his life scattered around the room. Now and then, she would pick up a framed picture or a trinket he'd acquired somewhere as if trying to solve the mystery of his past. He couldn't help but feel exposed to her scrutiny as he tried to look at everything through her eyes.

"Did you ever teach music somewhere?" she asked, looking at his framed college diploma on the wall.

"That was the plan to start with, and I tried it once," he said, coming up behind her. "I was fresh out of college with a master's degree under my belt and a lot of new ideas in my head. I quickly learned the school I worked for didn't want anything new. They didn't approve of my job at the club either. I'm still not sure if I left or they fired me."

She continued moving around the room, and he noticed her glass was nearly empty. Before he could offer to refill it, she silently handed it to him. When he returned from the kitchen, she was looking out the glass door leading to the small balcony.

"The fireworks will be over to your left," he said as she took the refilled glass. They stood there, staring out at the sunset until their glasses were empty once more. By then, she was leaning back against him, and he swayed them back and forth to the music. He kissed the top of her head and inhaled the scent of sunlight still clinging to her hair. When the last song played and the turntable automatically shut off, Benny left her in the doorway to turn the record over, adding a couple more to the stack to reduce the interruptions.

"I want to dance again," she whispered in his ear, startling him.

He hadn't heard her follow him across the apartment and was surprised and delighted at the look of absolute love and trust on her face. They danced through one song before a flash of light caught their attention, closely followed by a popping sound, muffled by the glass door. Instead of stopping their dance, Benny shuffled them close enough to open the door so they could dance out on the balcony while the fireworks lit up the sky above the surrounding buildings. Peg sighed happily as they held each other close, swaying to the music and watching the dancing lights. Then

Benny gently tipped her face up to gaze down into her cloudless blue eyes.

"Will you marry me, Peg Bennett?"

Her eyes blinked rapidly and began to fill with tears as her breath caught in her throat. Benny panicked and pulled back from her, taking her face between his hands so she couldn't look away. It had been such a perfect day, but now he was afraid he'd ruined everything.

"I'm sorry, Peg. I'm sorry. Please don't cry. I wasn't originally going to ask you tonight, but after today, I knew I couldn't wait. I don't even have a ring to offer you yet. I know we're so different, that you're too good for me, that I'm too old for you, that you're planning to go off to college soon, that you're used to a much richer life than a jazz musician can offer you—but I don't care about all that. I love you and I don't want you to leave me to go back home at the end of the month. I want to be with you, be by your side, have you all to myself…forever. I'll do whatever you want—move to Eagle Creek, quit playing music and get a different job, wait until you finish college even if it kills me—just please don't leave me. Don't leave me alone again."

Her tears flowed freely down to wet his hands, and he silently berated himself for scaring her. He didn't even realize he was crying himself until she reached up to wipe his wet cheeks. It wasn't until she smiled that he felt the iron band on his chest loosen and was able to breathe normally again.

"Yes," she whispered.

"Yes?"

She nodded her head between his hands. "Yes, I'll marry you. I love you, too, Benny Hunter. And I don't care where we live or what job you have as long as we're together."

Benny's heart soared and he picked her up, swinging her around in a circle as he kissed her soundly while the fireworks continued booming overhead as if in celebration for just the two of them. She wrapped her arms around his neck and kissed him back until they were both dizzy from spinning and lack of air.

As the turntable dropped another record and a new album began to play, they held each other tightly, swaying to the music in perfect unison, completely oblivious to the sparkling lights above them. Benny held her hand and kissed each knuckle before pulling back and shaking his head.

"This has been driving me crazy all day," he said, pulling her scarf from her top and slowly sliding it off her neck. As he bent low to kiss the exposed skin, he whispered, "Now, this is better."

Chapter Twenty-two

"Oh, my!" Mary Jean closed the cover of the journal I'd handed her and fanned herself with it.

"He did have a poet's soul, didn't he?" I took the journal back from her to return it to the file cabinet.

"Thanks for letting me read it. Now I know why you didn't want to tell me yourself. That thing reads better than a romance novel. Did he write any more like that?" she asked hopefully, but I shook my head.

"That's the last of the juicy stuff. Although I don't know why he felt the need to be quite so detailed in a journal he started for his daughter. I mean that was my mother he was…you know…and even though she told Claire they didn't have to get tipsy to do it, I'm sure it certainly helped them…relax. He could have left the part after the proposal to the imagination."

"But Benny *did* ask your mom to marry him, and she said yes," she pointed out. "So, doesn't that make it okay, even back then? And I think he probably wrote it all out more to keep his memory of it alive than specifically for you. Did he get a chance to buy a ring before he left on tour?"

I pulled the necklace from the inside of my top and let the simple, delicate ring dangle at the end of the chain so she could inspect it. "He got it while on tour but didn't get a chance to give it to her. I found it stashed in the back of the file cabinet behind all his tax papers. It's nothing fancy or very expensive, but he could have sold it at any time for a little extra money. I think he just couldn't make himself give it up."

"I can respect that. He wrote about several stolen moments over the next couple of weeks before leaving with the band, but do you know when you might have come into the picture?"

"Not exactly," I said, falling back into the chair. "I mean, they evidently never used protection—at least he didn't write about any—so it could've been anytime. Maybe I'm just being romantic, but I want to believe it happened that Fourth of July."

She gave me a knowing smile. "Sounds like that's a pretty special holiday in your family."

I rolled my eyes. "I told you nothing happened between me and Liam that night. We just agreed to try dating."

"Whatever," she teased, giving me a wink before returning her attention to the story. "So, what happened next? Why didn't they get married and live happily ever after? Did your grandpa forbid them to go through with the wedding or something?"

"According to Claire and Benny's journals, neither one told anyone about their plans. Benny wanted to properly ask Grandpa for her hand in marriage and all that old-fashioned stuff but was going to be gone for that three-week tour. He didn't want to leave, but Mom insisted he couldn't let the band down. They'd already booked a lot of fairs and festivals and they were all counting on the extra money and exposure. They figured they'd have plenty of time after he got back to visit her dad, make a formal announcement, and plan out the wedding, but when Benny got back, she was gone. No warning or explanation. Even her aunt and uncle were closed-mouthed about her disappearance. They'd been instructed by my grandpa not to tell him anything."

"Why would he do that if he didn't know about the proposal yet? He didn't even know about Benny, did he?"

"Grandpa didn't know about him, but he found out about me and came to his own conclusions about Benny's character. Claire said my mother was very depressed when Benny was away and only left the house a couple of times to visit his parents at the store. The rest of the time she slept a lot and wasn't eating much. One day, Claire and Ali finally talked her into playing a round of croquet and she passed out on the lawn. She wasn't out long, but her aunt went into hysterics and called Grandpa to come as soon as he could. He insisted on taking her to the hospital. When they got back, Claire said he stormed in, dragging her crying behind him, talked privately with her aunt and uncle, then just drove off without even packing her things."

"Well, it's pretty obvious your grandpa wasn't very happy about finding out she was pregnant."

"It was more than that," I sighed. "Grandpa was a well-respected judge with a well-respected lineage. The very thought of having it tarnished by an unwed mother was more than he could bear. So, that's why Grandpa called Dad—David, I mean."

“Are you telling me David married your mom just to save your grandfather’s precious family tree?” MJ was shocked at the very thought. “And he agreed to do it?”

Chapter Twenty-three

August 5, 1969

"Thank the good Lord you're here," Judge Bennett said, grabbing David by the shoulder and pulling him inside the house. He gave a quick glance up and down the street like he was worried someone might be watching them before closing the door and leaning against it as if it were the only thing keeping him on his feet.

"I got here as fast as I could. What's wrong with Peg? Is she hurt? Why couldn't you tell me over the phone?"

The phone call had been brief and frantic, two things David had never associated with the Judge. In all the years he'd spent time at the Bennett house, Peg's father was the epitome of composure and his lengthy conversations—or lectures—were legendary in the community. Having the man he'd idolized and feared since picking Peg up for their first date acting this out of character caused David to panic.

'I need you to come over right away. Peg needs you,' was all the Judge said before hanging up the phone. When his parents asked him why he looked so pale, he couldn't even answer them. As he left his suitcase half-packed for college on his bed and ran the few blocks to Peg's house, he couldn't even imagine what might have happened to Peg...or why he felt this level of panic for her well-being.

Of course he cared for Peg—you couldn't date a girl for four years without at least liking her—but they'd agreed when he came back for spring break to stop seeing each other. Even when he was over at her house just to hold her while she cried over her mother's death, they both knew it was only out of friendship. He was going to the University of Wisconsin-La Crosse and this fall she would be going to Mount Mary University in Milwaukee. They'd learned this past year that their relationship wasn't strong enough to last long-distance and had agreed they were both free to see other people.

So why did he have this knot in the pit of his stomach? Why did the thought of something happening to Peg make him run the whole way to her house? Why did the thought of her needing him make him feel so good?

"I never should have sent her to Detroit," the Judge said, ushering him into the sitting room. It looked completely different than the last time David visited. Gone were all of his wife's knick-knacks and flower vases sitting on lace doilies. In their place on the shelves and side tables were leather-bound books—expensive and important David was certain, but not something meant to decorate a sitting room.

"What happened in Detroit?" David asked, sitting on the sofa that no longer boasted hand-made afghans and embroidered pillows. He rubbed his damp palms nervously along his brown, corduroy pants.

The Judge paced back and forth between his new leather recliner and what had to be the ugliest wooden Indian statue, its paint faded and chipped as if it had sat out in the elements for decades. "The worst thing imaginable. My baby girl has been…violated."

From the way he ground out the last word from between his teeth, David understood exactly what he meant. His stomach clenched, threatening to expel his mother's pot roast, and he felt suddenly hot and cold at the same time. He wiped his shaky fingers across his forehead and found it slick with sweat.

"She was…raped?"

David had never personally known any girls who had been raped. Oh, he'd heard rumors of it happening, especially at a co-ed college, but the guys were all adamant the girl in question was willing at the time and just regretted it afterward. Subconsciously, he'd always wondered if that was entirely true, but it certainly wasn't something he'd question his fellow fraternity brothers about.

"I'm afraid it's even worse than that," the Judge continued. "The…incident…resulted in an unfortunate complication."

It took David a minute to understand exactly what the Judge was trying to tell him without actually speaking the words he deemed too horrible to say aloud. He'd stopped pacing and just stood over David with his arms crossed, waiting for him to realize how serious the situation had become. When David felt the color drain from his face, the Judge nodded.

"So, as you now see, this is a situation that cannot easily be forgotten." He started pacing again, his hands clenching and unclenching as if wanting to strangle someone. "Never before has this family had anything remotely as shameful as this happen to such a proud and noble lineage."

"Does she know who..." David couldn't even complete the sentence.

The Judge nodded. "She does. And if I could, I'd have him strung up from the nearest tree and left there for the vultures. But..." he sat down on the edge of his recliner and leaned his elbows on his knees, staring intently into David's eyes, "...the vermin did something to her. Brainwashed her. I heard he was some kind of musician. Probably fed her some drug or another so she didn't know what was happening at the time, and now she's delusional. She's saying things like he's going to marry her and that if I have him arrested or make her give up the product of his assault, she's going to kill herself. I had to lock her in her room and make sure there wasn't anything in there she could hurt herself with. Now does that sounds like the Margaret we know and love?"

David shook his head. It didn't sound anything like Peg at all. She was the kindest, sweetest, gentlest girl he'd ever known. They'd gone to Bible study together and had discussions about all the ways a person could be barred from heaven. It was one of the reasons they were able to keep their kissing from going any further—the other being his completely reasonable fear of the Judge. Having sex outside of marriage was a sin, but suicide sent you directly to hell. The Peg he knew would never even consider killing herself. Something was definitely wrong with her.

"We have to help her, David. You have to help her."

"You mean talk to her?"

"What's happening inside her isn't something that talking can help," the Judge said, raising one eyebrow to see if David understood his meaning. "And I will not allow our family name to be dragged into a scandal because of that... degenerate. She must be convinced to deal with the consequences of her immorality in the eyes of God."

"You're not thinking of her getting an... I mean she can't just... That's...murder."

The Judge dropped his head and shook it. "No, even if what's growing is part of that monster, I cannot in good conscience go against God and the church and end an innocent life." He suddenly looked up and David flinched at the frightening look on his serious face. "That son of a whore who did this to her, though, can rot in hell for all I care."

"So, I don't understand what I..."

The Judge's hand shot out and grabbed David's wrist with the speed of a striking snake. He wanted to pull away, but the older man's strength was undeniable.

"We need you, David. Margaret needs you. I need you. *God* needs you. You're the only one who can save our family from scandal, save Margaret's life, and keep her from going to hell. Will you help us?"

David looked from the hand wrapped around his wrist like an iron band to the intense eyes staring at him from inches away. "I still don't know what you want from me, Sir, but if Peg needs help, I'll do whatever I can."

A slow smile spread across the Judge's face. "I knew I could count on you. You and your family are good, upstanding people and an asset to our community. And I know you wouldn't want anything to jeopardize that." He raised his eyebrow again and David had a feeling there was some kind of threat buried beneath the compliments even if he wasn't quite sure what it was yet.

"What exactly do you want me to do, Judge Bennett?" he asked, wanting him to say out loud what he had in mind just to be sure they were thinking the same thing.

The Judge gave him a big smile as he released David's wrist, giving his knee a friendly pat before sitting back in his chair. With the confident air of someone who knew everything was going according to plan, he left David sitting in silence as he dug his cigarette pack out of his shirt pocket, shook one out, and lit it from the ornamental lighter on the side table. He took a long drag and blew the smoke toward the ceiling before speaking.

"First and foremost, I count on your discretion to keep this little talk just between us. It's up to you what you say to Margaret because it's obviously her secret that needs to be secured but let me remind you of her fragile mental state right now. I think we both know it would be best if we did everything in our power to alleviate some of the pressure and hardship that has been thrust upon her. Don't you agree?"

David nodded. "I wouldn't tell anyone what happened to her, anyway. I've heard how people can treat victims of…these kinds of crimes…and I would never want that to happen to her. I will keep her secret to keep her safe."

He gave one definitive nod and took another drag, then pointed the cigarette at David. "Good boy. Now, for the most important thing you can do." He leaned forward again, and David felt drawn toward him as if what the man was about to say was of dire consequence. "Marry her."

They sat in silence for a full minute, the Judge waiting patiently for David's reaction while

David was unable to process the two-word sentence enough to react.

"Marry…Peg? But we don't want to get married." Even as the words left his mouth, he realized the flimsiness of the argument against the bigger picture. Of course, her father wanted her married. Of course, a marriage would hide the legitimacy of a child's parentage. Of course, he was the best—possibly only—choice to make such a sudden marriage believable. "Did she say she wanted to get married…to me?"

The Judge gave him a look full of incredulity and pity. "She's a scared, teenage girl who has just survived an attack of who knows what proportions and is now suffering the shame and physical hardships of carrying her attacker's seed. She can't possibly know what she wants. It's our job as men who care about her welfare to know and do what's right. And since we can't get rid of the problem without risking her eternal soul, we'll just have to do the best we can. Right?"

"But I'm heading back to college tomorrow. When would we…"

"You know as well as I do that time is of the essence. I can marry you tonight, right here. As for college…" he waved the hand holding the cigarette and the smoke made spirals in the air, "...the whole reason for going is to get a job. Right? Well, I can save you the time and tuition and get you a job at the courthouse. It might not be what you planned to use your business major on, but it's a steady paycheck with opportunities to advance. Who knows? Work hard enough and you could even try for an elected position." He stabbed the butt of his cigarette into the ashtray beside him until there were no remaining embers. "I will even buy you two newlyweds one of those new houses that just went up on Birchwood Drive as a wedding present. A new job, a new house, a new wife…a new family. What do you say?"

David's head swam. Part of him knew this was the best plan to save Peg and her reputation. Part of him wished he would wake up from what had to be a nightmare. Was he really considering dropping out of college, getting married to someone he liked but didn't love, working a job he didn't want, moving into a house he didn't choose, and raising someone else's child? Things like that just didn't happen. Especially with so little notice.

"Can I ask," he began hesitantly, "what would happen to Peg if she refused to marry me? I mean you can't really force her to agree if she doesn't want to go through with it."

"Can't I? I am her father, and she has to honor me," he replied with complete surety. "But if she thinks she can defy me and refuse our help, I will have no choice but to have her committed to one of the mental hospitals the church runs. Of course, they would make sure to re-educate her in the faith, but she would have to stay there longer than nine months or people would talk. Probably a year at least depending on how well her lessons go.

Then when—or if—they deem her ready, she will return home…alone…and possibly live the rest of her life with people thinking she's crazy. You wouldn't want that for her, would you? No, if she insists on keeping it, she will have to agree to the marriage."

"But what about the guy?" David persisted. "What if he does want to marry…"

The Judge's face flared with anger, his neck turning a concerning shade of red. As the Judge glared at him, David felt more and more uncomfortable, imagining this was the way criminals felt in his courtroom. David expected him to yell, so pressed himself back into the sofa, but when the Judge spoke, it was with such measured control he didn't even sound like himself.

"*If a man seduces a virgin who is not betrothed and lies with her, he shall give the marriage present for her, and make her his wife. If her father utterly refuses to give her to him, he shall pay money equivalent to the marriage present for virgins. Exodus 22:16-17.* Do you think for one moment that I would allow someone who could do something like that to my daughter actually join my family? *My* family? I would rather die first."

"I…I…understand…Sir," David said, his voice cracking with fear. "And the…the job… everything…well, it sounds…great."

"Wonderful," the Judge said, slapping David's knee as he stood up. "I knew you would make the right choice. Let's go up and get Margaret and we'll get this over with."

David imagined the Judge dragging Peg out of her room and forcing her to say the right words to make their marriage legal. That wasn't the way he wanted to start a marriage—almost a literal shotgun wedding. Before he even realized what he was doing, he laid a hand on the Judge's shoulder to stop him from going up the stairs.

"Can I talk to her first? Try and make her see what we're doing is the best thing for her?"

The Judge shrugged his shoulders and stepped aside to let David climb the staircase alone. David had never been up to Peg's bedroom but knew it was the first door at the top of the stairs. Even if he hadn't known, it would have been obvious by the key dangling from the lock and the chair wedged under the handle. Taking a deep breath, he knocked on the door.

Chapter Twenty-four

"Peg? It's David. Can I come in and talk?"

Peg's voice was muffled, but he could tell she must have been sitting against the door. "David! Thank heaven! Let me out!"

He moved the chair and turned the key in the lock. Before he could reach for the doorknob, Peg flung the door open and ran into his arms.

"Thank you! Thank you! How did you know? Never mind. I need to get out of here before Dad finds out. Can you give me a ride to the bus station? I've got to…"

Her voice trailed off and she stepped away from him, her eyes fixed on something over his shoulder. David glanced back to see the Judge standing in the middle of the stairway, his size and crossed arms barring any escape. She looked from her father to David, her face screwed up with the pain of betrayal. Shaking her head, she backed into her room until her legs hit her bed and she sat heavily on the bare mattress.

David stepped inside the stuffy room and closed the door quietly behind him so they could talk without the Judge looming over them. "Your dad called me. Can I sit?" he asked, motioning to the open space beside her. She shrugged her shoulders and dropped her head, staring down the length of her legs, bare in her shorts, at her feet. David took the gesture as an invitation and slowly walked over to perch on the edge of the mattress next to her.

"He told me everything," David began, reaching for her hand. When she didn't pull away, he added an arm around her shoulders, the skin left bare by her tank top as smooth as he remembered. "I am so sorry this happened to you, Peg. I can't begin to imagine what you're going through."

"You mean being dragged home, locked up, and ignored?" She ran the heel of her hand across her cheeks and looked up at him with eyes red and puffy from crying. "He won't even listen to me. He's got it all wrong. I wasn't attacked. I love him."

David remembered what her father said about her delusions, but thought she sounded sane to him. "So, tell me what really happened, Peg. I'll listen."

Peg began to ramble on about someone named Benny, jazz music, sneaking out with Claire, the Fourth of July, a hardware store, concerts in the park, a picnic with black people, going to the doctor, a band's tour, holding a sleeping baby, and a Jamaican woman named Mama who told her to make him happy. The more she talked, the less David understood the story.

"He proposed and I said yes," she exclaimed. "He's a good guy, David. He's almost thirty, so he's mature and I know he meant it."

"So, where is he? If he loves you, why am I here holding you instead of him?"

She lifted her head from his shoulder and noticed his arm against her back, his hand still stroking her upper arm, and then looked down at where she held his other hand with both of hers. She tried to untangle her fingers from his, but he lifted them up to his lips, brushing them lightly across the back of her hand.

"You've been through a lot this summer, and I've always been here for you. Haven't I? Well, I'm here to help you through this, too."

"You mean you're going to help me get back to Detroit?" she asked, her face lighting up with hope. "Find Benny and convince Dad to let us get married?"

David took a deep breath and let it out slowly. "Peg, I'm going to ask you some questions and I want you to be perfectly honest with me. Are you pregnant?"

"That's what the doctor said," she agreed.

"How long and how well did you know this guy before he…took advantage of you?"

Her eyebrows drew together. "He didn't take advantage of me."

"How long and how well did you know him before?" he repeated patiently.

"Let's see. We talked at the club for a few weeks, at the park a couple of Saturdays, met at his parents' store, then the picnic. So, I knew him for about a month, but I knew enough about him to know I loved him."

"Did your aunt and uncle invite him to dinner like your dad always invited me? Did you sit and talk about your childhood, your faith, and your dreams for the future like we did? When you were at this club, did he encourage you to drink alcohol? Did he hold you too tight or try to touch you inappropriately when he thought people weren't looking? Did he try to get you alone? Was it his idea to take you somewhere private? His apartment, maybe?"

Peg's mouth opened and closed as she thought of a response. "You're making it sound like he had some kind of an elaborate plan to... what...lure me into a den of iniquity? That's not how it happened at all. We fell in love."

Keeping her hand locked with his, he stroked one finger lightly across her cheek as his eyes captured hers. "After such a short time? We've known each other all our lives. I know everything about you. You know everything about me...except I never told you how much I love you and want to marry you."

Claiming her lips was as natural as breathing after their four years together. Only this time, he deepened it immediately instead of waiting all those frustrating minutes of tender pecking. Peg tensed but for once he ignored her subtle signals. Tightening his arm to draw her even closer to him, he pushed her back onto the mattress, trapping her beneath the weight of his chest. He threw one leg over both of hers but stopped just short of pressing himself against her.

Peg's sound of surprise was muffled in David's mouth as she ineffectually tried to push and kick him away. He continued kissing her until she finally wrenched her head to the side, gasping for air. He used the opportunity to move his lips down to her neck.

"David, stop. David? What are you doing?"

"Your dad invited me," he said, his voice deep and husky as his lips and breath tickled across her skin. "You and I have talked before about our dreams for the future. Now, I finally have you alone, I've talked about love and marriage, and I'm holding you too tight. What do you think I'm doing?"

She went completely still, and David froze with his face buried in the crook of her neck. "You're trying to make a point," she said. "I get it. But Benny didn't force himself on me…like this."

David raised his head to look down at her and she looked defiantly back, her trust that he'd never do anything to hurt her unwavering. "Even if he didn't do it physically, a guy that much older and experienced can talk a young, innocent girl into doing things she normally wouldn't do. That's not love, Peg."

A smile tugged one side of her lips. "But I know he does love me. Just as I know you really don't. Now, get off me." She threw her weight into him, and her bare thigh brushed against the rough corduroy stretched over his groin. Feeling his obvious arousal for the first time, she gasped.

"You don't have to be in love with someone to feel desire for them," David said, staring into her eyes and letting her see a hint of the fire he felt inside. Finally, he saw understanding dawn on her face of the dangerous position they were in and how helpless she was against his strength. "I may not love you, but I've always wanted you. Luckily, I also liked and respected you enough to stop myself from doing anything that could possibly ruin your life. Too bad someone else didn't," he added as he suddenly rolled off her and sat up. Moving over so they were no longer touching, he leaned his elbows on his knees and took deep breaths in an attempt to reign in his body's response. It was the closest he'd ever come to losing control and it scared him how easy it could have been.

Peg laid absolutely still for a full minute before pushing herself off the bed and pacing back and forth in front of him. Her arms were crossed tightly across her stomach and David worried he'd gone too far. She stopped in front of him and when he looked up into her face, he saw confident determination and knew it hadn't worked after all.

"There's nothing you can do or say to make me believe what happened between me and Benny was anything but love. And there's nothing my dad can do or say to change my mind, either. I don't care what he wants. I don't care what anyone thinks. I want to go back to Detroit, and I want to marry Benny."

David heaved a heavy sigh and ran his hands through his hair in frustration. "You know he'd never let you do that." Standing up, he grabbed her upper arms so she couldn't turn away from him as he stared into her eyes, willing her to understand what had to be done. "Your dad will never let you marry Benny, Peg. You know that as well as I do. He cares too much about appearances to let you end up with a lowly musician. And if you try running back to him, the Judge will use whatever connections he has to have Benny arrested and thrown in jail. He hates this guy so much for getting his only daughter pregnant, I wouldn't even put it past him to make up charges to keep him there as long as possible. If you really love him, you don't want to ruin his life like that. Do you?"

Her eyes were wide as she slowly shook her head.

"And now think about you and the baby. If you go against your dad and he gets Benny locked up, you'd be all alone. You couldn't possibly support yourself and a child. How would you make enough to pay for a place to live, food, and all the medical expenses? You wouldn't be able to work after the baby was born. And think how you both would be treated. Being a single mother with a bastard child isn't the kind of life you want. Is it?"

Tears began pooling in her eyes and she tried to blink them back as she silently shook her head.

"Right now, you only have two choices, Peg. One is to marry me." She shook her head harder, but David persisted. "I can take care of you, and we can raise the baby as our own. No one will know any different. We may not love each other as much as other couples, but at least we care about one another enough to want to do what's best. Right?" She didn't respond, but he knew she understood. "The other choice is to refuse to marry me. If that's your choice, the Judge said he would have you declared mentally unstable and send you to a hospital where you lose both your freedom...and the baby."

She began to cry, softly at first but increasing in intensity as she finally realized the hopelessness of her situation. David held her and stroked her hair as his shirt soaked up her tears. He knew how she felt. He was feeling trapped and helpless as well, his plans for his own future dissipating like smoke before his eyes. At least they would be trapped together.

Chapter Twenty-five

"So, they were married just like that?" Mary Jean snapped her fingers. "How was that not suspicious?"

"Remember, this was back in 1969. It was acceptable to elope, just not to conceive a baby out of wedlock."

"That's outrageous! He basically sold his only child with a bribe of a job and a house. That's downright barbaric!"

"I wonder if things would've been different if Benny hadn't gone on that tour. Once they found out about me, they could have eloped and pretended the pregnancy happened after the wedding. Then there wouldn't have been anything Grandpa could've done about it without causing a scandal. But Benny did go on the tour and Bo said it would've been impossible for Mom to contact him while they were on the road."

"If your grandpa even let her try," MJ pointed out.

"And since Grandpa didn't want a piano player as a son-in-law, he convinced David marriage was the best way to deal with the 'consequences of her immorality in the eyes of God.'"

I rolled my eyes as I air-quoted Dad's exact words as he'd quoted my grandfather. "MJ, you go to church. Is that the kind of God you believe in? One that makes you feel guilty about everything? The thought of living with such pious ideals is incomprehensible to me. I mean, I know we didn't go to church much when I was little because Mom was sick, but I feel I've got a pretty good grasp of what's right and what's wrong, even without being told by some Bible-thumping preacher. And being made to feel that guilty for giving yourself to the one you love just because there isn't a ring on your finger seems wrong to me."

MJ slowly shook her head. "It wasn't God that said that about your mom. It was your antiquated, male-chauvinist pig of a grandfather. The Bible does say you're not supposed to have sex before marriage, but that was also back when marriages were arranged, and women were sold off to men with several wives. Both of which are now, thankfully, no longer common practice. Now, I think it's more of a warning to keep your mind, body, and heart safe from the wrong person so it can be given to the one you're committed to."

I took a deep breath to let go of the anger thinking of that part of the story always seemed to elicit. If my mother had just been able to marry my biological father, she would have been much happier. If she'd been happier, would she have lived longer? Had her sickness been brought on by a broken heart and the separation from her true love? What would my life have been like then? These were the questions I now asked myself late at night when I couldn't fall asleep.

"In any case," I continued, knowing I had to move on if I was going to get through the story in one night, "Grandpa, being a judge, married them that night with Dad's parents as witnesses."

"What did David's parents think about all this? Did he tell them the real reason for the rushed wedding?"

I rolled my eyes. "Of course not. They were surprised but since David and Peg had been dating for so long, his parents assumed they'd get married eventually. They just didn't like that he'd dropped out of college and did it so suddenly. They agreed to a small church wedding to appease the community after they got back from their honeymoon—a couple of weeks in New York paid for by Grandpa, of course. Everyone was so used to seeing them together and thought the elopement romantic. By the time I came along, it was all proper and no one was the wiser."

"Well, that certainly sheds a better light on why there was a serious lack of love in your family," MJ said. "And why you have your issues. Especially in the relationship department."

My mouth dropped in shock. "What issues?"

She gave me that look that said I was somehow being dumb on purpose. "What issues? You date the wrong guys, or they're good guys but you don't put in the effort to make it work, or great guys but you somehow sabotage the relationship before it gets too serious."

"I don't know what you're talking about. Yeah, I've had a lot of bad relationships, but they didn't all end because of me."

"Did you or did you not date scumbags in high school just to upset your dad?"

I opened my mouth to argue but she continued.

"And then in college, you finally meet some decent guys but since you didn't have Dad to criticize them you did it yourself, picking apart every little thing until you drove them away. Not to mention your serious trust issues. Not every guy is perfect, Ter. Sometimes you have to help them change what you can and deal with some of the habits you can't."

"What about you-know-who?" I asked, pointing a finger at her. "Everyone kept saying what a great guy he was, but he cheated on me. You can't blame that on me."

She rolled her eyes at the memory. "He gave his ex-girlfriend a little kiss under the mistletoe at a staff Christmas party. You're the one who blew it all out of proportion and threw all his stuff out on the sidewalk in the snow. He tried to apologize every day for a week, but you wouldn't even listen. Your loss, I guess, because now he's happily married and coaches his son's T-ball team. But now you're on the verge of a new relationship with Liam, and you're already looking for flaws and an excuse to keep him at arm's length even though he's clearly into you. You may not be able to see it, but he doesn't look at any other woman the way he looks at you."

"I still don't see what my failed relationships have to do with my parents." Even I hated to hear the pouty twang in my voice as I said it.

"They got married and stayed together out of social propriety. Not love. Oh, I have no doubt they cared about each other's health and welfare even though it sounds more like a business arrangement than a real marriage. I'm sure they both loved you, but since they couldn't love each other, you weren't taught how relationships are supposed to work. How love can be shown in so many different ways—loving another person, loving yourself, and loving a higher power. I'm sorry you had to grow up like that—and I know your parents did the best they could under the circumstances. That doesn't mean you can't learn to make relationships work now. All it takes is a little help, but you need to want to accept it, too."

I rubbed my temples where a headache was threatening to bloom. I rationalized it was from the wine or not drinking enough water that day, but deep down I knew this happened every time I thought too much about myself.

"So," MJ began, recognizing my stress and steering us back to the conversation, "did David say how your mom dealt with everything? The pregnancy, being ripped away from Benny, the shotgun wedding, and having to keep such a big secret?"

I heaved a deep sigh. "He said no one else seemed to notice how unhappy and stressed she was all the time. She was depressed throughout the entire pregnancy, not wanting to go anywhere or talk to anyone. The doctor kept telling him it was perfectly normal because of the hormones, but David said he knew better."

"She was heartbroken."

I nodded. "And then complications set in, and she ended up bedridden for the last month and I came even earlier than expected. David said for a while he wasn't even sure she'd survive the birth." I smiled, thinking about what he'd told me during our frank discussion. "He said Mom snapped out of her depression the minute she saw me. She was always happiest when she was holding me and loved being a mother."

"It's too bad you had such a short time with her," MJ said in a consoling voice. When I didn't reply, she jumped up and disappeared into the kitchen, returning with the other bottle of wine. "I have a feeling we're going to need this soon."

"Probably," I agreed, knowing the hardest part was still to come.

She poured herself a glass and took a sip before asking, "But before we get to that part I have to know. What about Benny?"

Chapter Twenty-six

August 8, 1969

"Can't you at least tell me when she left?" Benny pleaded with Peg's uncle, Peter.

"Sorry," he replied as if he, and his sour-faced wife standing behind him, weren't sorry at all. "I think you'd better leave now." The door closed in Benny's face just as a flash of lightning jumped between the dark clouds that had been gathering along the horizon and heading directly toward Detroit. The accompanying rumble of thunder gave him an ominous feeling in the pit of his stomach.

He slowly walked back to his car, extremely confused. What happened? When he left for the tour, he and Peg were so happy. They'd planned to drive over to Eagle Creek as soon as he got back so he could talk to her father about their engagement. He even picked up a ring at a discount jewelry store they happened upon while on tour.

Now he was back, anxious to see her…and she was gone. And why were her aunt and uncle suddenly treating him like the enemy? They wouldn't tell him anything. Not where she went, not why, how, or even when. They didn't even let him in the house.

He drove back to his apartment in a depressed fog as the first drops of what promised to be a severe thunderstorm pelted his windshield. He thought about driving straight to Eagle Creek, but the storm warnings and tornado watches on the radio advised against it. Even without the weather, Benny was too tired from the trip home to safely travel anymore that night. In his need to see Peg, he'd convinced the rest of the band to drive all night and day to make it back as quickly as possible. Even if he wasn't the one driving, he hadn't been able to sleep. He'd been too excited about giving Peg the ring which now sat heavily in his pocket. All his weary brain knew for certain was that he loved Peg, and she'd left him without a hint of explanation.

As he entered his apartment, his hair dripping cold rainwater down his back, he noticed an envelope that appeared to have been slid beneath the door. He quickly turned on the light and was relieved to see Peg's beautiful handwriting. Maybe this explained everything. He opened it and held the single sheet of paper close to the lamp to read it.

Dear Benny,

I need to talk to you as soon as possible. There's something very important I have to tell you.

Peg

He read the note over and over as the wind, rain, and thunder rattled the windows around him. He didn't want to believe it, but he couldn't stop thinking about her uncle's icy demeanor. In his exhausted mind, he thought he knew exactly what the note meant. She didn't want to see him anymore.

"And why would she?" he asked his empty apartment. Hadn't he been expecting something like this in the back of his mind since the night they first met? He'd left her alone to go on that blasted tour and she'd come to her senses, realizing he was nothing more than an old piano player. "She can do so much better than me."

Benny dropped the paper and sat down hard in a chair. He tried to tell himself it couldn't be true, but his tired and depressed brain wouldn't listen. He put his head in his hands and tried to figure out what went wrong. Did he do anything to drive her away?

He'd thought everything was so perfect between them. They had so much in common, and he thought she'd loved him as much as he loved her. She'd accepted his proposal, and they were going to tell her father as soon as the tour was over. She warned him that her father might not approve of his age or profession, but he'd told her he was willing to go back to teaching and would move anywhere she wanted to live. The only thing he couldn't change for anyone was his age.

A sudden flash lit up the sky immediately followed by a deafening crack of thunder as lightning struck close by and plunged the apartment into darkness. Benny barely noticed as his sadness had now turned to anger. His pride was wounded that she'd left while he was away. Did she plan on breaking up with him even before he left on the tour? Was that why she insisted on him going? Did she leave the note saying she wanted to talk, then decide she didn't want to talk to him after all, fleeing back to Wisconsin where she knew he didn't have her phone number? Did she do that on purpose so he couldn't talk her out of it? Maybe the month of happiness he thought they shared was only one-sided. Maybe she didn't mean to marry him after all. Maybe she was using him for some kind of summer fling, stringing him along while she just had fun. Maybe she had someone else back home. Maybe...

Suddenly, he crumpled the note and threw it across the room where it disappeared into the darkness. If she could be so heartless, he was better off without her. He'd just have to get on with the rest of his life and thank God he hadn't married her after all.

That night, Benny did something he'd never done before. Even though he was dog-tired and sleep-deprived, every time he tried to sleep, all the hurt and anger washed over him like the rain cascading from the sky. When he closed his eyes, all he saw was Peg's face. Regardless of the power outage and raging storm, he trudged to the liquor store a block away and bought himself a bottle of whiskey. He knew the only way to get her out of his mind was to drown it. Since he hadn't eaten much, it only took half the bottle before he passed out across his bed.

Chapter Twenty-seven

October 18, 1969

The next couple of months were pure hell for Benny. He didn't want to work, he didn't want to play at the club, and he didn't even want to leave his apartment.

"I'm quitting the band," Benny announced when Bo called to find out why he hadn't shown up at the club.

"No, you're not," Bo replied calmly.

"She's gone, Bo. And I've lost the passion to play. Honestly, I don't know if I'll ever get it back."

"I'm still not letting you quit, Benny. I'm sorry this happened, but you can't let it ruin your life. Take as much time as you need, but you're not quitting."

During the day, Benny sulked around his apartment, barely eating unless his mother insisted she wouldn't leave until he did. Every night, he'd stare at the piano he couldn't bring himself to even touch as he drank himself to sleep. He grew thin and weak, and there were gray hairs in the beard he didn't bother to shave.

"Good God, Benny, you look like you've aged ten years."

"Get out, Bo. I'm not coming back to the band."

"Have you heard anything from Peg?"

Benny grabbed an empty bottle and threw it at him. "Mind your own business and leave me the hell alone!"

~~~~~

When Benny still hadn't come back to the club after three months, Bo seriously worried about his friend's declining health and state of mind. He was afraid Benny may never come back from the dark abyss he'd fallen into or to the music he'd once loved. So finally, he worked up the courage to go back to Benny's apartment and confront him. The door was locked, but Benny had once given him a key to use whenever his wife was mad enough to kick him out of the house.

The stench nearly drove Bo back out to the hall. Sometime in the last couple of months, Benny had taken up smoking as well, and the apartment was hazy with it. Along with the smoke, he could smell whiskey coming from the many empty bottles strung around, forgotten spoiled food from the kitchen, and a very pungent aroma wafting from the direction of the bathroom. He swallowed hard and crossed the room to open the sliding glass door to let in the fresh, cool, autumn air and sunlight before venturing into the bedroom.

When he first saw Benny lying face down on the floor, the drawn shades making the room as dark as night, Bo feared his friend was dead. He
~~~~~

was wearing clothes that hadn't been changed for at least a week and was nearly as thin as a skeleton. His skin was pale and tight over his sharp cheekbones.

"Benny?" When he didn't stir, Bo called his name louder. "Benny!"

Kneeling down, Bo held his breath against the stench of body odor while he listened for the raspy breathing coming from Benny's open mouth.

"Well, at least you're not dead," Bo said to the unconscious Benny. "So did you pass out on the floor or fall out of bed this time?"

Not expecting an answer, Bo went back to hang his coat on an empty hook by the door before rolling up his sleeves and heading into the bathroom. He turned on the faucet in the tub and firmly plugged the drain. When he carried Benny in to dump him in the water, Bo could feel every rib and had to fight to keep down his lunch from the rank smell.

It didn't take long for Benny to wake up from the dip in the cold water. "Damn it, Bo! What the hell did you do that for?" he sputtered, fighting to get himself in a sitting position so he wouldn't drown. Drenched and hungover, he managed to shut off the water and lay back in the tub, scowling with hatred at his unwelcome intruder.

"All right, I'm awake. Now leave," he croaked. His body ached from being abused by the alcohol and cigarettes, and his head felt like it had been split open by an ax. The last thing he wanted to see was a smiling Bo.

"He lives! Hallelujah!" Bo shouted like a raving Baptist preacher. "Thank God Almighty, brothers and sisters."

Benny held his head which threatened to explode at any moment. He glared at Bo through his puffy, red-rimmed eyes, but had no strength left to fight with him. Instead, he closed his eyes and tried to sink back into the darkness he'd worked so hard the night before to reach.

"Oh, no you don't sleepyhead," Bo said. He turned the cold water on full blast and hit the shower lever. This time the shock hit Benny like a thousand knives into his flesh and his heart skipped a beat as he pawed at the knob, finally getting it turned back off again.

"What do you want?" he sputtered, wiping the water from his face.

"Well for starters, I want you to get cleaned up. You smell worse than a garbage truck during a heat wave. Then, I want to see you eat something."

At the mention of food, Benny's stomach lurched, and he struggled out of the tub, flopping like a fish onto the floor to reach the toilet in time. Bo helped by holding his head, and he wasn't surprised to see spots of blood come up with the remaining undigested alcohol. Finally, Benny sat back on his heels, laying his cheek against the filthy rim as he gasped for breath, his face even whiter than before. Bo prayed he wasn't too late to save his friend.

"What have you been doing to yourself, man?" Bo asked seriously, handing Benny the cleanest of the dirty towels. "Are you trying to kill yourself?"

"So, what if I am," came the muffled response from behind the cloth, sounding lost and hopeless.

"Well, you're going about it all wrong," Bo announced suddenly, realizing there was only one way he could think of to help him now. "At this rate, it'll take months, even years before you succeed."

"So, what's your point?"

"My point is that if you really want to kill yourself, you're doing it all wrong."

Bo grabbed Benny's arm and yanked him upright enough to stare calmly into the bloodshot eyes. It took a minute for the other man to register the deadly seriousness in his face.

"Let me go," Benny whispered, pulling weakly against the iron grip on his arm.

"The way you're going about this is only hurting the people around you. Is that what you want? To make everyone else suffer right along with you? Why don't you just shoot yourself or something and save the rest of us the suspense and agony?"

Bo could see Benny's eyes were beginning to sharpen, and he was slowly coming alive at the thought of his death.

"That's right, you don't have a gun. I didn't think to bring one with me, either." He sighed, tapping his chin in thought. "Let's see what else we can think of. You don't have an oven to gas yourself. Jumping off the roof is never a sure thing unless you hit the ground just right. You'd probably even mess up slitting your wrists yourself, now that I think about it. You were always a bit squeamish when it came to something as simple as gutting a fish."

Benny sat speechless, staring in open-mouthed disbelief at the way the other man was so casually talking about ways to end his life.

"I've got it," Bo declared, snapping his fingers as he stood up over the dazed Benny. "It's relatively quick and clean, but since I know you'd just botch it up, I'll have to help you. Don't worry. I'll tell everyone you were already dead when I got here so Ginny and the kids won't think I just stood there and watched my friend die."

With a quick jerk, Bo yanked Benny around on his knees and stood behind him, grabbing a handful of his stringy hair in one fist. Benny didn't even have time to react before he found his face held just inches above the water still in the tub.

"Now, I'll hold your head under and all you have to do is breathe it in. Do you think you can manage that much at least?" Bo said in his ear.

Before Benny could do more than gasp, Bo plunged his head under the water until his forehead was pressed firmly against the bottom of the tub.

Benny flailed his arms and tried to push against the slick, wet porcelain. After a few seconds, Bo pulled his head back up and Benny sputtered and coughed the water out of his mouth.

"Can't you even do *this* right?" Bo yelled. "I thought the point was that you wanted to die. So here I am, trying to be sure you don't ruin it like you've been ruining your life for the last three months. I told you, no one wants to watch you kill yourself slowly because it's also killing the ones who love you. Now, come on, let's try it again." Benny's head was shoved under the water once more.

This time he was ready for it. With more determination and strength than he'd shown in months, Benny set his hands on the bottom of the tub and pushed his face up out of the water. He reached up and grabbed the hand still holding his hair and gave it a sharp twist. Bo let go of his hair, but Benny didn't let go of the hand. He pulled it hard and hauled Bo over his shoulder to land in the tub with a splash. Grabbing the front of Bo's shirt, he pulled back his other arm, ready to pound him. The fist never found its mark as Benny froze in shock at the wide smile on Bo's face.

"Welcome back, Brother," he said and laughed at the confused expression. Benny finally realized what his friend had done for him, and his fist dropped to his side.

"I was ready to kill you," Benny admitted, giving Bo a helping hand up to sit on the edge of the tub. His brief flare of adrenaline spent, Benny let himself slide sideways until he was propped against the wall with one shoulder. “You could have killed me.”

“I could have,” Bo agreed. “Lucky for both of us you decided life was worth living after all.”

Benny groaned, leaning his aching head back against the wall. “I don’t know why I stopped you. There’s nothing worth living for anymore. She’s gone, Bo. She ripped out my heart and stole every ounce of hope and joy and light in the world. How am I supposed to just go on living with all this pain and emptiness?”

Bo picked up an empty whisky bottle and waved it back and forth like a pendulum in front of Benny. “So, you thought this could fill that void in your heart? It’s nothing more than a poor distraction from your main problem.” He tossed the bottle across the room where it made an echoing clatter against the dirty linoleum.

“Oh, yeah? And what, pray tell, is my problem, oh wise one?” Benny asked, rolling his eyes.

“That’s it right there,” Bo said, jabbing a finger toward him. “Pray.”

Benny stared blankly at him for a minute, waiting for more. He knew he was still drunk, but the other man was making absolutely no sense to his tortured brain. “Pray? That’s your big solution? What am I supposed to do? Pray that she comes back to me? Pray that I forget her? Pray that I go completely numb inside for good so it doesn't hurt so much?"

"No, but you can pray for help, for strength, for the courage to face another day. I know you're in pain, Benny. And I'm sorry I wasn't able to stop this trainwreck you're going through, but I can't help you if you don't want to help yourself. Even then, I can't give you what you need most. But there is someone who can give it to you if you only ask."

"Are you seriously telling me to ask God for...what was it...help, strength, and courage to stop drinking?" Benny snorted and closed his eyes. "I'm too tired for a temperance revival sermon, Reverend Beauregard Bailey."

"*When the righteous cry for help, the Lord hears, and delivers them out of all their troubles. The Lord is near to the brokenhearted, and saves the crushed in spirit. Many are the afflictions of the righteous; but the Lord delivers him out of them all.*"

Benny opened his eyes and stared at the ceiling. Could it be that simple? Asking for help and being rescued? Even God couldn't take away this feeling of emptiness...could He?

When he didn't scoff at the Bible verse, Bo continued, "At least let me introduce you to Pastor Jim. He's got experience dealing with depression and has given some great sermons about asking God for help with all kinds of life's troubles. If he can't help you, he'll at least be able to find you someone who can. And you've got to do something," he insisted, getting to his feet.

"Because watching you slowly kill yourself is torturing the rest of us who care about you. Now, I'm going to see if I can dig up some dry clothes...preferably cleaner than those filthy rags you're wearing, then you are going to eat something before we muck out this pigsty you've created. Once you start living like a human you might start feeling like one, too."

As Bo left him to dry off and change, Benny thought about what he'd said. It was true he'd wanted to die, but something had stopped him when the opportunity presented itself. Something deep inside him wanted to live even if he had to do it without Peg. He was skeptical about God being the answer to all his problems but decided he might as well try something. He felt like he was at the bottom of a deep well anyway, so there was nowhere to look but up.

Now that he'd been forced to look outside himself, he began to regret his actions over the past months. Bo and his parents had tried to talk to him, comfort him, and bring him back to life, but he'd ignored or yelled at them, pushing them away so he could wallow in self-pity and lose himself in a stupor of alcohol. He felt embarrassed when he thought about the way he'd treated his family and friends—and himself. How would he ever be able to face any of them again?

Bo was busy in the kitchen when Benny finally emerged from the bedroom. He'd made toast and coffee and was tackling the stacks of dirty dishes he'd collected from around the apartment. Benny quietly ate the offered toast, not knowing how to thank his friend for saving him or if he should take him up on the offer to meet with his pastor. Bo talked about this and that as he worked, trying to cover up the tension he could sense in Benny and giving him the time he needed to sober up. When the dishes were finished, Bo grabbed an empty grocery bag and tossed another one to Benny.

"I'll pick up the living room, you get the bedroom."

They worked the rest of the day to put the apartment back into reasonable order, and Benny realized he was starting to feel better. When Bo finally declared the place clean enough, he sent Benny in to take a shower and shave off his scruffy facial hair. He started the shower but paused when he heard Bo talking in the other room. Opening the door a crack so he could hear better, he also heard his mother's voice and realized she must have stopped by with another offering of food to tempt him into eating.

"It took a bit of tough love, but I think he may finally have turned a corner," Bo was saying. "I'll make sure he eats this when he gets cleaned up."

"Well, the apartment looks amazing," his mother said. "I tried to clean it up a few times but he just...you know." Benny's face heated in shame as he remembered his reaction to her attempts to help.

"I know. I'm going to introduce him to Pastor Jim as soon as possible. He'll be able to give him some tools to help when he starts to feel the need to drown his pain."

"I tried," she began, then Benny heard her sniffle back her tears. "I tried to help him, but I couldn't. I failed him, Bo. I'm his mother and I couldn't help him."

"I know, Mrs. Hunter. We do the best we can, but sometimes people need more help than what we can give."

Benny could just imagine his mother crying into her handkerchief while Bo comforted her and felt even worse than when he first read Peg's note. This wasn't just about the pain someone caused him. This was a pain he'd inflicted on those he loved. Unintentional as it was, it was still something he was embarrassed and ashamed to admit he'd done.

Closing the door and stepping into the shower, he let the hot water pound down over him as he sat beneath it with his arms wrapped around his knees. He cried as quietly as possible so he wouldn't be heard over the water, letting the tears and pain wash out of him and run harmlessly down the drain.

Bo ushered Benny's mother out of the apartment with a promise to keep her updated on their progress, hoping she hadn't noticed the sound of crying coming from the bathroom. She was feeling guilty enough as it was without having to listen to her son breaking down in the shower. At least this was a healthier option than the alcohol that had kept him in a constant downward spiral. Hopefully, the tears would wash away the toxic feelings he'd kept inside for much too long.

It was nearly five minutes before the sound of crying stopped, but the shower continued to run steadily. The absence of movement worried Bo more than the outpouring of grief. He pressed his ear to the door, listening to make sure Benny hadn't done anything stupid after all. Just as he was about to knock to check, the sound of the water changed, and Bo breathed a sigh of relief that Benny was finally moving around normally as he scrubbed the sweat and alcohol off his skin.

"Your mom dropped off some chicken dumpling soup," Benny called through the door once the water was turned off. "Want me to dish you up some now or wait until you get rid of that sorry excuse of a beard?"

"I'll shave first," Benny replied.

Bo was disheartened to hear the amount of sadness in his voice instead of the biting comeback he'd hoped for. He looked around the apartment, searching for inspiration for lifting Benny's spirits and his eyes fell on the dusty piano. He'd never seen Benny's piano in such a neglected state and realized not only had his friend given up playing at the club, he'd given up on music altogether.

"Music hath charms to soothe the savage breast," Bo murmured to himself as he sat down before the keys. If only he could get Benny interested in his music again, he knew he could use it to release at least some of his emotions. A smirk tugged at his mouth as an idea came to him. "If this doesn't get him to play again, nothing will."

Bo began to play a snappy tune on the piano. A few lines in, he made a mistake and started the song all over. At the same point, he made the same mistake and began the song again. By the third mistake, Benny opened the bathroom door and stood there in only a towel with shaving cream on his face, glaring at him. Bo played past the mistake and Benny went back to his task of shaving. He'd only gotten through one stroke of the razor when Bo made another mistake and began the song once more.

"Play it right or don't play it at all," Benny called from the bathroom.

"I don't know, man. I think maybe the piano's out of tune."

It was then Bo played his ace in the hole. He struck a wrong chord that would sound like fingernails on a blackboard to any trained musician. Even though he knew what was coming, he could hardly keep the smile from his face when a string of curse words came from the bathroom.

Benny stormed into the living room, shaving cream on one half of his face and a trickle of blood running down his neck where he'd nicked himself with the razor. "Are you trying to kill me again?"

"Sorry," Bo said, as innocently as possible. "I've had to do a lot of the piano parts lately, but some of the songs just give me the worst trouble."

"Don't tell me you've been playing like that in front of people," Benny said in disgust.

"Well, we didn't have much choice. It was either me or Stubby." Bo had to start playing again so he would have an excuse to look down at the keys so Benny wouldn't see his face. This time when he made a mistake, it wasn't on purpose, it was because he was shaking too much from barely contained laughter.

"They were going to let Stubby play? Stubby can't play *Chopsticks* without messing it up. What's wrong with you guys?"

"What's wrong is we don't have a piano player," Bo said, starting the song yet again. He knew if he kept it up long enough, Benny wouldn't be able to help himself. He would have to play the song right just to show Bo how it was done.

"You do now," Benny said and shoved Bo off the seat. Still in his towel, half shaved, and bleeding slightly from his cut, Benny sat down and played the entire song without a single mistake. Bo sat back and smiled. His friend was back.

Chapter Twenty-eight

March 21, 1970

"Thank you for the beautiful baby blanket, Claire," Margaret said, running a hand along the soft, quilted fabric. "And thank your mom for the casserole and pie. I'm sure David will really appreciate them. He's been having to do most of the cooking for months now since I haven't been able to get around much."

Claire smiled down at the sleeping infant cradled in her arms and sighed. "I'm just glad to see you're feeling better. You sounded so tired whenever I called, and you never wanted to talk very long. I tried visiting every time I came home, but David always said you were resting. I started to wonder if he was holding you hostage or you were on some kind of house arrest or something."

"It did sort of feel like that toward the end," she admitted, then stroked the fine, blonde hairs on her daughter's head, "but the long bed rest was all worth it once I laid eyes on this precious gift. She's the most important thing in the world to me now. And because of that, I have a question. David and I want to have Teresa baptized next month and we wondered if you would stand up as her godmother."

"Godmother? Me?" Claire was both honored and shocked. Although she went to church with her family whenever she was home, she didn't consider herself a model Catholic. Then again, she'd do anything for her best friend, especially after all she'd been through in the last year. "I would love to. Just let me know when and what I have to do."

"Thanks. We really appreciate it." Margaret smiled and relaxed.

"You were worried I'd say no, weren't you?" Claire accused. "Why?"

"Well," she began hesitantly, plunging her hands deep into the pockets of her shapeless, post-maternity jumper dress, "you can be pretty pessimistic about faith sometimes. I was afraid since going off to college and having all these new experiences you'd give up on religion altogether."

Claire felt a wave of sadness at the accusation and was surprised it touched her so much. "I know I sometimes bash the church or even the Catholic faith, but I still believe in God." She smiled down at the baby in her arms who was looking back intently as if memorizing everything she said and did with those green eyes. "I mean, how can you not believe in a higher power when you look at this little miracle?"

"So, how is college?" Margaret asked and Claire could tell she wanted to change the subject but wasn't certain if she wanted to steer away from the topic of faith or her daughter.

"Oh, pretty much like high school, but without as much immaturity," Claire replied. She didn't want to tell the truth that she loved the freedom and opportunities to expand her mind that college offered. Peg—no, *Margaret,* she'd been corrected several times by David—no longer had the chance to attend college now that she had a child to care for.

"So, how's David?" Claire asked, lightly.

"Fine," she answered without elaborating any further. When the baby started to squirm in Claire's arms, Margaret took her back and laid her gently in the bassinet beside the couch. She rubbed her back a few seconds, smiling lovingly down at Teresa before turning her attention back to her guest.

"What?" she asked when she saw the look of pity on Claire's face.

"Do you realize this is the first time we've gotten to really talk since you passed out at your aunt and uncle's house? That was July, Peg. I've got a lot of questions."

"It's Margaret now," she responded automatically.

"Then that'll be my first question." Claire made herself comfortable on the couch, tucking her paisley bell-bottomed legs under her to prove she was not about to be dismissed. After a few seconds, Margaret gave a resigned sigh and sat beside her, her posture rigid and defensive.

"I'm a wife and mother now, Claire. My high school nickname doesn't feel right anymore."

Claire wanted to say she looked and acted like a completely different person as well but didn't know how she'd take it. It was like her best friend was gone, replaced by this pale, thin imitation.

"Does Benny know?" Claire asked quietly. When her friend winced at the name and looked away, she knew the answer. "I'm not an idiot. Even though your uncle wouldn't give up any information no matter how much I badgered him all the way back from Detroit, as soon as your dad told me you and David were married and off on your honeymoon…I put two and two together. David knew before he married you, didn't he? About Benny and the baby."

She stared down at her hands, clenched tight in her lap. "He knew."

Reaching over to lay a hand over Margaret's, Claire squeezed just hard enough to assure her she understood. "How is…married life…with David?"

She took a deep breath before letting it out and turning her sad eyes to Claire. "Fine. David is steady and stable. We have a lot in common and he knows me so well. He'll be a good provider and I know he'll always be there for Teresa."

"My God, that sounds like your father talking. Do you even love the guy?"

"David's a good man," Margaret argued, but Claire noticed it was more in defense than out of love. "Even after…everything…he was there for me. It may not be a passionate kind of love like with…" she trailed off, unable to say the name, "...but he does care for me…us."

"But what happened between you and Benny? I know you loved him because it was the happiest I've ever seen you, and any fool could see he worshipped the ground you walked on. You obviously did more than just listen to him play at the club and attend Fourth of July picnics." She nodded her head toward the satin-lined bassinet. "Those eyes are a dead giveaway. So why settle for dull, stable David when you had someone like Benny? What happened when your dad dragged you back from Detroit?" She held up a finger in warning. "And before you even try dodging the question this time, know that I am not leaving this house until you tell me and I'm satisfied you're more than just 'fine'."

Margaret rubbed her furrowed forehead as if thinking of the past caused her physical pain. "It all happened so fast. I knew my period was late and suspected I might be pregnant. I wanted Benny with me before finding out for sure. He would've been so happy, but he was off on that tour. Then there was that whole thing with me fainting." She smiled sadly at Claire. "When the doctor told me, I was so happy. I knew Benny would be, too." The smile slid from her face. "Then Dad burst in and started yelling at me right in front of everyone, demanding what I'd been doing all summer and calling me a sinner. I tried to tell him about Benny—about how he was a hard worker with two jobs and was nearly thirty so he was mature and dependable, and that he wanted to marry me—but he just wouldn't listen."

"Hold up," Claire interrupted. "Benny asked you to marry him? For real? And you didn't tell your best friend?"

She smiled wistfully. "He wanted to do that whole asking-for-the-father's-permission thing in person before we told anyone. I didn't want to come back home yet, so we planned to do it after he got back. We thought we had all the time in the world," she added, and Claire noticed her eyes were shiny with unshed tears.

"But your dad didn't believe you when you told him your plans?" Claire asked softly.

She shook her head and returned to staring at her hands. "All the way home he kept telling me how ashamed he was, how ashamed my mother would have been, how the entire town would call me a sinner, how God would turn his back on me for fornicating with an older man. He said the proposal was just a figment of my imagination and that even if it were real, he would never let me marry a musician who seduced young girls, got them pregnant, and then ran off. By the time we got back home, he almost had me believing I really was a harlot, that I really wasn't in love, and that I'd just been coerced by an older, more experienced, ungodly deviant."

"That's horrible! I knew your dad was fanatically old-fashioned, but I never would've thought he'd treat his own daughter like that." Claire leaned forward so she could study Margaret's eyes. "You know it's not true, right? That everything your dad tried to make you believe was all B.S.? Benny's not like that at all! He may be a square, but he's a good guy."

Margaret nodded. "In my heart, I knew all along, but I was so scared and confused. There was nothing I could say or do to convince Dad to let me go back to Detroit and he said if I ran away, he'd have him arrested. Then he started trying to talk me into giving up my baby." She laid one hand possessively on the rim of the bassinet, peering in at the sleeping infant as if needing to ensure she was still safe and sound. "I told Dad if he even tried to take her away from me or do anything to her father, I'd kill myself."

Claire gasped. "You really weren't..."

"No, of course not." Then a contemplative look came over her face. "At least I don't think so. It was pretty immature, I suppose, and it really didn't help. Dad thought I'd gone crazy and locked me in my room. The next time the door opened, David was there to save the day."

"And he wanted to marry you? And you agreed? Just like that?"

"I was given two choices. Marry David and keep the baby's real father a secret, letting everyone think she was his, or be shipped off to an institute and lose our baby. After a year or so, I would then be sent back home where Dad could continue his constant barrage of guilt."

"That wasn't a choice at all," Claire exclaimed.

"I was not about to give up the only thing I had to remind me of…him. I couldn't lose the only thing that reminded me of what life could be like. What it felt like to love and be loved. I agreed to marry David because it was my only option, but then it felt like all the color went out of the world and I began to wonder if I'd ever feel happy again. Before her eyes turned from blue to green, I'd almost convinced myself last summer was a dream."

"But if you miss Benny so much…and I'm sure he misses you…why not go to him? Tell him about his baby. He has a right to know, doesn't he?"

"What good would that do?" Margaret asked. "I'm married, Claire. I can't just leave my husband and I can't just get a divorce. Telling him about David would only hurt him. Telling him about Teresa without letting him be a part of our lives would only hurt him. Letting him be a part of our lives without being able to be with him would hurt me. I got married in the first place to keep a secret. How would it look to suddenly have another man claiming to be her father? What would people say about me? How would they treat her? What's she supposed to think about having two dads around? No. Telling him would only cause everyone pain."

Claire sat in shock, her heart aching for the wrongness of it all. She opened her mouth to say something, but the baby started fussing, waking from her nap hungry just as the front door opened and David returned home from work.

"I have to feed her," Margaret said, quickly retrieving her daughter before she started to fully cry. She looked down at her baby girl and a genuine smile of love spread across her face. "This is my life now, Claire. She's my life, my world, the only thing I can love now. Can you tell David about the food you brought? He can heat that up for supper for the three of us."

"Thanks, but I promised my parents we'd go out to eat tonight. But I can get supper ready before I go. You just take care of that precious little one." Claire hugged her around the baby and whispered in her ear, "Just think about telling Benny, okay? It's not right for him not to know." She gave Margaret a final squeeze before pulling away. "It was so great to see you. Let me know the plans for the baptism and I'll come home whenever you need me to. I'll be back for the whole summer, and we can spend more time together. Right?"

Margaret nodded her head, but Claire could tell she didn't mean it. She was a wife and mother now and didn't have time to waste hanging out and going to parties with her college friend with nothing but free time on her hands.

Claire found David in the kitchen, his discarded suit jacket hanging on the back of a chair, his tie pulled loose, and the top button of his shirt undone. He was staring at the contents of an open cupboard as if mentally trying to piece them together into a meal. He glanced over his shoulder, then turned back to the perusal of meal options. "Hey, Claire."

"Hey, David. How's work?"

"Same old, same old, I guess."

Claire opened the refrigerator and took out the casserole dish, setting it on the counter. "Supper. Compliments of my mom."

David gave a sigh of relief and moved out of the way as Claire took over the preparations. "Thanks. That looks delicious. How was your visit?"

"Good. Peg…sorry, Margaret…is feeding the baby and I've got to get going soon." She looked over to where David sat at the table sorting through the mail. "What's with the sudden change with her nickname anyway? Was that your idea?"

He paused with one envelope held over the garbage can, then let it fall before answering. "No. That was all her. She told me it was because the name sounded too immature for an adult, although Peggy Lee seems to be doing alright with it." He watched Claire put the dish in the oven and turn on the timer. "Personally, I think she just needed a break from…before…you know, separate her life now from…before."

Claire could tell by the muscle in his jaw and the strained way he paused before the last word that he had strong feelings about Benny. She sat in the chair across from him and folded her arms in front of her, being careful that her voice didn't travel far enough to reach upstairs where Margaret was nursing the baby. "Can I ask you a question? Are you really okay with all of this? I mean, marrying Margaret so fast like you did and raising someone else's child?"

David's back straightened in defense, but he didn't seem surprised that she knew the truth. "It's not just 'someone else's child'. She's Margaret's child...and now she's mine, too. I was the one who helped her through morning sickness, took her to all her doctor's appointments, rubbed her aching back and legs, and felt the baby kick for the first time. I took care of everything when the doctor put her on bed rest because she was having labor pains too early. And when I saw that little pink bundle for the first time in the nursery...well, I knew it was all worth it. I promised them both I'd always be there for them. Then..."

He paused and ran his hands through his hair. Claire waited for him to continue, but he seemed to have trouble finding the words. She could finally see how this whole arrangement had affected him as much as Margaret. He'd also given up going to college to be a husband and father, his freedom gone just so the truth of the baby's conception wouldn't ruin her life.

"Then?" she prompted quietly.

David dropped his hands and clasped them on the table, his knuckles white with tension. He stared down at them as he spoke. "Then I—we—saw her eyes. The greenest eyes I've ever seen. I know every time Margaret sees them, she's reminded of who Teresa really belongs to."

"You don't really believe what her dad said about Benny, do you? That he took advantage of her? I'm telling you, I saw them together and there's no way both of them could have faked that level of emotion. She looked at him like he hung the moon and he looked at her like she was the most precious thing on earth. They really were in love."

He nodded without looking up. "I know. I knew the moment the Judge said she was pregnant she had to have loved the guy to let it get that far. I also believed her when she said they planned to get married because she's not the kind of girl to have just a summer fling." He looked up at Claire and she wanted to cry from the pain in his eyes and the injustice of it all. "The truth and what I believed didn't stand a chance against the Judge's wrath. He didn't care about her feelings at all. The only thing he cared about was if her condition sullied his good name, and I've hated him ever since. I had to do what I did, or Pe— Margaret would've suffered. Luckily, he doesn't have much to do with us anymore. Other than the few social events we both attend, he's pretty much left us alone and that's the way we like it. Now we're just trying to do the best we can with the situation and hope it's all worth it in the end."

Claire reached out and covered his hands with one of hers. "Thanks. For sacrificing yourself to help her and for taking such good care of both of them. I think you're going to be a great dad to your little girl. And who knows, maybe she'll have a little brother someday."

His face crumbled, on the verge of tears and he folded his hands together, pressing them hard against his lips in an attempt to hold back his emotions. "She had a hard pregnancy, Claire. Really hard. The doctor said unless she gets a lot healthier and stronger, we shouldn't even think about trying to have another baby because she may not survive it again. I'll be there and do anything I can for both of them, of course, but I also know that my little girl will always be looking at me with those green eyes. I also know that every time my daughter does or says something that reminds Margaret of him, I'll have to hear 'Just like her father'."

Chapter Twenty-nine

March 31, 1970

When the letter came and Benny saw the familiar handwriting, it made his blood run cold. It had been months since Bo dragged him kicking and screaming from his self-induced torture and back into the light. His life had finally returned to normal since then, but the sight of the familiar script set off flashbacks from that personal hell.

Without even taking off his coat or snow-covered boots, he dropped the mail on the table and went to the kitchen sink for some water to soothe his suddenly parched throat. It wasn't what he craved, but he'd given up drinking alcohol and cut down the smoking to half a pack a day. It was the only habit held over from that time, and he was finding it the hardest to break.

Bo had been his main and constant source of strength while he worked to sort out his life and learn to cope with the depression that sent him over the edge. Not only had he pulled Benny back from the shadow of death, but he also introduced him to their pastor. Benny was shocked to learn the well-spoken, clean-cut leader of the Methodist Church who led such passionate, inspiring sermons had been in a similar situation after he returned home from serving a tour in Vietnam. Pastor Jim had worked through his own depression and addiction to pain medication with the help of his faith and now led Bible studies for men who needed a little extra help navigating through life. Benny became a regular at both the church services and study sessions and was planning to get baptized and officially join the church with Bo as his sponsor. With the help of his friend and faith in a higher power guiding his path, he was finally happy and healthy once more.

He closed his eyes and prayed aloud the verse he kept taped to his kitchen cupboard for strength. "*I love thee, O Lord, my strength. The Lord is my rock, my fortress, and my deliverer, my God is my rock, in whom I take refuge.* Please, Lord, let this be nothing more than one of those hallucinations I used to have. If not...Lord give me strength."

When he opened his eyes and saw the letter still there, he knew he hadn't imagined it. He knew who it was from even though there was no return address. Peg. With shaking hands, he ripped the envelope open and slid out the single sheet of paper. He could tell even before unfolding it that the letter was very short. Finally, he took a deep breath and read the message.

Your daughter has Hunter-green eyes.

It took a while for the words to sink in and realization to dawn. He has a daughter. He and Peg have a daughter. She knew it was his because of the color of her eyes. Hunter-green eyes, just like his.

It took even longer to understand what she was telling him. She'd been pregnant when she left. Did she know at the time? Is that why she left? Why didn't she tell him? Why was she telling him now?

He had a lot of questions, but no answers. Whenever he felt like this, there was always an accompanying growing darkness inside threatening to overtake him, and he was far enough away from that particular experience to know he didn't want to go back there ever again. When he started feeling this lost, there were only two people he could call on to help him work through the worst of the gravitational pull the void seemed to have over him…and one of them was taking his daughter, Cheri, on a college visit today.

"Benny. Is anything wrong? My secretary said you needed to talk to me right away."

"I'm sorry to interrupt, Pastor Jim, but…yeah, something's wrong."

Just hearing the caring sound of his pastor's voice began to drive the darkness back and Benny was able to think rationally again. He honestly felt sorry for having to bother such a busy man, but Pastor Jim had told him time and time again, 'Relying on someone to help you through the valleys of life does not make you a weak person. It takes courage to ask God for help and even more courage to ask your fellow man.'

Pastor Jim waited patiently for Benny to form his thoughts enough to continue. "I got a letter in the mail today," he began. "From Peg."

When Benny was silent for over a minute, Jim prompted, "And what did the letter say?"

"I…Peg…I mean…we…have a daughter."

Benny could hear the sound of Pastor Jim exhaling and briefly wondered what he'd expected Benny to tell him. Whatever it was, this wasn't it. "Wow," he breathed into the receiver. "That…that's some news. What else does it say?"

"That's it," Benny said, picking up the single sheet of paper and reading it out loud for him. "That's the entire letter. It's not even signed, but I know it's her writing. No explanation, no other information other than she knows it's mine because of the eye color. Not when or how they're doing. Nothing! So, she was pregnant when she left but I don't know if that's why she left."

"You said she'd slipped a letter under your door before she disappeared. That she needed to talk to you about something."

"Yeah, but I don't know if this is what she was going to tell me." Benny sighed and rubbed his forehead where he could feel a tension headache threatening to explode. Now that his initial panic was ebbing, he realized how warm he was getting still wearing his coat. Without taking the phone from his ear, he shed the extra layer one-handed. "I guess I thought for so long that the note meant she was leaving me, it's kinda hard to think it was anything else. Maybe she did know. Maybe she was going to tell me. But if she knew and was going to tell me, then why did she leave?"

"Did you ever think maybe she didn't want to leave?" Pastor Jim asked quietly. "That she was taken away from you against her will?"

Benny nearly dropped the phone as his body went numb. He'd never even considered the possibility that Peg hadn't wanted to leave him. That she may have still loved him. When she simply vanished without a trace, he'd naturally thought the worst. When months went by without a call, letter, or even a rumor about her, he'd resigned himself to the fact they would never see each other again. And then decided being alone was probably for the best after all. If one, brief love affair could drive him to the brink of death, it wasn't worth pursuing anything more substantial. His mind and body…his soul…couldn't take another trip to hell.

"Benny? Do you want to come by and talk about it face-to-face? Or I could come there. Either way, it doesn't sound like you should be alone right now."

"No, no, I'm fine," Benny said. "I mean, I'm okay at least. I don't feel like drinking or anything like that. It's just…"

"You don't know what to do next?" Pastor Jim guessed.

Benny felt a wave of calm assurance come over him that he'd only ever felt in church after a prayer of confession. The kind that he'd always imagined as an angel's wings wrapping around him to tell him he was safe, loved, and forgiven.

"I know what I want to do," Benny said, his back straightened as he took in a deep, cleansing breath. "Find Peg and our daughter."

His first thought was to immediately drive to Eagle Creek. He even started planning what needed to be done before he left—get a message to Bo that he wouldn't be playing at the club for a while, let his parents know he wouldn't be working for a while, his car needed gas, he needed to pack, hunt down a map and find the route—then an unbidden image stopped him in his tracks and he stood petrified beside his bed with an empty suitcase open before him. It was an image of his beautiful Peg lying beside him in the corn at Bo's picnic, her extended belly carrying their child. His child. Before his legs could buckle beneath him, he let himself drop onto the bed.

"Peg had my baby," he whispered to the empty room. "Peg and I...we...one of those times...we created life." The amazement of it all made him smile and he felt the first stirrings of fatherly pride welling up from deep inside. "I have a daughter. I have a..."

Another image darkened the first and the smile immediately fell. It was of Peg, alone in the dark. "No, she had a daughter. She had a baby without me. I wasn't there for her."

The darkness began to swirl once more, and Benny felt sick to his stomach like he used to feel after waking up from his alcohol-induced comas. He raised one shaky hand to wipe the cold sweat from his face and started to regret not taking Pastor Jim up on his offer to visit. But he didn't want to bother him again. He wasn't even sure if he could physically make it back across the apartment to the phone. There was only one other way to drive back the demons eager to reclaim their hold. Sliding off the mattress to his knees, he closed his eyes and clasped his hands so tight he could feel his blood pulsing through his fingertips.

"Dear God in Heaven. Be with me now and give me strength against my doubts and fears. Please let Peg and the baby be okay. Don't let me find out she went through all this alone and scared, or that she gave up our daughter because I wasn't there for them. But why is she telling me now? Does she want me to come to find them?"

Benny could still feel the darkness, but its hold on him was slipping as he was finally able to verbalize what he would've allowed to eat at his insides before. Getting him to share his burden and allowing God to steer his life in the direction it was meant to go was the best thing that came out of his sessions with Pastor Jim. More than once his frantic prayers to the Father had been his life preserver. So, Benny sat in silence, forcing himself to relax, and prayed silently, "God, I open my heart to hear Your answer to my prayer. Help me to understand and accept Your word...even if it's not what I want to hear. Amen."

He stayed on his knees for another few minutes and let his mind go as blank as he could, but he could still see Peg, bright as day, behind his eyelids. It seemed as if all their interactions were running backward as if his imagination were a film reel in fast reverse. Peg lying beside him in his bed, dancing with her, sitting under the tree at the picnic, looking out from the stage to find her blonde hair and white face in a sea of black, holding her hand as they walked at the park, drinking champagne together until her cousin and friend came to drag her away.

"That's it!" Benny exclaimed, silently thanking the Lord for showing him what he needed to do. "I'll ask them about Peg! They can at least tell me if Peg and the baby are alright. Maybe they can even tell me why she waited so long to tell me or why she left in the first place!"

The obvious first choice was to call Ali, but when Peter answered, Benny's hopes were quickly dashed.

"Allison is away at college," Peter said in a tone of superiority Benny never thought he'd hear from the conservative man. "And, no, I am not going to tell you where. In fact, I don't want you to contact her at all. Don't you think you've hurt this family enough?"

"Look, I still don't know what I did to make you so angry with me," Benny began as calm and civil as he could manage with the frustration and a growing sense of urgency making his heart beat double-time. "But whatever it was, I'm sorry. I wouldn't hurt you or your family on purpose for anything in the world."

"It's so easy to apologize when it's too late to do anything about it, isn't it?" Peter continued. "We trusted you and you betrayed that trust. Luckily, things worked out for the best in the end so we can at least thank God for that. Don't call here again."

The heavy click on the other end of the phone was reminiscent of the door slammed in his face last summer. Although Peter hadn't been as rude as before, Benny could detect a small amount of sympathy. Whether that was for him or Peg, he couldn't tell, but it made him even more determined to find them.

He went down to the store to tell his parents he was leaving, and they quickly closed up to join him in his apartment while he packed.

"But if she didn't tell you about the baby before she left, why is she telling you now?" his father asked.

"I don't know, but there must be a reason," Benny answered from deep in the closet. "Maybe she didn't know she was pregnant when she left. I was afraid maybe something was wrong with them, but Peter said things worked out in the end so that has to mean they're both fine. I think something prevented her from telling me before. Now that she's finally able to, it has to mean she wants me to look for them."

"You don't even know where she is," his father continued, trying to be the voice of reason. "Don't you think if she wanted you to find her, she would have at least given you her address?"

"If she didn't want me to look for her, she wouldn't have told me at all," Benny responded as he took the small satchel he found in the back of the closet into the bathroom.

"What if she's married?"

His mother's quiet, practical voice worked like a bucket of ice dumped on top of his head, dousing his hope with reality. He paused in the process of collecting items from the bathroom counter and leaned against the doorway in shock.

"You must have known it was a possibility," she continued more gently at the ashen look on her son's face. "I mean she couldn't very well have had the baby on her own, could she? It just isn't done."

"And if she wasn't married, she may have been sent somewhere for girls in her condition," his father added. "Those places that pretend to be a kind of finishing school or college that lasts less than nine months, but it's really a convent or something. That would explain why she couldn't contact you. I hear those places keep the girls locked away from their family and friends until after the baby has been given to a deserving couple."

Benny felt his world tip out of balance. Peg's uncle had said things worked out for the best, not that the result was a happy one. Did that mean he really wouldn't be able to see his daughter? Ever? That the result of his and Peg's love for each other was beyond reach for both of them? Would he really never know his own child with his same Hunter-green eyes?

"No!" Benny said firmly, pointing a warning finger at his father. "Don't even think that. Peg would never have given up our baby. At least not voluntarily," he added, weakly, then shook his head. "Even if she did, once I find her, we can get our daughter back and finally be together."

Chapter Thirty

"So that's why you laughed when I told you about Liam and what he went through," Mary Jean exclaimed. "I thought you'd grown heartless or something."

I shook my head, smiling at the irony. "Nope. Just amazed with the number of parallels between Benny and Liam. I mean, come on, he's from Michigan, plays piano in a band…"

"Both like the Fourth of July," she interrupted with a smile and a wink.

I glared at her but continued, "...and he had his heart broken and went into a self-destructive depression. Now tell me those aren't the biggest coincidences you've ever heard."

"Are you saying you believe meeting Liam was fate?"

"Are you saying it wasn't?" I countered, completely confident in my belief.

"You forgot one coincidence," she began, leaning forward slightly with one raised eyebrow. "They were also both saved by someone leading them to faith. Yes, maybe meeting Benny and learning his story was just a way to prepare you for Liam coming into your life. Maybe it was the other way around and meeting Liam somehow made the story about Benny and your mom more real for you. But maybe it was also all part of a bigger plan laid out by God."

I opened my mouth to protest her religious theory, but something made me pause. Was I really sure that God *didn't* have a hand in my story? All those Bible verses Benny wrote in his journals or had hanging in his apartment did seem to call to me and I found myself searching them out all summer, writing every one I found down in my own notebook. I chewed on a thumbnail as I mulled over the idea of a higher power guiding people in and out of my life. I believed in God, but was I ready to think He believed in me enough to bother caring about what happens in my life?

"Do you want some more coffee?" MJ asked to break the silence and pull me back from my deep contemplation. "I think I might go get some water."

I glanced at the clock and saw it was almost two in the morning. I hadn't stayed up this late in a long time. I wasn't as tired as I thought I'd be, but my throat was dry from talking more at one time than I think I'd ever done in my life. "Water sounds good. I didn't expect the story to take this long. I guess it's a good thing neither of us has to work tomorrow…I mean today."

"Don't worry about me," she said, already on her way to the kitchen. "I'm used to these hours. You're the one who has to get yourself back on track again. By the way, how did you manage to get the day off anyway…especially on a Friday?"

I groaned, remembering my heated conversation with Jerry. "I've been working doubles to cover someone who went on vacation and Jerry nearly burst a blood vessel. He called me up to his office again and I told him I was the last one called just like he wanted me to be, so it was either me or no one. He said I had too many hours and he didn't want to see it happen again. So, I told him I would drop the second shift on Thursday and take Friday off and he could cover it himself."

"Woah, you go, girl! What did he say to that?"

"After asking 'Why? Do you have a date?' I told him my personal life was none of his business and if he ever asked me that again I'd file a formal complaint with HR. I swear, if it weren't for Jess, I'd have probably quit the first time he asked me."

"No, you wouldn't have," MJ said, setting two full glasses of ice water between us and settling back down on the couch. "You've always put other people's feelings ahead of your own and apologized even when you didn't do anything wrong. But I've noticed you've changed recently. Like you've gotten stronger. I don't know if it's because you've gained some strength from Benny's story or because of Liam…but I like this new Teresa. You're like the old you without something holding you back."

I paused to think, realizing I'd been feeling different lately as well. "I guess you're right. Jess said almost the same thing. It could be because of my parents' story…life is short, and you never know what's going to happen…but Liam also invited me to go to church with him and his sister. You know what? It wasn't as boring and preachy as I remembered as a kid. I've also been reading Benny's Bible verses over and over, too." I pulled the faded verse that once hung in Benny's kitchen from my notebook and handed it to MJ.

"*I love thee, O Lord, my strength. The Lord is my rock, my fortress, and my deliverer, my God is my rock, in whom I take refuge, my shield, and the horn of my salvation, my stronghold,*" she read aloud.

"I can see now how it brought him a sense of peace when he needed it. But I think I felt the biggest change—like a weight was lifted off my shoulders—when I reconciled with my dad…David. I understand a lot better why he did what he did and how he did love me…at least as much as he could when he was reminded every day we didn't share any genes."

"You know, Benny, Liam, and David all had something else in common," she pointed out, handing the paper back to me. "They all lost their families. David lost his daughter when he saw your eyes, then his wife died. Liam didn't even get to see his child, then his wife left. What about Benny? Did he finally get to see you and Peg after getting that letter?"

Chapter Thirty-one

April 1, 1970

When Benny reached Eagle Creek, he found a reasonably clean and respectable motel and immediately began to go through the phone book. He was surprised at the number of Bennetts listed there. He wished for the hundredth time that he'd asked her more about where she lived and her family. Even the name of her high school would have helped, but the thought of school just reminded him of the difference in their ages.

With no other option, he started at the top of the list and began dialing numbers. With each call, he asked if Peg was there or if they knew where he could contact her. By the time he neared the bottom of his list, he was getting very discouraged. Most of the people on the other end of the line were polite and said they were sorry they couldn't help him. Two just said no and hung up on him before he could ask if they had at least heard of her. Three didn't answer and three more he hadn't tried yet.

After he took a break to eat at a nearby mom-and-pop diner, he sat back next to the phone and dialed the next number on the list. A gruff man answered, and Benny asked the same question he'd asked so many times already. This time, though, the man paused before speaking.

"Peg, you said?" he asked in a tight, gruff voice.

"That's right, Sir. Peg Bennett. Does she live there, or do you know where I can contact her?" Benny's hopes grew as he realized he hadn't been rejected immediately.

"No," the man said after another pause. "There's no Peg Bennett living around here."

Benny's hopes were dashed. He thanked the man and slowly hung up the phone. When the man paused, he was sure he'd finally found Peg's home. But now, he sadly felt as if he would never find her. He tried the last numbers with no luck and then fell back onto the bed in exasperation.

Now, what should he do? Eagle Creek wasn't as big as Detroit, but it was big enough to make it feel like he was looking for a needle in a haystack. If only he knew someone else here that could help him. Someone who maybe even knew Peg.

He sat up as a thought suddenly occurred to him. What about that friend who came to Detroit with her? They were best friends, so she would certainly know where to find her. There was only one problem, though.

"What was her name!" Benny shouted in frustration. He'd spent so much time focused on Peg that he couldn't remember the friend's name. Peg had introduced her to him. They'd gone places with both her cousin and her friend. But now he couldn't remember her name.

"Think! Think!" he said aloud as he paced the floor with his head in his hands. He just had to remember that name. It was his only hope.

He tried to think of her face. She was short like Peg but looked more like Ali. She acted like Ali, too. Always looking for a party or some guy to hang out with. "We'd joked about her last name being the same as…what?" he asked himself, eyes squeezed so tight he saw flashes of light behind the lids reminding him of fireworks. "That's it! Sherman! Something…Sherman. Claire!"

He let out a bark of laughter as he grabbed up the phone book once more, nearly ripping the cover off in his excitement. There were almost as many Shermans as there had been Bennetts, but this time luck was on his side. The first number he tried had the answer he needed.

"Claire? Yeah, she's my cousin," the teenage-sounding voice said. "But I think she went back to college after the spring break, so you won't find her at home."

Benny got the name of the college Claire attended from her cousin, and within minutes an operator had him connected to the correct dorm's front desk. As he waited impatiently for someone to locate Claire to inform her she had a phone call, Benny paced the tacky motel room carpet as far as the phone cord allowed.

"Hello?" came an out-of-breath voice from the other end of the line.

"Is this Claire Sherman?" Benny asked although he was certain it was.

"Yeah. Who's this?"

"This is Benny Hunter…from Detroit." There was silence from the other end, and he was afraid she would give him the same run around as Peg's uncle until he heard a definite snort.

"You're looking for Peg," she stated rather than asking. Did he detect hostility in her voice? Or was that amusement?

"Yes, I am. Do you know where I can find her?" He made a quick prayer that not only did she know but was willing to tell him.

"I do," she affirmed. "But I'm not sure if I should tell you."

"Please, Claire," he begged, hating the way he sounded but unable to steady his voice anymore. "I need to find her, and no one else will help me. I asked her uncle, I came all the way to Eagle Creek and tried all the Bennetts in the phone book—you're my last hope." As he said the last, his voice broke, and Claire gave him a sigh of pity.

"I don't know…" she said, her voice wavering with uncertainty.

"Please."

Claire sighed. "Why, Benny? Why do you need to find her?"

Benny sat heavily on the bed. "I love her, Claire. I loved her the minute I saw her, I loved her when I thought she didn't love me and left Detroit, breaking my heart…and I still love her now."

"Wait a minute. You think she left because she didn't love you?" She whistled softly. "Boy, are you way off the mark. But why look for her now? Especially after all this time?"

He didn't know how much he should tell Claire, but if he wanted the truth, he had to give it first. "I got a letter from her yesterday."

He heard her swear under her breath before she switched the receiver over to her other ear. "She must've changed her mind. How much did she tell you in the letter?"

"Not much, but enough," he said, not wanting to admit how little she actually said. "Hunter-green eyes, Claire. That's why I have to find her. Will you help me?"

"I have a feeling this is probably my fault. I told her you deserved to know, but if you're asking how to find her, she must not have invited you. It may not be a good idea…" There was a slight pause and Benny held his breath. "Fine, I'll give you her address, but I have to warn you…you may not like what you find."

His heart fell into his stomach. "Why? Is something wrong with her? Is something wrong with…" he stopped himself, unable to even voice the thought.

"Peg's fine," she reassured him quickly. "And she seemed happy enough when I visited during the break. I'm just saying don't expect to be welcomed with open arms after…" She stopped herself as if not wanting to give him any information he didn't already know. "I know you just want the best for her, and I always thought you were a good guy, Benny. Just don't expect…anything. Okay?"

Chapter Thirty-two

The next morning, Benny was a bundle of nerves as he got dressed in his best blue slacks and green jacket that highlighted his eyes. He was anxious to see Peg but was a little scared as well. Claire hadn't said anything about the baby, but then again, he hadn't asked, either. What if Peg had sent him the message right before she gave the baby away? What if she blamed him for ruining her life? What if she no longer loved him? There were so many questions and only one way to find the answers. He had to go to the address Claire gave him and learn the truth for himself.

The directions from the motel's front desk clerk took him to a newly developed neighborhood at the edge of town. Signs of fresh construction were still evident around the perimeter of the three-block project where the melting snow no longer hid the unlandscaped dirt between the houses and the sudden beginning of a thick forest. No doubt the developers planned to continue excavating the trees once the ground thawed enough.

The rows of split-level, modular homes were the kind of mass-produced construction that spoke of convenience before aesthetics. Each boasted attached garages and actual, honest-to-goodness, white picket fences surrounding small yards that were undoubtedly meant to be trimmed obsessively all summer long. The only evidence of individuality were the color of the front door and the way they were decorated. The house Benny stood before had a blue door with matching flower boxes waiting for spring so the blooms could add a brightness to the drab, brown siding. Peg told him she grew up in a large, old house passed down for generations. She clearly didn't live with her father anymore, but even Benny understood this community was much too expensive for a single mother.

"So, she's married after all," Benny whispered to himself, glad the sidewalk was empty so no one could hear him or see the stricken look on his face. It felt like a knife had just been plunged into his stomach. Part of him knew it was inevitable, but he'd still hoped he could be the hero to rescue her and their daughter and live happily ever after.

Now the question was in the timing. Did she marry before she knew she was carrying his child? Did she marry because of it? If so, why not marry him like they'd planned? Was her marriage a happy one or just convenient? Did she come back home and sleep with other guys until she realized she was in trouble? Did she honestly not know the baby was his until she saw the green eyes?

By the look of things, she was at least living in style. But was this why she didn't come back to him? Did she want more for her child than a lowly musician? Did she already have a rich boy waiting for her back home when they were together? Did she know she was pregnant when she left and choose wealth over love?

Benny shook his head to clear his thoughts. He could question things all day, but the only way he was going to get answers was to ask Peg herself.

With shaking hands, he let himself into the yard and walked up to the front door. Within a minute of his knock, the door opened. A stocky, dark-haired man with chiseled features stood before him, scowling slightly at the stranger on his doorstep.

"I'm here to see Peg Bennett," Benny announced, plastering a smile on his face that probably looked as forced as it felt.

The man's brow furrowed in confusion and then widened in shock when he noticed Benny's green eyes. He opened and closed his mouth silently several times and looked nervously behind him, uncertain of what to say or do.

"I…I don't think…" he stuttered, and Benny instinctively knew that he was at the right place.

"Is she here? I'd like to talk to her," Benny asked, knowing he should feel guilty for enjoying the other man's discomfort but finding it satisfying instead. The other man finally snapped out of his confusion.

"I think you'd better leave," he said defensively and puffed out his chest slightly to stand up straighter. Even then, his eyes only reached Benny's chin.

"And who are you?" Benny asked, looking him up and down, wondering what—other than money—this man had that Peg preferred over him. He hadn't come this far to be turned away from his goal that easily, even by this man in his obviously more expensive button-down shirt and khakis.

"This is my house, and I would appreciate it if you didn't bother me…or my *wife*. You have no reason to be here."

So, this was the husband, after all, Benny thought sadly. For a moment, he felt like going home with his tail between his legs to lick his wounds until he finally forgot her. But then he remembered the note he still had tucked in the pocket of his coat. There had to be a reason she sent it to him. Maybe it was a loveless marriage, and she was looking for a way out of it?

"I understand, but first let me show you this. Then you can decide whether I have no reason or not," he said, holding the envelope so the other man could see the handwriting. When he removed the paper and held it up for him to read, the dark-haired man looked both angry and hurt and Benny took on a more sympathetic voice. "Please believe I didn't come here to make any trouble. Could we at least go inside and talk? I'm thinking this is a conversation better left private."

He looked from Benny's face to the note to the neighborhood as if anyone could overhear their secrets. Finally, he sighed and reluctantly opened the door wider for him to enter. The inside of the house was as impressive as the outside with a full set of matching living room furniture and artistic prints on each wall. Benny was led downstairs to what appeared to be the man's office. Sitting behind the heavy, oak desk, the man held his hand out for the paper. When Benny handed it over, he smoothed the note flat between them.

"Benny Hunter," he said, leaning slightly over the desk to offer his hand.

"David Billings."

David glanced up at the friendly gesture but refused to shake as he scowled down at the single sentence. Benny slowly straightened back up, let his hand drop back to his side, and stood waiting for David to process what the letter meant. Finally, he jerked his chin toward the other chair as an invitation for Benny to sit.

"Why are you here?" David asked, clearly confused.

"It's true, isn't it?" Benny countered.

Benny could tell David toyed with the idea of lying to him, but his earlier reaction had already given away the truth. He just wanted the other man to say it out loud.

"Yes."

The single whispered word was full of pain and sorrow. Benny recognized the feeling immediately as it was the same way he felt when Peg disappeared. Betrayal.

"I just... Why she... When... She... I thought..." David struggled to control his emotions in front of what Benny imagined he thought of as the enemy to him and his family.

"Can I talk to Peg?" Benny asked, trying to keep his voice as non-threatening as he could.

"She's sleeping."

"Then can I at least see my daugh—?"

"No!" David snapped, then winced at the unintended volume. He quickly got up and closed the office door, then walked back to lean over the desk, his hands on either side of the innocent-looking sheet of paper. "She is *my* daughter. And my wife doesn't go by Peg anymore. Her name is Margaret. Margaret Billings. And how dare you just show up after what you did to her? Haven't you caused her enough pain?"

"After what I..." Benny slowly stood up to his full height, towering over David, yet keeping his voice as controlled as he possibly could. "I don't know what everyone thinks happened between me and Peg..."

David crossed his arms over his puffed-out chest in an attempt to make himself look bigger. "It's pretty obvious to me. You took advantage of an innocent, impressionable, young girl—one who was in mourning over the loss of her mother, I might add—and violated her."

Benny's jaw clenched as defensive anger overtook him. His fingers curled into fists and he had an overwhelming urge to bury one of them in

David's accusatory face. Now he understood why Peg's aunt and uncle refused to speak to him and treated him like a leper.

"Listen, I don't give a damn what you think of me, but don't you dare presume I'm the kind of man who would do…that. Not that it's any of your business, but nothing happened between us until after she agreed to marry me. We loved each other."

"She may have thought she was in love, but that didn't give you the right to use her and leave her alone and pregnant."

"Leave her? I was only gone for a three-week tour with my band. She knew that. We were going to announce our engagement after I got back. When I came home, she was gone, no one would tell me anything, and I was left alone with a ring, a broken heart, and absolutely no answers."

"Don't come in here acting like the injured party," David warned between clenched teeth.

Benny knew he should back off, but the memory of all that pain also brought back all the anger he didn't realize he still harbored deep in his heart. One thing he'd learned during his time in the darkness was that anger made him mean, but he just couldn't stop himself.

"I guess now that I'm here I'm understanding the situation a little better. Who could blame her for leaving me when she had someone like you waiting for her at home? Someone with money." He gestured around the room. "I wouldn't have been able to compete with all this. All I could offer her was love and a small apartment over a hardware store. Guess that wasn't enough for her, was it?"

In a flash, David was around the desk and grabbed Benny's shirt front. He raised one fist, then paused as he glanced toward the closed door. Lowering his arm, he seemed to settle on pulling Benny down to his eye level.

"Listen, Bud. You don't know Margaret at all if that's what you think. She was devastated after what happened and I've spent the last eight months trying to pick up the pieces for her. Your pieces. I'll bet you never even tried contacting her in all that time, did you?"

"I didn't even know about the baby until yesterday." Benny's voice was tight in an attempt to control his raw emotions. "I've been to hell and back trying to pick up my own pieces, convinced she never loved me in the first place."

"How can you possibly compare your problems to hers? You can't even imagine how distraught—how depressed—she was when her father brought her home in such a serious predicament. Luckily, when he called me, I was willing to step in or who knows what would've become of her while you were off playing music with your bar buddies."

"Wait a minute," Benny said, holding up his hands. "You mean she didn't leave me because she loved you instead?"

David loosened his grip as he realized what he'd just admitted. With a sigh, he let go and went back to his seat at the desk.

"No," David said, putting his forehead in his hands.

"Then why?" Benny asked quietly and let himself sink into the other chair. "Why didn't she wait for me? Why marry you?"

"Her father found out about her condition and immediately brought her home. He told me the guy responsible had robbed her of her innocence and then left. He said she deserved better. I agreed and Judge Bennett married us that same night so no one would know her secret."

Benny sat forward in his seat. "But didn't she tell her father about me? Didn't she tell you she was already engaged? That I would be back soon for her?"

"She did," David admitted in a defeated voice. "At least she tried. But…" he trailed off before looking up at Benny with a bitter twist to his lips. "You don't know the Judge. Her father can be very…persuasive. He made me doubt her. We both made her doubt herself."

"She didn't leave me," Benny whispered as it slowly sunk in. Then he remembered the note he'd found after she disappeared. "She *was* going to tell me about the baby." He looked at David. "Why didn't she tell me before now? She knew where to find me."

"My guess is she was trying to spare you—or me—any more pain. Keeping you safe from her father's wrath and me from the embarrassment of a scandal. That sounds just like Margaret."

They sat in silence for a while as they each lost themselves in their own thoughts. Benny's was how he'd nearly killed himself because he thought she didn't care.

"She'd been taken away by her father all along," he said, rubbing his cheeks wearily.

"I thought she was depressed because of the unwanted pregnancy," David said, chewing on a thumbnail while one knee nervously bounced up and down. "I thought I was saving her from a delusional, one-sided affair. Now, I'm thinking it was because her father forced us to marry." He shook his head sadly. "That son-of-a— He played all of us to make it come out the way he wanted."

"Is she…happy?" Benny asked.

"She wasn't to start with," David admitted reluctantly. "Then she had some health issues toward the end of her pregnancy. But now that the baby's here, she's happier than I've ever seen her," he added with a genuine smile.

"Good," Benny said. They'd both been through a lot of pain, and he was glad to hear she'd been able to get through it as he had.

"I don't know why she sent you this letter," David said, handing the note back to Benny. "But I think we both know it would be best if you two didn't see each other. She's still not completely healthy yet and I don't know if she could take such a shock. Don't you think she's been through enough?"

Benny sighed but nodded in agreement. "I still want to see my daughter."

"She's my daughter, not yours," he said sternly. "Look, I'm sorry for what happened, but your being here is a threat to my family. They're both well cared for and safe with me. Isn't that enough for you? Now, I think it's time you left." David stood up, but Benny didn't.

"She will always be my daughter," Benny said. "And I will always care for her, whether you let me see her or not. I just want to do right by her."

"Then leave," David said with his hand on the office door. Benny still didn't move. "Do you think you'd be helping either of them by getting involved now? Margaret's life is finally stable. Do you realize what seeing you could do to her? What people would think of her if they found out what really happened? She wouldn't be able to handle a scandal like that."

"What about the baby?" Benny asked, standing up. "I'm responsible for her."

"No, you're not. I'm raising her as my own daughter, and she'll have everything she needs. It would just confuse things with you around. Think how it would affect a child to grow up knowing her mother had a baby with someone other than her husband. How would they both be treated by the community? Isn't it bad enough we're both reminded of what happened every time the baby opens her eyes? If you care about them, you'll leave us alone. And if you don't, I'll be forced to call the police."

David opened the office door with a look that said their conversation was through. Benny knew David would do anything to protect his family and respected that. He didn't want Peg to suffer any more than her father already caused. He loved her more than that. With a nod, he left the office and walked back down the hallway with David close behind. At the front door, he turned back for one last request.

"I won't bother you, but would you please do one thing for me."

David looked skeptical but didn't immediately say no, so Benny took that as a good sign.

"Let me have a picture of them," Benny said and held up his hand as David was about to object. "Please, listen first. I spent the happiest days of my life with Peg. When I thought she left me, I spiraled deep enough to almost kill myself. I never want to feel that low again. Now, I find out she didn't leave me on purpose and that I have a daughter. If I had a picture…I could use it to remind myself of something worth living for when times get hard and I'm on the verge of…slipping back toward that darkness."

David studied Benny, wanting to refuse. But Benny gave him nothing but sincerity. He went back into the house and returned shuffling through a stack of photos. Choosing one, he handed it to Benny who eagerly studied it right there on the front step. The black and white image showed the three of them—David's arm protectively around Peg who was glowing with happiness as she smiled down at the bundle in her arms. Benny's breath caught at the sight of the most beautiful baby he'd ever seen. She was sleeping, swaddled in a blanket with soft wisps of light hair peeking out from beneath a tiny bonnet. He wished he could see the color of her eyes to confirm she was truly his.

"They're both so beautiful," he said with a tear in his eye. "You're a very lucky man."

"I remind myself of that every day," David agreed.

"I won't cause any trouble. Just promise me you'll take good care of them and if they need anything you'll let me know." He took a Hunter's Hardware Store business card from his wallet and held it out until David reluctantly accepted it. "They don't even have to know it's me, I just want to be sure you understand I still feel responsible for them both and would do anything for them."

David stood silent for so long Benny didn't know if he would answer or not. Finally, he gave a single nod before quietly closing the door. Benny nodded back, then turned and left with nothing but a picture of his true love and his baby daughter.

Chapter Thirty-three

"That's when he decided to start the journals," I said and poured the last of the wine into Mary Jean's glass.

"That is so sad," she said, shaking her head as she looked at the old, slightly worn picture of me and my mom that had been tucked into one of Benny's many journals. "I understand where David was coming from, but don't you think Benny deserved a little more involvement in your life?"

"I don't think Mom could have mentally handled it. She felt bad enough just having to leave Benny in the past—I'm sure of it now that I know the whole story. Imagine how she'd have felt if Benny came back in her life, and she wasn't able to be with him because of David."

"I see your point." MJ finished off her glass in one last gulp and handed the picture back to me. I placed it safely back inside my notebook. "So, Benny didn't go back to Detroit? What did he do all that time?"

"He decided to stay close to us just in case. He got a job teaching music at a high school in a nearby town and started the bank account, putting in anything he could. He said the picture of our family helped him through a lot of bad times, but then he started going out for drinks with some of the other teaching staff. He was careful not to let himself drink too much or do anything that would draw attention to himself. All he wanted was to blend in and hope, by some chance, he'd be able to see me and my mom one day."

"Personally, I think he should have gone back to Detroit," MJ said. "At least he could've still played in the band and been with Bo and his parents. It must've been a pretty sad life to live just hoping to catch a glimpse of someone. He didn't even know your name, did he?"

"Not then," I agreed. "The day he did find out…well, it ruined his life."

"What do you mean? What happened?" MJ had finished all of her wine, but I'd kept my glass for this particular part of the story. I took a sip before I started.

"I was 10 years old. My mom had a bad case of pneumonia the winter before and was still fighting the weakness. Every now and then, she'd run a high fever and be delirious for an entire day. She'd talk about things that happened when she was young and say things to me I didn't understand. I know now she thought I was Benny because of my eyes. Dad, I mean David, had to hire a nurse to take care of her while he was at work and was very worried about her declining health. Life at our house was stressful. It scared me to see my mom that way, so Dad encouraged me to play at my friends' houses whenever possible. I was coming back home one evening and decided to take a shortcut down a street I'd been forbidden to go. There were a few bars on that stretch, but I thought I'd be fine. You know, the fearlessness of kids who think they're invincible. I was running down the sidewalk when a man walked out of one of the doors. I couldn't remember a lot of what happened back then but reading about it in Benny's journals brought it all back."

Chapter Thirty-four

April 11, 1980

Benny had been going out with the same group of teachers every Friday after school for the last few years. He hadn't told any of them about his nearly fatal experience with alcohol, still too embarrassed by what he considered a weakness of character. At first, he'd offered to be the designated driver, sipping on sodas while longing for something stronger. He missed hanging out with Bo and the rest of the band and wanted to find anywhere to fit in. Eventually, he gave in to peer pressure and told himself as long as he had enough willpower to stop at only one—maybe two—drinks one night a week, he couldn't call himself an alcoholic.

The rest of the group were all single and had nothing better to do on a Friday night. The math and economics teachers were divorced and bitter, the science teacher was a grieving widower, and the rest were simply too pathetic or too self-absorbed to care about finding a significant other. They were much younger than Benny and seemed content to talk and complain about relationships instead of pursuing one.

They usually visited the same bars on a rotating basis to fairly and evenly distribute their patronage, staying near campus so they could begin their so-called "meetings" as soon as possible. That night, Sarah, the economics teacher, suggested they do something different. She'd heard about a new place in Eagle Creek and, before he knew it, Benny was dangerously close to the neighborhood he'd promised to avoid. He thought about catching a cab back home, but the rest of them talked him into staying for at least a little while. Finally, he gave in, rationalizing that the odds of David seeing him in a crowded bar were pretty slim.

Sarah groaned and laid her head on the table. "Why are all the good ones either taken or gay? Why aren't there more handsome, nice guys out there? Like Benny, here." Benny snorted and rolled his eyes. "No, really. If you didn't turn down every woman who asked you out, I'd ask you out myself."

Benny forced a nervous laugh. He hated being reminded of his marital and dating status when the only woman he wanted was out of reach. It had been a topic of conversation for years now among the staff with several attempts at matchmaking. "I'm just not looking for a relationship right now, that's all."

"I still say he was left at the alter and it scarred him for life," Dalton said, tipping his beer bottle toward Benny in a salute.

"No," Kerrie mused, studying him through the smoke of her cigarette. "I think he was the one doing the leaving. Fear of intimacy and all that. Thinks some girl will trap him into a loveless marriage by getting herself pregnant, so he's sworn off women altogether. That's my bet."

Benny forced a smile as the conversation about his lack of love life evolved into a debate around him. He avoided eye contact as he lit a cigarette and kept his focus on his beer for fear of someone reading the truth. As always, there was a painful, empty hole in his chest every time he thought of Peg. He knew if his co-workers found out his tragic story, they'd talk him into reuniting with her no matter the consequences…and knew he'd probably let them do it.

As the group's conversation morphed into their own personal, tragic love stories, their mood—and Benny's—sank deeper and deeper. He was only partially paying attention to what was being said as his imagination took him back to that summer with Peg. It was so long ago, yet still fresh in his mind as if it had just happened yesterday. And when one of them bought a round of shots for the table, he automatically downed the bitter drink without thinking. A few minutes later, another glass appeared before him, and he drained that as well. When he stood up to use the bathroom an hour later, a wave of dizziness came over him and he finally realized how much he'd had to drink.

"Well, this has been fun and educational, kids, but I think I'm going to call it a night," he said, dropping a few dollar bills on the table for a tip. "See you all Monday."

They nodded and waved as he made his way to the bar to pay his tab and ask the bartender to call him a cab. His mouth was dry from the extra cigarettes he'd smoked while drinking, so he dug into his trench coat pocket for a piece of hard candy. The candy had become a new addiction for him since working at school while he attempted to give up smoking. He figured if it worked for Kojak, he'd give it a try. There was always a bowl of it on top of his piano for the times he felt the urge to smoke, and whenever a student had a good lesson, they were rewarded with a piece.

As he walked outside to wait for the cab, popping the peppermint in his mouth and looking up at the early evening stars, Benny was hit from the side by someone running down the street. The force of the blow knocked the candy from his mouth and made him stagger sideways. The impact also knocked the runner down onto the pavement. When he'd recovered his balance, he saw it was a young girl who had collided with him. She was sitting with her sweater sleeve pulled up, inspecting her elbow which was bleeding from a nasty scrape.

"Are you alright?" Benny asked. She didn't answer but continued her careful examination of the elbow. She was late elementary or early middle school age, lean and lanky with fine, golden hair hiding her face.

"Can I see that?" he asked as he knelt beside her. He took out his handkerchief and dabbed at the blood. Underneath, he found the cut was small enough not to need any stitches. "There, you see? It'll be alright. But you really should watch where you're going."

Just then, the girl looked up to thank him. His heart and breath stopped as he looked into his own eyes. Could it be her?

"Who's your mother?" he asked, but the fiercely intense look on his face frightened the girl. She tried to slide back away from him, but he reached out and grabbed her arm to stop her.

"Your mother? What's her name?" he asked more forcefully.

She tried to pull away, but he didn't even notice. Her green eyes were wide with fright and locked on his own which were wide with desperation.

"Is it Peg? Is that her name? It is, isn't it?" he asked, louder than he'd meant to. His need for her to answer was so strong, he could almost taste it.

He didn't realize how much he was scaring the girl. Tears started streaming down her cheeks as she clawed desperately at the hand that held her.

"Did she tell you about Detroit? Or me? Benny? Benny Hunter?"

By this time, he was yelling loud enough to attract the attention of some of the people inside the bar. And still, she wouldn't answer. She began to sob and pull back with all her strength. The crying finally registered in his frustrated mind, and he began to see how terrified she really was.

"Shhh, don't cry. I'm sorry." Then he remembered the candy in his pocket. He pulled out a handful and held it out to her. "Here you go. Just tell me. Are you Peg's daughter?"

Suddenly, Benny was grabbed around his neck from behind and hauled to his feet. In his surprise, he let go of the girl's arm and the candy flew across the sidewalk.

"Run home, Teresa. Run as fast as you can," the man who held him hollered. The girl quickly jumped up and ran down the street with her shiny, blonde hair streaming behind her.

Benny tried to yell after her to stop, but the arm tightened around his neck cutting off his air supply. He struggled to breathe and tried to dislodge the arm, but the man was much stronger. With the last of his strength, he drove his elbow into the man's stomach. The arm loosened enough for Benny to slip free, but he could do nothing more than gasp for breath. Before he was able to walk away, the other man grabbed the hair at the back of his head and tossed him into the brick wall of the building. The last thing he remembered before he slid, unconscious, to the sidewalk was the exploding pain as his head made a hollow thud against the brick.

Chapter Thirty-five

"Where's Teresa?" David asked the nurse when he checked on the sleeping Margaret.

"She hasn't returned yet, Mr. Bennett."

"I gave her strict instructions to be back by the time I got home from work. Now it's completely dark," he grumbled to himself as he headed for the phone. He was just picking up the receiver to call her friend's house when he caught a flash of blonde hair through the window, reflecting the glow from the streetlight. He smiled at her attempt to beat him home by running as fast as she could. He was glad she took his rules so seriously even though he would obviously have to punish her somehow for breaking them.

But as she turned into the yard, he noticed her terrified face. She looked as if the devil himself was after her. He hurried into the hallway just as she hit the door. She was so terrified that she wasn't able to turn the knob and began pounding frantically at it. He quickly opened it and she threw herself at him. She was gasping for breath as she clung to his waist and crying too hard for him to understand what she was saying.

He looked up and down the street but couldn't see anyone or anything out of order.

Confused, he closed the door and held his hysterical daughter tightly. It took a long time for him to finally understand what she'd been saying over and over again.

"I'm sorry, Daddy. You were right. I was so scared. I'm sorry, Daddy."

He had no idea what she was sorry for, but he stood there stroking her hair, waiting for her crying to reduce itself into sobs. When she was showing signs of calming down, he steered her into the living room and sat beside her on the sofa.

"Teresa, what happened?" he asked gently. "What are you sorry for?"

"You were right, Daddy," she said, clinging to him with her head on his chest. "I should've listened to you. I shouldn't have gone. Oh, Daddy, I was so scared."

Gently he held her and rocked back and forth while he listened to her disjointed story. He winced when she showed him her scrape but knew it would look better when they cleaned it up. When she finished her frightening tale, they sat quietly as he sorted out everything she'd said.

"Tell me if I understand you right," he said with more calm than he was feeling. "You were running down a street we told you to stay away from and bumped into a man. That's how you got the cut on your elbow. The man kept asking you questions and offered you candy. Then someone grabbed him and told you to run home. Is that right?" She nodded against his chest.

"He looked so scary, Daddy. He wouldn't let me go no matter how much I pulled." She rubbed at her upper arm, and he pushed her sweater sleeve up to find the marks that would turn blue and purple by tomorrow. His anger grew, but he fought it down for her sake. Teresa was frightened enough already. She didn't need to see her father lose control of his emotions.

"Teresa, honey? I need for you to tell me exactly what questions he was asking you." David was afraid to hear what she might say. He knew there were a lot of disturbed people in the world, and he'd worked very hard to keep them from his family. To think a dirty, old man was asking lewd questions of his daughter made him want to vomit. He hoped the man was behind bars already because at that moment he felt as if he was actually capable of finding and killing another human being.

"He asked about Mom," she said, sniffing loudly. "And something else...but I can't remember. He asked if Mom told me about...something. I can't remember. I was so scared."

He hugged her tightly and kissed the top of her head. He was very confused now. Why would someone attack a little girl just to ask about her mother? Suddenly, David's stomach felt like ice as a thought occurred to him.

"Do you remember anything about what this man looked like?" he asked, already knowing what she was about to say.

"Yeah. He was tall and skinny. His hair was almost white." She looked up at him with those eyes that belonged to someone else. "And his eyes were green. Just like mine."

Chapter Thirty-six

When Benny awoke the next morning, the first thing he noticed was the unbearable pain in his head. He'd experienced bad hangovers, especially in the months after Peg had left, but nothing like this. Without moving the rest of his body, he lifted his hand to the back of his head. His fingers discovered the cause of the pain before he remembered the reason. There was a gash on his scalp that must have bled freely because there was a considerable amount of crusty, matted hair.

He finally managed to pry his eyes open but didn't recognize what he saw. He knew he wasn't on his bed because this one was harder and had a rough blanket instead of his soft one. He knew that wasn't his wall because it was made of stone and his was paneled.

Taking a deep breath, he steeled himself against the stabbing pain and turned his head to see what was on his other side. The sight of the steel bars brought everything back in a rush. The girl, being choked, thrown against the wall, shaken awake by the police, and fingerprinted. The only thing he couldn't remember was if they had asked him questions or what, if anything, he had answered.

"Come on, sleepyhead," called a guard as he knocked on the bars with his stick. "There's someone here that wants a word with you."

Benny could feel the vibrations all the way down his spine but couldn't find the strength to complain. He heaved himself off the cell's cot and fought down a wave of nausea as he struggled to his feet. Even the sound of the keys in the lock drove spikes of pain into his brain.

The guard ordered him to turn around and then snapped the handcuffs securely around his wrists. The pinch of the steel helped take his mind off his aching head, and the walk down the hallway brought him more awake. He was taken to a small interrogation room which was furnished with only a square table and two chairs. On one wall was a mirrored surface which Benny knew must be two-way glass. He caught sight of his reflection and was shocked at just how bad he looked. There was dried blood smeared through his hair and across his scruffy cheek, and his eyes were bloodshot red. He had no memory of what happened to his trench coat, but there was evidence on his sweater vest that he'd vomited at some point, either from the alcohol or a possible concussion.

He was told to sit at the table after his handcuffs were removed and then left alone in silence for nearly ten minutes. He took the time to fully wake up and gather his wits before a very large officer came to join him. The sergeant was older, probably near retirement, with deep wrinkles around his eyes and pure white hair fringing his balding head. He took one look at Benny and turned back to the door.

"Why the hell hasn't this man been cleaned up yet," he shouted down the hall. Then he came back and sat on the chair across the table from Benny. "Boy, you look like something chewed on you then had the good sense to spit you back out."

"Well, that's pretty much how I feel, too," Benny replied, grateful for the sergeant's concern.

Another guard entered the room with a pan of hot water and clean towels. Benny had to grit his teeth when the filthy sweater vest was unceremoniously jerked over his throbbing head and concentrate on his breathing to keep from screaming as his wound was roughly rubbed clean. By the time the guard was done and Benny was able to relax his eyes open, the sergeant had placed a cup of steaming coffee in front of him.

"You look like you need this," the sergeant said and leaned his chair back so far that Benny was sure it would break in two from his considerable weight. "Do you remember anything from last night, Mr. Hunter?"

Benny nodded and sipped at the hot coffee. He could feel it warm its way down to his stomach and begin to clear his head.

"Would you like to tell me about it?" the sergeant continued.

"I went out to a bar with some co-workers, and I guess I must have had too much to drink,"

Benny said simply. He could not think of anything he had done that was bad enough to land him in jail, though.

"What about the girl just outside the bar? Do you remember what happened there, or were you too drunk?"

"She ran into me," Benny said defensively. "I was coming out the door and she must've been running down the sidewalk. I didn't knock her down on purpose. She ran into me."

The sergeant set his chair back down and leaned over the table toward Benny. "Do you know why you're in here?"

The way the officer stared intently into his eyes for the truth made it obvious there was something Benny was missing. Something very important or something very wrong. Benny just shook his head.

"Several witnesses testified you were kneeling over and intimidating a terrified, young girl lying on the sidewalk, offering her a handful of candy. Add on the fact that you were drunk, and you know what you get?"

Benny's eyes widened in surprise. He couldn't believe what the sergeant was accusing him of. Did they really think he was capable of…that?

"That's right," the sergeant said, nodding at the conclusion he'd come to. "You are on the verge of being charged with the solicitation of a minor, a Class D felony, topped with a Class B misdemeanor of drunk and disorderly. That is unless you can tell me something to change our minds."

"I…I," Benny stuttered, "I could n-never… That's not what happened at all."

"Then why don't you tell me what happened?" the sergeant said, taking a notepad and pencil from his uniform pocket.

"I…I was coming out of the bar a-and this girl ran into me. She fell and s-scraped her elbow. I knelt down to help her because it was bleeding and…" Benny paused. He'd promised not to divulge the true parentage of his daughter to anyone, but couldn't lie to the police, either. Especially since he didn't know what other people may have overheard. "And then I thought…I recognized her. S-so I asked her what her mother's name was. I didn't mean to scare her. She must've…misread…my intentions, though, because she started to cry. I couldn't s-stand to see her c-cry, so I apologized and offered her some of my candy to show I was s-sorry. The next thing I knew, I was being strangled from behind and couldn't breathe. I hit the guy in the stomach so he would let go, but then he threw me against the wall. I must've been knocked out then. That's all that happened," he insisted, willing the stone-faced sergeant to believe him. "That's the truth. I would n-never hurt that child."

"Do you know who that child is?" he asked, tapping the notebook with his pencil.

Benny shook his head, truthfully. He was almost positive it was his daughter but didn't get the proof he needed. Instead, he'd managed to terrify her, get knocked out, and thrown in jail.

"Who did you think she was," the sergeant asked, narrowing his eyes at him. Benny tried to think of a lie but knew he wouldn't be able to pull one off. He settled on telling a half-truth instead.

"I thought she was the daughter of someone I used to know. She looks a lot like her." Benny was relieved when the sergeant nodded and hauled himself out of the chair.

"You can just stay put there for a bit. Someone else may want to ask a few questions of their own. Then we'll get an official signed statement from you."

Then he was gone, and Benny was left to absorb his situation and finish his coffee in peace, praying to God for help. When the door opened again, he thought it was just another officer so didn't waste the energy to turn around.

"I knew it was you," a gruff voice said behind him. Even though it had been nearly ten years since he'd last heard that voice, he knew exactly who it was.

Chapter Thirty-seven

"It was her, wasn't it?" Benny asked without turning.

"It was," David confirmed, still not moving from the door. "And you scared her pretty badly."

"I'm sorry," Benny said, staring into his empty coffee cup. "I didn't mean to scare her." David walked around the table and sat in the chair the sergeant had vacated.

"What did you think you were doing?" David asked in such a deadly whisper, Benny finally looked up at him. He wasn't surprised by what he saw. Even though the other man had put on several pounds, softening the angles of his face, David still wore the same dangerously protective look Benny would've had if it had been him in that chair. When Benny looked pointedly at the mirrored glass instead of answering, David waved a dismissive hand. "I told the officers to stop the recording and go on a coffee break until I was done. Honestly, I think they were hoping I'd beat the shit out of you. Can't deny it didn't cross my mind, so I'll ask you again...what did you think you were doing?"

"I'm sorry," he said again. "It's just...when I saw her eyes..."

"You thought that gave you the right to accost her?" David finished. "And what? Tell her about you? Make friends with her? To kidnap her?"

"No!" Benny snapped, offended he would even think such a thing. "I just saw her eyes and had to know if it was her. I wouldn't have told her anything. I swear. I didn't realize at the time how much I was scaring her until it was too late. You know I'd never do anything to hurt her, don't you?"

David stood up and paced back and forth while he fought for control. "I was watching when the sergeant explained your charges and saw how shocked you looked. So, either you're a really good liar and acting innocent…or you're telling the truth." He took a deep breath and let it all out in one big whoosh, shaking out his clenched fists. "And I don't think you're that good at hiding your true feelings, so I believe you. But the protective parent part of me still wants to punish you for putting my baby through this mess."

"Is she alright?" Benny asked. "Will she be alright?" His obvious concern forced some more of David's anger to drain away.

"She had some trouble getting to sleep last night. But once she did, she slept fine. She was much better this morning. The bruises should heal in a week or so."

"Oh, my God," Benny whispered, the blood draining from his face. "I gave her bruises?" David nodded and Benny laid his head in his arms on the table feeling a sudden wave of dizziness and nausea overcome him. "Oh, my God."

The other chair creaked slightly as David sat back down. Benny gave a quick prayer of forgiveness and asked God to give him the strength to never let anything like this happen again. David was silent, giving him the time he needed to think about what he'd done.

"Does Peg…I mean Margaret…know it was me?" he asked from inside his arms.

"No. She…she doesn't know anything."

Benny caught the slight pause and detected a deep sadness in David. Raising his head, he looked at the other man closer. There were dark circles under his eyes and tension in his neck as if he'd been under a great deal of stress for a long time. He recognized the hopelessness in his eyes and the depression that surely accompanied it.

"What's wrong with her?" Benny asked, guessing the cause of his pain. David gave a deep sigh and slouched back in the chair as if admitting defeat.

"She's very sick," he said at last. "She had pneumonia a while ago and just can't seem to get completely healthy again. I feel like she's slipping through my fingers and there's nothing I can do to stop it." His voice broke as he said the last words and covered his eyes with his hand to fight back the tears.

Benny sat, speechless. He couldn't believe what David was telling him. He'd always held onto the hope that Peg would always be there, just on the other side of the city. That was the only reason he stayed. It was like he needed to be as close as he could get to her and their daughter to be able to carry on with his life. If something happened to her, what would he do?

He looked over at David, the man he considered his rival all these years, and the pain he was obviously experiencing. It was then he realized although he would be losing the chance to be together with Peg again, this man was losing his wife and that little girl was losing her mother. Guilt joined the grief that tore at his heart, and he blinked back the tears, berating himself for being selfish and petty.

"I'm sorry," Benny said quietly. "I wish there was something I could do to help. I know how much you must love her. Staying by her side all this time and all."

David's jaw clenched as he dropped his hand and looked across the table at Benny. "You still love her, don't you? After all this time and having married someone else?"

"I never stopped," Benny admitted openly.

"I don't think she did either," David said. "There are times, when she's delirious, that I think she's talking to you…and then she looks so happy," he added with a slight crack in his voice.

"Then let me go to her," Benny said, leaning forward and pressing his chest so hard against the edge of the table he knew he'd probably end up with a bruise. "Let her see I still love her and am here for her. Maybe it would give her the hope and strength she needs to fight this thing and come back to us. If not…then maybe I could at least give her a little comfort before…" He trailed off, not able to even think the worst.

David pinched his lips together and stared down at his hands as if contemplating all possible scenarios before making a decision. Finally, he began to shake his head. "Even if I could get you out of here, I can't do that to either of them. I can't give Margaret false hope that there's a chance you can be together again, just to cause her more heartbreak when she realizes you can't. And after last night…well, let's just say your face at our house isn't a good idea for so many reasons."

They both lapsed into an awkward silence, not knowing what to say to the other. Finally, David reached into his jacket pocket and pulled out a card.

"I assume you don't have a lawyer," he said, handing Benny the card. "Here's the only man that'll be able to help you now."

"What do you mean?" Benny asked, taking the card. "This was all just a misunderstanding. You're really going to charge me for…that?" He couldn't bring himself to say those horrible words.

"Well, if I know Margaret's father, he's probably already found out about this incident. Judge Bennett will move heaven and earth and call in favors to get one of his other judge buddies assigned to your case. He'd happily lock you up and throw away the key himself if he could, but since his granddaughter's involved, it would be a conflict of interest. That doesn't mean he won't be pulling the strings from behind the scenes to get the outcome he wants, even without revealing the truth. If you go with a public defender, you might as well kiss your freedom goodbye."

"But I didn't do anything," Benny objected. "At least I didn't mean to."

"That won't matter. I'll refuse to go through with the charges, of course, but you'll still end up on trial for drunk and disorderly along with any other charges Bennett can cook up against you—such as talking the guy you elbowed into claiming assault. The Judge doesn't take kindly to anyone hurting his family, whether they meant to or not, and he's a man used to getting his way. You should know that already by the way he took Margaret from you. He is not a man to be crossed," David warned seriously.

"Do you think this guy can help me?" Benny asked and tapped the card David gave him.

"He's the only man I know in the area that's not afraid of him and the strongest defense lawyer you could probably afford. And if you can't, I'm going to help you. Anonymously, of course." When Benny started to protest, David put up his hand to silence him. "I know what you did started out purely innocent, even though it got carried away. I probably would've done the same thing if I were in your shoes. But you did what I asked by leaving us alone and keeping our dirty laundry private, and that goes a long way in my book. I've had a lot of time to think about what the Judge did back then and how weak I was to stop him. I don't want him to ruin your life any more than he already has just because of what happened over 10 years ago. He's punished us all enough."

David pushed himself out of his chair and walked around the table to stand beside Benny, looking down at him with a mixture of pain and pity. "Besides, I owe it to Margaret. I never told her you came that day or that I knew you were still in Eagle Creek. I was afraid she'd let you visit and mess up what we'd all sacrificed so much for. And now..." He took a deep, shuddering breath. "Even though she'll probably never know anything about this, I owe it to her and her daughter to help you."

He opened the door, but Benny called out before David could leave. "I'll pray for your wife's health. And for God's peace for your family. I'm truly sorry. For everything. You have a beautiful daughter, David," Benny added to let him know he intended to keep their secret. "Can I ask her name?"

"Teresa," David said, his smile full of gratitude. "Teresa Marie Billings."

Chapter Thirty-eight

"I can see why your mind would block that out," Mary Jean said sympathetically. "And it certainly explains why you never like walking around town alone."

"It makes more sense to me now, too," I admitted. "Somewhere deep in my subconscious, I remembered how helpless I felt during that incident and never wanted to feel like that again…even if I couldn't remember specifically what happened."

I picked up the empty glasses and MJ grabbed the coffee cups and ice cream dishes, following me into the kitchen. The first rays of sunlight were shining through the window over the sink as I filled it with hot soapy water. We'd talked all night, but strangely it didn't feel like it took that long. Without being asked, MJ heated up the frying pan and got the eggs from the refrigerator.

"Did you have to go to court and testify against Benny?" MJ asked, whipping up some scrambled eggs while I washed dishes.

"It never made it that far," I explained. "Grandpa worked his angles, but the lawyer David helped Benny get was very good. David refused to press charges, and no one could prove Benny had any illicit intentions toward me. Grandpa was mad at David for ruining his chance to punish Benny for what happened with Mom, but David stood his ground. He didn't even file for a restraining order like Grandpa wanted him to. It was finally settled out of court by Benny pleading to the lesser charge of drunk and disorderly behavior."

"How bad was the sentence?"

"He spent a month in jail. Dad…David…said Grandpa got him denied house arrest but couldn't legally force him to leave town when he got out. His journals don't say much about his time there, though. It must've been too hard or embarrassing for him to write about."

"I'll bet."

By the time I dried the last dish, MJ had plates ready for us at the table. We sat down and ate our eggs and toast, using the quiet time to think about the events of the past.

"So, was that the end of Benny's journals?" MJ asked, breaking the silence as soon as her plate was cleared. I shook my head while I finished chewing.

"Not quite, but the last one reads more like a confessional and covers all of the last twenty or so years. He did write about Pastor Jim coming all the way from Detroit to visit him, both in jail and after. There was a piece of paper stuck inside the journal with a Bible verse on it, but it wasn't in Benny's handwriting, so I assume it came from him." I jumped up from my seat and went to fetch my notebook so I could show her what I had read and reread several times since finding it.

MJ took the notebook and read the verse aloud. "*We rejoice in our sufferings, knowing that suffering produces endurance, and endurance produces character, and character produces hope, and hope does not disappoint us, because God's love has been poured into our hearts through the Holy Spirit which has been given to us."*

"I don't know if I completely believe it," I admitted, "but it must've given him at least some comfort because he kept it. And he needed all the comfort he could get. Not only from being incarcerated, but because Mom died while he was there, and he couldn't even attend the funeral."

"What? No!" She paused as her eyebrows drew together in confusion. "Wait a minute. I completely forgot I already knew the end of this story. But it still stinks that they never got to see each other at least one more time after everything they'd been through. I bet Benny took that really hard."

"That wasn't all he had to deal with either," I said, clearing the table and putting the dishes in the waiting sink. "Since he'd been accused of soliciting a minor, even though he wasn't charged for it, he lost his job at the school. He was fired before he even pleaded the lesser charge. David visited him personally to tell him about Mom's death, and shortly after he was released, his parents told him they'd sold the store. They were getting too old to run it any longer, so they retired."

"Wow. That's a lot for an average man to take all at once." She picked up the towel to dry and put away what I washed. "How did a sensitive soul like Benny cope with it all?"

"Not well, it sounds," I admitted. "Even though he vowed never to drink again after his arrest and prayed for God's help every day, he still fell off the wagon quite a few times. Our picture stopped him from sinking too far, but it wasn't until he started going to AA meetings that he was able to get a handle on it."

"Thank heaven, even if the damage was already done."

We settled back at the kitchen table as I tried to wrap up the rest of my night-long narrative on my months' worth of investigation.

"Benny convinced David to let him add my name to the bank account as a memorial to Mom and a kind of payment for the pain he'd caused us, and that seemed to help bring him back a little. I think it finally gave him something to live for, even though by this time his health was seriously compromised. Since he couldn't get a job working with kids anymore, he played in bars and clubs when he could find an opening, but his heart just wasn't in it anymore, and his music showed it. That's when he started writing his melancholy-er songs. I'll have to play them for you sometime."

"I'd like that. It looked like he'd written a lot of songs, and you know I love hearing you play the piano."

"The saddest ones were written right after his parents died. I think I was about fifteen at the time. While he was back in Detroit to sell their house, he decided to make out his will. He knew how sick he was getting and wanted to be sure everything was left to me. He came back to Eagle Creek after that and 'simply existed by God's good grace' as he put it in his journal."

"But don't you think it's an odd coincidence that he lived where he did? Right where you'd walk by on your way to work?" MJ asked.

"Oh, that wasn't a coincidence," I said. "He found out that I worked for the clinic from a newspaper article—the clipping was in the journal. He followed me home one day, intent on introducing himself."

"Creepy," she mumbled.

"He knew he didn't have very much longer to live and wanted to explain the truth to me before he died. But once he got here, he was afraid I'd remember him from that incident before and chickened out. While he was driving away, he saw the rent sign for that apartment. Since he was too sick to work, he sold his car for the down payment. He was there for years knowing I was so close and trying to decide whether or not to tell me who he was. His mind was made up for him when he could no longer ignore the blood that came up when he coughed. That was when he came to the clinic…"

"And all of this began," MJ finished for me. "It's just amazing. But also, very sad. Have you decided what you're going to do now with all this new information?"

"I have some ideas," I said, not ready yet to divulge all my secrets. "I'm still working out the details, but I promise to let you know if and when I decide to do them."

"Fair enough. As long as you don't keep me in the dark so long this time," she warned, shaking her finger at me.

Chapter Thirty-nine

Mary Jean ordered me to get some rest after the all-night story session. It was physically and emotionally draining on both of us, but I still didn't go straight to bed after she left as I led her to believe.

First, I took Benny's Psalm 18 verse from the notebook and taped it to my kitchen cupboard just as it had been in both his apartments. After reciting it aloud twice, I called Liam.

"Do you have time to stop by on your way to work?" I asked. "I'd like to ask you something in person and if I wait until this afternoon, I might talk myself out of it."

There was a brief pause as if he was trying to guess the question, but his voice was confident when he replied, "Of course. I can be there in five minutes."

While I waited for him to arrive, I found myself pacing and wringing my hands as my nerves threatened to overcome my sudden burst of courage. To calm myself, I took out the sheets of music I'd stashed in the piano bench and laid them out across the music stand. The song was still unfinished, but I knew now how it should end.

I played through the whole thing almost by heart—the two of them meeting, falling in love, the tragic ripping apart of their relationship, the birth of a child, a great loss, pride in their daughter—and when the notes ran out on the paper, I closed my eyes and continued—another loss, a discovery, acceptance and a newfound sense of love. The last phrase was a mirror of when they met, only played in a higher register as if they were finally together again in heaven with a final run a little lower to indicate the continuation of their daughter.

As the last notes lingered and faded away around me, I knew that was the end of the song. The perfect ending I'm sure Benny intended. But as I lifted my fingers off the keys and opened my eyes, a feeling of panic overcame me.

"No. No no no no!"

I stared down at my fingers and the keyboard. I couldn't believe I just played something so perfect, so pure…and now…now…

I struggled to breathe around the tightening in my chest. Just as I began to hyperventilate, the doorbell rang. In a trance, I walked to the door fighting against the dizziness and the blackness that was gradually narrowing my vision. But when I opened it and saw Liam standing there, I slammed it shut again, not wanting him to see me so weak and in the middle of a panic attack.

"Teresa?" Liam called through the door. "Are you alright?"

I tried to answer, but my voice wouldn't raise above a whisper because my throat was too constricted. I backed away from the door until I bumped into a small table, knocking the vase of artificial flowers from it to break against the hardwood floor.

"Teresa!" The door opened and Liam stood in the doorway, framed by rays of morning light like an angel in my failing eyesight. He looked around the room as if surveying for danger, his gaze taking in the table and broken glass. He held out both his hands but didn't immediately rush in which, even in my haze, I recognized and appreciated. "Don't move. There's glass on the floor right by your feet. Is it all right if I come in?"

I nodded, leaning against the table as I tried not to run, knowing even if I didn't cut my feet on the broken glass, I would probably end up passing out cold before I'd made it two steps. Liam entered, walking slowly and carefully around the mess as if wanting to be sure not to frighten me.

"I want to get you somewhere safer," he said, his voice soft and comforting. "Do I have your permission to pick you up?"

His calming presence and the way he didn't just rush in and take over to handle things gave me a sense of security. The steel band around my chest began to loosen and I was able to get more oxygen to my brain. I nodded and held my hands out to him, thinking he was going to sweep me off my feet like a child. Instead, he wrapped his arms around my waist as if hugging me and lifted me effortlessly in the air, taking a step back as he turned and placed me back on the floor out of range of the shattered vase. He loosened his hold but didn't let go of me, using his hands on my waist to steady my balance.

"Just breathe. In through your nose, out through your mouth."

He demonstrated a few deep breaths and I found myself breathing slower and deeper along with him. The darkness around my field of vision dissipated and I found I was able to think clearer. Strength returned to my legs, but I didn't want to drop my hands from his shoulders or step out of his strong arms just yet.

"That's better," Liam continued in his deep, soothing tone. "Just keep breathing. You've got this."

I took a deep breath, held it, and then blew it all out, sending the last of the tension along with it. I felt drained and twitchy, but somehow stronger because I'd survived the attack. Glancing up into his concerned face, I felt myself start to blush and finally stepped back away from him.

"Thanks. I'm sorry. I don't..."

"Hey. Don't apologize." He bent down slightly to capture my gaze so I could see how sincere he was, and I couldn't help but stare into those beautiful, brown eyes. "I've been there. I'm just glad I could help. Now, first things first, did you get hurt at all?"

We did a quick assessment with Liam insisting I sit on the piano bench so he could check the bottom of my feet himself and found I made it through the accident without even a scratch.

"Now," he began, sitting on the edge of the bench beside me yet giving me as much room as he could, "do you know what prompted the panic attack? Can you tell me?"

I looked down at my hands, clenched tight in my lap, and felt a faint echo of the attack threatening to bloom once more deep inside me. Liam must have sensed it because he covered my hands in his and held them between us.

"Whatever it is, I want to help."

The word *want* caught my attention more than anything. Not *I'm here to help*, or *Let me help you,* not even I want to help *you*…simply I *want* to help. The tiniest change in motive made all the difference and I found I wanted him to help even if I didn't think he could solve my problem.

"The sheet music on the piano was written by Benny…my real father…and the song is about…well, it's sort of a long story I planned to tell you later…about Benny and my mother and me…" I knew I probably wasn't making much sense, but it was the best I could do considering the amount of adrenalin coursing through my veins and the way his hands were still gripping mine, giving me his warmth and strength. "Anyway, the song wasn't finished. I don't know if he didn't know how to end it or didn't get a chance before he…you know. Mary Jean and I were up all night, and I was telling her the whole story about what happened between them, and then…I started playing it and when I got to the end of what he'd written I suddenly just knew what should come next. I played through all the way to the end…and it was perfect…it was the perfect ending to a perfect song…it showed my parents finally together in heaven and then me here remembering them…" My voice broke as I felt tears begin to slide down my cheeks. It was like I was losing my parents all over again. "...and I didn't record it and don't know how to write the notes down to finish the song. I don't even know if I can remember exactly what I did. How can I transfer onto those empty lines on the paper what my fingers just played automatically?"

Liam's hands gently cupped my face, his thumbs brushing away the tear streaks. "I have a confession to make." The statement was so out of the blue, the words didn't register right away. When I wrinkled my eyebrows in confusion, he gave me a sheepish grin. "I was standing outside listening to you play. I didn't mean to eavesdrop, but I also didn't want to interrupt. And you're right, it was a perfect ending to a perfect song. If you want me to, I could help you finish writing out that last part."

"But what if I can't remember how it goes?"

His smile spread even wider. "I'm in a cover band, remember? Listening to a song and copying it is what I do. But I think if you start from the beginning again, you'll more than likely find your fingers remember the notes better than you think. Why don't you give it a try?"

Skeptical, yet willing to give it a try just because he seemed so confident in my abilities, I turned around to face the keys. He joined me, his leg flush against mine, yet sitting back far enough to leave my arms free to reach the lower keys. I took a deep, steadying breath and began the song again.

As the notes flowed from the piano strings, I found myself getting lost in the story of the music once more. When I reached the end of Benny's notes, I allowed my hands to take over and discovered Liam was right. My fingers remembered the right keys even if my brain hadn't transferred them to visual notes, rests, and chords yet. When I came to the last phrase, my right hand reaching for the high melody that indicated my mother in heaven, my heart skipped a beat as I felt a warmth slide along my back and Liam's hand appeared beneath my arm to play the part meant to be my father joining her. I held my breath as my left hand added another, lower layer to the high notes to represent myself, the culmination of their love. The notes gradually slowed, and Liam matched my pace exactly as together we reached the end of my composition, but just before the final notes, his left hand joined in, playing a very slightly altered version of the melody on the low keys that sent a shiver down my spine and gave me goosebumps. We held the last note until we could no longer hear the vibration of the strings, then lifted our fingers in unison, letting them rest lightly on the keys in silence. When I was finally able to talk, I could only bring myself to speak in a hushed tone of reverence.

"That last part was…" I struggled for the perfect words to describe something so amazingly beautiful I didn't want it to end.

"I hoped you might like it," he whispered back, his breath playing along my neck since we were still sitting so close. "If you don't, we can write it your way and end with just your melody."

I turned my head enough to look up into his eyes. "It was you, wasn't it? Those last notes? That was you coming into my life so my notes wouldn't be left without harmony."

He didn't nod to take credit or even smile sheepishly to look humble. He merely gazed down into my eyes and waited to see what I was going to do or say next. Whether he would be accepted or not. It was then I noticed that even with us being pressed so close together, he wasn't looking at me like an object of desire or staring as if trying to bend me to his will like almost every other man in my life. Inside these perfect little chocolate-colored circles I saw doubt (as if he didn't think he deserved me), hope (that I felt he was deserving), fear (that he might do something wrong)...and a deeper love than I'd ever experienced.

One of Benny's many Bible verses popped into my head and a strange calmness suddenly flowed through me. *There is no fear in love, but perfect love casts out fear. For fear has to do with punishment, and he who fears is not perfected in love.* I thought I knew what it meant until this very moment, looking at and feeling perfect love for the first time. All the tension from my own doubt and fear was pushed away and I felt a warmth in my heart I didn't realize I'd been missing.

"I don't just like it, I love it," I said, smiling at him and letting my eyes convey all the feelings of gratitude, faith, happiness, and love I had no words for.

Liam smiled back and his eyes reflected his pure joy at my acceptance of both him and his offer through the music to be a part of my life. He bent his head, giving me the softest of kisses. Turning in his embrace, I wrapped my arms around his neck and deepened the kiss. He held me gently as we tasted each other, our breath deepening as we proved at least a fraction of what we were feeling—what I never believed I was even capable of feeling for someone else. He shifted his hands down to my hips to pull me even closer and his elbow hit the piano keys, the discordant sound startling us both. As we realized how powerfully frightening the wave of blind passion had over us, we began to laugh, the noise a welcome distraction as if warning us not to dive head-first into something without at least some control. Settling for resting my forehead against his neck, we caught our breath while Liam stroked my back.

"Well, I am certainly glad you called this morning."

I gave a little laugh. "This isn't exactly what I planned," I admitted. "But it's even better."

He leaned back away from me, and I looked up into his confused face. "This isn't what you called me for?" he asked in mock pain. "So what, pray tell, did you want to ask me?"

I laid a palm against his cheek and gave him a light kiss to brush away the frown. "I've spent all night telling Mary Jean the story about my parents. Before I started, all I could see was a sad ending and two people suffering needlessly. Then I realized that everything went the way it was supposed to go. If anything had happened differently—Mom giving me up, David not marrying her, me growing up knowing my dad wasn't my real dad, or Benny breaking up their marriage—things could have been so much worse and my parents could have ended up resenting each other. As it was, they did what they had to do because they loved the other enough to give them up, suffering themselves to save the other one from more pain."

"Love can be painful sometimes," he agreed hesitantly, his eyebrows drawing in again as he tried to guess where my train of thought was leading.

"But it's worth it," I exclaimed happily. "Isn't it? To take a leap of faith and love someone? I mean, I wouldn't be here if my parents hadn't let themselves love each other because they were worried about the possibility of suffering because of it."

His lips tugged up slightly, but he still looked confused. "Is that what you wanted to ask me? If loving someone was worth suffering? I don't think I'm the right person to answer that question," he added, starting to pull away from my touch.

Just as he stood up, I grabbed his hand with both of mine. "Mary Jean told me about what happened to you and your wife."

He paused, searching my face for my reaction. When I gave him only understanding instead of pity or revulsion, he allowed himself to sit back down beside me. His voice broke slightly when he prompted, "And?"

"And my question is…" I began, holding his hand tightly like a lifeline between us, "...are you willing to risk suffering by loving someone again? Because I know how hard it was for you the first time. I've never done this before so I'm going to need a lot of help and patience from you."

It took a minute before the intent of my words sunk in. "You mean, you…want to…love…me?" I nodded my head emphatically and his face transformed into that of pure joy. A look I vowed to keep there…for as long as I lived.

"And you realized this by retelling your parents' story? I would really love to hear the whole thing sometime. I mean the way it sounds in the song was amazing."

"And I'd love to tell you," I said, standing and pulling him to his feet. "But you are going to be late for work, and I have to clean up that glass, then get some sleep. I've been awake for over 24 hours now."

"But I don't want to leave."

He kissed the back of my hand and my breath caught in my throat.

"Not now."

He placed a light kiss on my lips, and I felt the electricity all through my body.

"Not ever."

He deepened the kiss, but kept a little distance between us, knowing we couldn't let it go further. At least not yet.

I smiled against his mouth and kissed him one more time before pulling back. "Work. Remember?"

He glanced down at his watch and groaned. "Can I come back after work? Maybe for supper? Hear more of that story? Help you with your song?" he asked, smiling as he backed himself toward the door until his boots crunched on the broken glass.

"You better," I warned with a laugh as he picked his way across the entryway to the door.

He turned back with his hand on the door handle and his eyes were blazing with the love I felt heating my own. “Maybe hold you and never let you go? Until death do we part?”

I stood across the expanse of broken vase from him and let him see my own desire to do just that. “If there’s one thing I learned from my parents, it’s that you have to claim your love while it’s right in front of you because you can’t guarantee you have all the time in the world to wait.”

Epilogue

March 2, 2003

And so here we are, at last, Dad. I'm glad I can finally call you that, even if it's so late. I can't believe it's been a whole year since you came into the clinic and turned my world upside down—for the better, I'm happy to add. Even though you didn't get a chance to know me, I feel like I know you and Mom pretty well now…and you're finally right where you belong.

You wouldn't believe all the red tape it took to get your ashes moved from Detroit, but I wasn't about to let you and Mom down. And now, I'm finally able to bring you two together here just as I like to imagine you are in heaven. You also have David to thank for making this possible. He pulled as many strings as he could at the courthouse until they were as sick of hearing from him as they were from me.

But don't worry about him, Mom. It was his idea to give up his spot beside you. He said it was only right for him to step aside now that we know the truth about you two, and I think he regrets being partly responsible for getting in the way of true love all those years ago. He does miss you and regrets all that time wasted on jealousy and bitter feelings from having to keep our secret. He's happy with his new wife and he's doing just fine. I think he may even finally be in love.

Dad, I also want to thank you for getting me interested in going back to church. All those Bible verses in your journals and the way you were able to find the strength you needed through God's love were more inspirational than any self-help book. I'm starting to understand how powerful and comforting having faith in God really is. I hung up the verses you had about strength, suffering, and love. I look at them every day to remind myself that help is just a prayer away.

David and Charlotte have also started going to church with us every Sunday. Now that everything's all out in the open, he and I are closer than we've ever been. Charlotte was confused by our sudden change of heart at first, but after we told her your story, they've both been so supportive over this last year. My new therapist helped us understand that my distancing myself from David was a reaction to the love-challenged environment I grew up in, and how hard it was for him to see the person you should have been with every time he looked in my eyes. You can't imagine how relieved we both were to discover we've actually loved each other all this time. We're still family, after all, even if we don't share DNA.

I hope you don't mind, Dad, but I finished the song you started writing about me and Mom. It was just too beautiful to leave unfinished. Don't worry, it has the perfect ending. Claire even helped me record it, along with your other originals, at her studio, and now I've got some professionally made CDs. I sent one to Bo to thank him for all his stories. He said it sounded just like your playing back in the day. I couldn't think of a nicer compliment.

I also wanted to tell you two about Liam. He works with Ron at the police department. Mary Jean pushed us together, of course, but after learning from your story, I was finally able to let my defenses down and love with my whole heart. I'm so glad I did. He's so handsome and kind and patient and funny and easy to talk to and talented—he plays piano in a band on the weekends—and best of all…I trust him. Mom, doesn't that remind you of Dad? We didn't want to let doubt ruin our chance for happiness—I mean, you never know what life may bring, right? So we got married last Christmas. I hope you don't mind, but we used the ring you were supposed to share. It helps remind us to never take love for granted. Although sometimes I still have to remind myself I'm worthy of someone's love and devotion, we've been deliriously happy.

I just found out today that we're starting a family of our own. I know Liam is going to be ecstatic when I tell him tonight, but I hope it doesn't bring back too many bad memories for him. Even though I sometimes wonder if I'm doing everything I can to be the wife he deserves, I feel in my heart I'll be the best mother to his child. I just can't help but hope our baby has Hunter-green eyes.

Author's Note

Thank you for reading *Hunter Green.* It's been an ongoing project for so many years now—the original version written on paper with an actual pencil. It's a relief to finally have it out in the world for others to enjoy.

When my children were young, I used to sing to them along with my favorite songs on cassette tapes. While singing the Tanya Tucker song *What's Your Mama's Name?* —realizing it was probably an odd song choice to sing to my own children—I wondered about the story behind the lyrics. I wrote out the story I envisioned between the young couple to answer what could have happened to split them apart and why they never got back together even though he followed his love to find his daughter. After years of sitting in a notebook, I came back to the story and then wondered what happened to the little girl, adding her story to that of her parents. After several editions, my mother suggested it would make a good Christian romance, and she was right. The hope of the father searching for his child and the child learning about the love of the father was so obvious. The rest just fell into place.

I want to thank my family for being so patient with me when I get caught up in my writing, especially my loving husband. I also thank all of those who read the many versions of this story and offered me critiques and suggestions. I couldn’t have fulfilled my dream of publishing this without all of your love and support.

Bible Verses

I love thee, O Lord, my strength. The Lord is my rock, my fortress, and my deliverer, my God is my rock, in whom I take refuge, my shield, and the horn of my salvation, my stronghold. Psalm 18:1-2

Rejoice in your hope, be patient in tribulation, be constant in prayer. Romans 12:12

For whatever was written in former days was written for our instruction, that by steadfastness and by the encouragement of the scriptures we might have hope. Romans 15:4

And after you have suffered a little while, the God of all grace, who has called you to his eternal glory in Christ, will himself restore, establish, and strengthen you. 1 Peter 5:10

If a man seduces a virgin who is not betrothed and lies with her, he shall give the marriage present for her, and make her his wife. If her father utterly refuses to give her to him, he shall pay money equivalent to the marriage present for virgins. Exodus 22:16-17.

When the righteous cry for help, the Lord hears, and delivers them out of all their troubles. The Lord is near to the brokenhearted, and saves the crushed in spirit. Many are the afflictions of the righteous; but the Lord delivers him out of them all. Psalm 34:17-19

We rejoice in our sufferings, knowing that suffering produces endurance, and endurance produces character, and character produces hope, and hope does not disappoint us, because God's love has been poured into our hearts through the Holy Spirit which has been given to us. Romans 5:3-5

There is no fear in love, but perfect love casts out fear. For fear has to do with punishment, and he who fears is not perfected in love. 1 John 4:18